T0147074

The Body from the Past

Books by Judi Lynn

Mill Pond Romances
COOKING UP TROUBLE
OPPOSITES DISTRACT
LOVE ON TAP
SPICING THINGS UP
FIRST KISS, ON THE HOUSE
SPECIAL DELIVERY

Jazzi Sanders Mysteries
THE BODY IN THE ATTIC
THE BODY IN THE WETLANDS
THE BODY IN THE GRAVEL
THE BODY IN THE APARTMENT
THE BODY FROM THE PAST

Published by Kensington Publishing Corporation

The Body from the Past

Judi Lynn

LYRICAL UNDERGROUND
Kensington Publishing Corp.
www.kensingtonbooks.com

LYRICAL UNDERGROUND BOOKS are published by

Kensington Publishing Corp.
119 West 40th Street
New York, NY 10018

All Kensington titles, imprints, and distributed lines are available at special quantity discounts for bulk purchases for sales promotion, premiums, fund-raising, educational, or institutional use.

Special book excerpts or customized printings can also be created to fit specific needs. For details, write or phone the office of the Kensington Sales Manager: Kensington Publishing Corp., 119 West 40th Street, New York, NY 10018. Attn. Sales Department. Phone: 1-800-221-2647.

Lyrical Underground and Lyrical Underground logo Reg. US Pat. & TM Off.

First Electronic Edition: September 2020
ISBN-13: 978-1-5161-1021-6 (ebook)
ISBN-10: 1-5161-1021-8 (ebook)

First Print Edition: September 2020
ISBN-13: 978-1-5161-1024-7
ISBN-10: 1-5161-1024-2

Printed in the United States of America

I have a lot of people to thank. Writing a book takes months, and my handsome husband, John, puts up with late suppers and fretting when chapters don't work with aplomb and constant support. He even sweeps and mops to help me eke out more writing time. He's a keeper.

My writers' club, the Summit City Scribes, meets twice a month, and when we get together and talk about our projects, we're always supportive of one another, even when we offer critiques. They constantly recharge my writing batteries.

M. L. Rigdon, aka Julia Donner, is my much-admired writer friend in whichever genre she's working on at the moment and my trusted critique partner. She, and my daughter Holly, read my first drafts, brave souls, and help me make them better.

My Jazzi books would never have found a home without my wonderful agent, Lauren Abramo, and my equally wonderful editor, John Scognamiglio, and the entire Kensington team that works on them. My thanks go to: Alexandra Nicolajsen, Larissa Ackerman, Lauren Jernigan, James Akinaka, Michelle Addo, and Rebecca Cremonese. And for my fantastic covers—Tammy Seidick.

I have to give a special mention to a dear friend of my husband and me, Ralph Miser, who is an expert house fixer-upper and all-around fount of interesting ideas for how to find clues for murder while working on a house project. Thank you, Ralph!

Chapter 1

Jazzi opened one eye to scowl at the alarm clock. She hadn't heard it go off before she felt Ansel's hand patting her fanny. How had she missed her wake-up buzz? The world was still blurry, so she squinted to focus better. And that was when it hit her. It wasn't six thirty yet. She opened her other eye and turned to glare at her husband.

Her tall, blond Viking grinned, unrepentant. "I thought we could get an early start on our new fixer-upper."

She groaned. She'd rather have had another half hour of sleep. Inky raised his head, looking irritated. Her black cat relied on the alarm, too. Marmalade, their *nice* cat, walked over Ansel's torso to snuggle between them. Ansel stroked her orange fur. Ansel's beloved pug, George, snored in his dog bed, as usual.

With a sigh, Jazzi swung her legs over the side of the bed. "I'm up. I'm moving."

Ansel was more excited than usual about this house. So was her cousin, Jerod. Jerod had found it in a quaint, small town southwest of River Bluffs, farther than they usually drove for a job, but they got it at such a good price, it was worth the extra effort. Merlot was a college town a half hour from River Bluffs, with a population close to six thousand. She and Ansel lived on the north side of town, so their drive would be longer than Jerod's.

They'd spent all summer and the start of fall working on a house north of River Bluffs in Auburn, Indiana. That town was quaint and charming, too. And they'd made so much money on their project that they'd all decided it was worth driving if they found a special house. And this one was even better than the last.

Jazzi pushed tangled, honey-blond hair out of her face. It had been damp when she fell asleep last night and it had dried funny. No matter. She always pulled it into a ponytail for work. Ansel was tugging on worn jeans and a T-shirt when she stumbled past him to the bathroom. She stopped to ask, "You aren't going to fall in love with this place when we fix it, are you? I don't want to move, no matter how awesome it is."

It *was* awesome. It looked like it could have been pulled right out of an English novel with its stone exterior, three chimneys, and arched windows. The main structure was three stories high and the wing on the side was two. The house was big, with lots of charm, large rooms, and as much curb appeal as their own stone cottage.

Ansel shook his head. "I love our place. It's plenty big enough for us, and we have enough property for our pond and gazebo. I never want to leave here."

Good. She felt the same way, especially since they'd renovated every square inch of it except the basement. And Ansel was already making noises about that. If she wasn't careful, they'd be turning half of it into a playroom, like they'd helped Jerod do with his.

Mollified, she hurried to get ready, and ten minutes later, she and Ansel were leading the cats downstairs to the kitchen. George, as usual, was carried by Ansel. The pug didn't like stairs. All three pets went straight to their food bowls, and while she fed them, Ansel poured coffee and started the toast. He barely gave her enough time to pack sandwiches and chips in the cooler for their lunch before he loaded everything, including George, into their work van and turned west toward Merlot. The drive took forty-five minutes.

Jazzi tugged her hoodie shut against the morning chill. Early October days were warm enough, but mornings and evenings were cooler. She glanced at the trees. Too early to see any color yet. In another two weeks, the woods would blaze with reds and golds.

The thought reminded her of their last Halloween. Not the best time for them. They'd been drawn into solving another murder, and that time, instead of finding her aunt's body in their attic, this one had been propped right on their front stoop. She sighed. She and Ansel had made a pledge: no more bodies.

When Ansel pulled into the driveway of the Merlot house, Jerod's pickup was already there. Her cousin was standing in the front yard, staring at their new project. Ansel went to join him, carrying George. Jazzi tugged the cooler out of the back of the van and, setting it beside the open door, went to join them.

"It's a beauty, isn't it?" Jerod asked. "With a new roof, it will look even better."

"I've been thinking about that." Jazzi licked her lips.

"When you do that, you've thought of something that's going to cost more money." Her cousin raised an eyebrow. "Spill it, cuz, but it had better be good."

"You know how much I love English mysteries. Well, I always like the descriptions of English gardens and thatched roofs."

"We can't do thatch here," Ansel said, interrupting.

"No, but we can do fake shake shingles. They'd give sort of the same effect."

Jerod rubbed his chin, studying the façade of the house. "You know, those just might be worth it on this place. It would fit the vibe of the rest of the house."

Ansel nodded agreement. "I'll give you a yes vote, too. This house deserves something extra."

That had been easier than she expected. Just wait 'til Ansel shared his ideas for the house with Jerod. There was a small room on the first floor that he was dying to make into a library. And he'd already shown her pictures of how he'd like to do the front foyer and create a small mudroom in the back hallway off the patio.

Finished looking, the guys grabbed their gear and Jazzi got the cooler, then they headed inside. Jerod called to order the shingles they wanted, and then he pulled on his heavy work gloves. The previous owner had warned them that she'd left some furniture behind. They had to clear it out. For once, the rooms downstairs and up were so large, they wouldn't have to knock out walls. The interior of the house was in good shape, except someone had gone crazy with wallpaper upstairs. Every room had some. It all needed to be stripped. The wooden floors could be refinished except in the kitchen, and they might have to refinish the graceful, curved stairs and railings, too. The kitchen and every bathroom needed to be gutted, and the basement's cement was crumbling. No structural problems, just old cement, worn with time. They'd have to add a new layer on the floor and walls, as well as a new furnace and central air. It sounded like a lot, but they usually had more to deal with.

This time around, they could focus on making every improvement add to the character of the house. Their first job? Clean out every room so that they could get started. Jazzi carried the cooler into the kitchen and tucked it against the wall where the kitchen table used to sit. For once, they'd decided not to gut the kitchen until later in their project. That way, they'd have a refrigerator and sink for their lunches.

Jerod scowled at the pine cupboards and linoleum floor. "The woman who owned this place loved to entertain. You'd have thought she'd spend the money to spiff up the kitchen."

Ansel shrugged, carrying George's dog bed to a corner of the room. He took the thickly padded oval from project to project. George immediately curled in it to supervise. "There's a big dining room. She probably only prepped food in here."

Jerod had talked to her. They hadn't. "She didn't cook. She catered."

"Well, there's your answer." Jazzi plugged in the coffee urn and turned it on. "She never spent time in this room."

"Sort of like my wife." Jerod constantly fussed about Franny's cooking. "I married a wonderful woman, but if I don't cook, it's safer to grab food on the way home."

"We all have different loves and talents," Jazzi reminded him.

"I guess. She's a whiz when it comes to furniture restoration."

"There you go." Jazzi looked out the kitchen window at the patio and backyard. The landscaping looked professional. And one of the added bonuses of this house was that a balcony led off the upstairs hallway, forming a roof for the patio beneath it. Two more great places to entertain.

Ansel followed her gaze. "I bet it was hard for the owner to leave this house."

Jerod shook his head. "Madeline gave lots and lots of parties, and that's how she met her new husband. After he attended one of them, they kept in touch. That's why she sold this place to us for the same price she paid for it originally. Once he popped the question, she wanted to sell it fast and move east to marry him."

Jazzi pursed her lips, trying to remember the house's history. "She got it at a good price, too, didn't she?"

Jerod nodded. "The same family owned it for years, passed it down through the generations, but the last of the Hodgkills sold it cheap and moved away the minute the ink dried on the contract."

Jazzi glanced around at the grand, old place. "How could you give up such a beautiful family legacy? It makes you wonder, doesn't it? There's probably a story behind that."

"Hey, it worked in our favor." With a shrug, Jerod reached for a gateleg table in the entryway. "But enough talking. Time to start working. Let's get this place ready to go." He picked up the table. "Anyone want this? It's a great antique."

Jazzi and Ansel shook their heads. "No place to put it," Ansel said. "Give it to Franny. She'll make it look good again."

It would be quick work getting the inside ready to paint. They'd decided to start on the roof first, though, because it was October and the weather might not hold.

The guys decided to tackle the downstairs, and Jazzi headed up to the bedrooms. There were five of them, and three baths. When they'd walked through the house, they'd seen most of them before the owner had to leave for a business meeting. They'd seen enough, though, that they knew the structure of the place was solid, and the house was a good buy.

The third step from the top creaked. She made a mental note to fix it, then started on the rooms on the left side of the wide hallway at the top of the stairs. Only a few night tables and a mirror were left in those, and she carried them into the hallway. Once that was done, she crossed to the last room on the right side of the hall, close to the French doors that opened onto the balcony. This room was the only one that was shut up. She pushed on its door, but it wouldn't open. The knob wouldn't turn. It was locked.

She went to the top of the stairs and called down, "A room's locked up here. Did we get a key for it?"

Jerod stopped what he was doing to come to look up at her, frowning. "I forgot about that. The owner told me about it, said it was locked when she bought the house. She had plenty of other bedrooms, so she just never bothered with it. And she never found a key."

"What do you want me to do?"

"Take off the door handle and hardware and break in. We have to get inside it, one way or another."

With a nod, Jazzi returned to the room and got busy, unscrewing the hardware and removing the knob. When they were off, she reached inside to the working mechanisms and clicked the door open. Then she stood and stared.

So much dust covered a double bed that its soft pink comforter looked gray. Strings of dust hung like Spanish moss from its pink canopy. Posters of movie stars who'd been popular when Jazzi was in high school were taped to the walls, their edges yellowed and curling. In the corner, tubes of lipsticks littered the top of a makeup table with an oval mirror—all buried under a thick gray coating. Cobwebs dangled to eye level and more dust coated the floor and its flowered rugs. Jazzi crossed the room to raise the blind on the wide window and sneezed. Dust flew everywhere. A hope chest sat under the window. She shivered, memories of Aunt Lynda's folded skeleton returning. She reached for its lid, then yanked her hand away.

The closet door stood open a crack. Cautiously, she pushed it wider with her toe, keeping a safe distance away. Clothes lined the rod that stretched across it. High heels sat under party dresses with matching colors, followed by slip-ons and gym shoes for jeans and flirty skirts. It felt like she'd walked into a time warp.

Why hadn't anyone ever emptied this room? Or at least cleaned it? She walked to the top of the stairs and called down to the guys. "You might want to see this."

Jerod carried a floor lamp to the door and started up the stairs. "Did someone leave a loose floorboard with a stash of money hidden under it?"

"Always the optimist. No. You've got to see this for yourselves."

Ansel climbed up after him, and she led them to the pink room. They stopped and stared. Jerod scratched his head and gave a low whistle. "Curiouser and curiouser."

Ansel's gaze riveted on the hope chest. "Have you opened it yet?"

"I didn't want to; at least, not alone."

He nodded understandingly and let out a long breath. "Let's see what's in it."

He lifted the lid, and Jazzi put a hand to her throat. "Treasures," she said. "Special moments in a young girl's life. Someone left them all behind." She reached down to ruffle through grade school pictures that showed the same young girl with long blond hair, serious gray eyes, and a willowy figure. She stood in the center of the back row where the tall kids were placed. Yearbooks. Jazzi reached for the newest and flipped it open to the girl's name—Jessica Hodgkill. Her picture smiled out at them, but no signatures peppered the page. She glanced at the front and back of the book. No friends signed it. A corsage with dead flowers. Swim team ribbons and tennis trophies. Report cards. Jazzi flipped through a few. All As and Bs. Stones, shells, and souvenirs from trips.

Why were her treasures still here, locked away? Why was this room left untouched all these years?

"Hey, no body!" Jerod said, relieved.

But something was wrong. Why had the family moved so quickly, they'd left everything in this room behind? Had something happened to Jessica?

Chapter 2

"What should we do with this stuff?" Ansel's gaze swept the room.

"We can't just get rid of it," Jazzi said. "We should ask Jessica's parents if they want it. They didn't when they moved away, but they might regret leaving it by now."

Jerod nodded agreement. "I'll call Madeline. She'll have the family's information, and I'll find out how to get in touch with them."

"Ask about the furniture," Ansel said. "They're antiques. They're probably worth something."

Jerod scrubbed a hand through his light-brown hair. "We might as well take a lunch break while I make the calls. What did you bring for us today, cuz?" On the job, when his thoughts weren't on working, they turned to food.

"Ham salad sandwiches and chips." He wrinkled his nose, and she gave him a look. "You like ham salad."

"I know." He dug his cell phone out of his jeans pocket as he started toward the stairs. "But we've had sandwiches all summer. Sometimes you change it up, is all."

"Are you in the mood for something different?" She didn't keep the sarcasm out of her voice. When they reached the kitchen, she might only give him one sandwich. Then he might appreciate them more.

Jerod purposely missed the sarcasm. He'd developed the skill when they were kids, bickering with each other. By now, he'd perfected a special ability to tune it out. "I was hoping you'd be in soup mode again. You usually are in the fall."

"It's not chilly enough outside. Give me a couple more weeks." But he was right. She'd made every sandwich type thing she could think of all summer long—paninis, tacos, burritos, and sloppy joes. She was getting tired of them. "It's not cold enough for potato soup." One of his favorites.

He grinned. "But it's perfect weather for your minestrone."

Ah. She should have known. The man couldn't get enough of that. When she wanted to spoil him, that was one of her go-to meals. She gave him an indulgent look. He loved to heckle her, but she gave as good as she got. That was why they got along so well. She glanced at her watch. "We're going to get home early enough tonight, I guess I could make you a pot."

That earned her a hug. Almost as tall as Ansel and heftier, Jerod always made her feel small, but she was above average height for a woman—five-eight and curvy. She always envied her younger sister Olivia's willowy figure, but Ansel liked her curves.

"You're the best," Jerod told her.

"Remember that when I bring peanut butter and jelly someday."

"Won't ever happen." He motioned to Ansel. "Your man burns too many calories. Those would only hold him for half an hour."

True. Her Viking was all muscle, and she swore he burned more calories than any human should. Oh, well, both men were easier to work with when their stomachs were happy. A pot of soup was worth the effort.

Jazzi started handing out sandwiches and bags of chips while Jerod made his call. Madeline picked up on the fifth ring, and Jerod asked her about the room upstairs. He put her answer on Speaker for them to hear.

"That room was shut up tight when I bought the house," she told them. "When I asked the Hodgkills about it, the wife told me she couldn't go into that room, not even to clean it. I always meant to call a locksmith or contractor to open it, but I didn't need it, so I just never got around to it."

"We have to clean it out," Jerod said. "Do you want any of the furniture? Anything in there at all?"

"Oh, no, none of it's my stuff. Do whatever you want with all of it. And I'm sorry I left it for you."

"No problem. My wife restores antiques. She might be interested in some of the furniture."

"Good. It would be nice if someone wanted it again, but not me."

Jazzi could understand why Madeline avoided that room. It had given her the creeps, too. And it wasn't like the woman hadn't had enough other bedrooms for guests.

Jerod asked, "Do you happen to have contact information for the Hodgkills?"

She looked it up for him.

"Thanks for the help. And congrats on your new life." Jerod ended the call and looked at them. "Should I try the Hodgkills?"

Ansel nodded. "Jazzi's right. Whatever happened took place a long time ago. Jessica's family might wish they had something of hers now."

Jerod made the call, and again, he put the phone on Speaker. When a woman answered and identified herself as Mrs. Hodgkill, he explained about the room.

"Throw everything out or give it away," she said. "That room holds too many sad memories. I can't face them. And please, never call here again. I've tried to put those memories behind me."

What memories? What had happened here? Jazzi wouldn't be able to resist looking up the family's history. And she couldn't throw away Jessica's treasure chest. It would feel wrong to trash so much personal history.

When they finally sat down to eat, Ansel frowned at her. "We made a pledge. No more dead bodies."

He knew her too well. "I'm guessing Jessica died and was buried a long time ago, and the mom was so broken up by it, they had to move away and try to put whatever happened behind them. Maybe she died in a car accident before she graduated from high school, or from some medical problem. Who knows?"

"That's the problem." Ansel pinched off a small bite of his sandwich to share with George, who'd come to beg. "I don't want to get involved in whatever happened. It couldn't have been good if the family had to run away from it."

"I can't throw away her treasure chest." Jazzi raised her chin, digging in. "I'm taking it home with us and looking through it."

Ansel closed his eyes and counted to ten. "And what if someone murdered her? What then?"

"They're probably in prison, and I won't visit them."

He sighed. "And you'll leave it alone? Even if the case wasn't solved?"

"I don't know Jessica. I'll feel sorry for her, but we're not involved with her past. It's not as if it's one of our friends or family."

His shoulders relaxed and he fed George another pinch of food. "I'm going to hold you to that."

"Fine. But it will drive me nuts if I don't dig around inside that chest."

He nodded, and Jerod shook his head. "I was a witness to this whole conversation. Ansel can use me as backup, cuz."

"First of all, you're *my* cousin, and *I'm* the one who cooks for you. But if you want to be like that, you two can be bosom buddies and do your thing."

Jerod rolled his eyes. "I'm not choosing Ansel over you. But the man has a point. You don't need to get involved in every murder that falls into your lap."

Pressing her lips tight, she raised an eyebrow at him. "Fine."

"When women say 'fine,' it's always a red flag." Jerod stood to throw away his paper plate. "If it comes to sticking up for you, Ansel, or choosing Jazzi's minestrone soup, she wins."

Ansel let out a puff of aggravation. "The last murder we looked into could have gotten us both shot. I'd rather have a happy marriage for as long as we can instead of having gravestones next to each other."

She capitulated. "I know you're just worried about me. I told you I wouldn't poke into another murder, and I meant it. But you have to admit, none of them has been my fault."

"I know that, and I'm grateful you helped clear my brother's name, and Thane's grateful you helped him, but I'd rather quit while we're still alive and undamaged." Ansel stood to help clean the card table.

"So." Jerod looked from one of them to the other. "Can we clean out that room now?"

"Do you think Franny would like the furniture?" Jazzi asked.

"I know she would. A kidney-shaped makeup table is right up her alley. And the maple canopy bed? She's going to be in an antique lover's heaven. Do you want any of it?"

Jazzi shook her head. "Only the hope chest."

"And the clothes?" Ansel asked.

"They're all dated." Jazzi went to get a box of garbage bags. "We'll give them to a used clothing shop."

It was no easy task carrying the heavy furniture down the stairs. While the men flexed their muscles, Jazzi emptied the drawers and closet, then carted the Shop-Vac upstairs and started cleaning. It took them the rest of the afternoon to finish the room. They all pitched in to sweep and dust the last bedroom and bath on that side of the hallway.

Finally, Jerod said, "Done. Tomorrow, we can start on the roof. The shingles are going to be delivered in the morning. These roofs are steep enough; we're going to have to pound in some boards for footholds."

They'd worked on worse. The house in Auburn had a turret they'd had to reshingle. But roofs were always dirty, heavy work. Yup, she'd make soup tomorrow. The men could use a little extra TLC.

Chapter 3

Jazzi helped Ansel carry the hope chest into the house when they got home. They put it in the living room for the time being. That way, she could sort through it while Ansel relaxed on the couch to watch TV. The cats came to sniff it. George was unimpressed, walking to his food bowl and sitting to stare at it, ready for his dry dog food. Eventually, their curiosity satisfied, Inky and Marmalade padded to join him, stopping at their food dish, too.

While Jazzi fed the beasts, Ansel headed upstairs to take the first shower. When he came back down with damp hair, smelling of soap and maleness, she lingered a minute, inhaling him, until he chuckled and motioned toward the stairs. "Your turn. You're coated with dust."

So much for her earthy beauty. Ansel and Jerod could humble her fast. She jogged up the steps to try to look human again. When she returned half an hour later, dressed in sweatpants and a baggy T-shirt, her hair wrapped in a towel on top of her head, Ansel grinned.

"Now you're the raving beauty I married." He opened the refrigerator, as if a magic genie would produce some wonderful enticement. "What's for supper?"

"Pork chops, hash browns, and sautéed apples. And I'm going to make minestrone for tomorrow."

"I'll help." Ansel loved cooking together. They peeled apples and started them, then diced vegetables for the soup. It was simmering on the stove before they sat down for supper. Ansel went straight for the sautéed apples. "We should make these more often."

She grinned. "You say that every time I make them." She'd removed the towel and thrown it down the laundry chute, so her hair was starting to wave and curl while it dried. She pushed a loose strand off her forehead.

George wandered to the kitchen island to beg while they ate. He was partial to pork chops. And chicken. And...Oh, well, the pug liked food almost as much as his master. Ansel snuck him morsels while they made small talk and enjoyed their meal. They were cleaning up when Jazzi's cell phone buzzed.

"Hello?"

Leesa, Jazzi's BFF since high school, burst into speech. "An old friend of Brett's called to tell him you guys were working on the Hodgkill house in Merlot."

Brett was Leesa's husband of five years, a financial analyst and a little on the aggressive side. Jazzi and Ansel got together with the two of them every once in a while for suppers out.

"Hold on a minute," Jazzi told her. "Ansel's right here, too. I'll put you on Speaker." This didn't sound like a social call.

"Good. He'll want to hear this, too." Leesa paused for a second when a voice interrupted her. "Just a minute, Riley. Mommy's on the phone."

The voice whined on. Jazzi smiled. Riley was two. Two-year-olds didn't care if Mommy was busy or not. No wonder Leesa often told them she went to her office on campus to make business calls. People would wonder if an English lit professor had to stop in midsentence to listen to her child. Finally, Leesa returned. "Are you still there?"

"If Riley wants a Popsicle, you should give him one," Jazzi teased.

"Just wait 'til you have one of your own. They're persistent."

"And that's why you wanted another one?" Leesa was pregnant with baby number two.

Leesa laughed. "What was I thinking? Oh, yeah, I might as well have them close together so I might have a life again someday."

Ansel's blue eyes glittered with humor. When they'd first gotten married, he'd talked about having a baby. Now, after meeting their friends' kids, he was ready to wait.

Jazzi tried to return the call to its original purpose. "You wanted to know something about the Hodgkill house?"

"Oh, yeah." Leesa sighed. "I swear, I'm losing it. I knew I'd called you for a reason." She took an audible breath. "Brett grew up in Merlot. That house holds horrible memories for him. Could you and Ansel come to supper here tomorrow night? Brett wants to invite his brother and his wife, too, so they can talk to you about it."

Jazzi frowned at the phone. "They want to talk about the house? Are they upset that we're renovating it?"

"No, nothing like that." Another pause. "You haven't heard?"

"Heard what?" What was the deal with this house anyway?

"Jessica Hodgkill lived there. Before high school graduation, during a party celebrating that she'd been named class valedictorian, she was pushed off the house's balcony and died."

Ansel's expression went as dark as a raven's wing. He gave Jazzi a look that said *don't go there.*

Jazzi took a long breath. "I'm sorry to hear that. We found Jessica's hope chest in her upstairs bedroom. It was filled with all of her childhood memories."

"If you look through any of it, you'll learn that Brett's brother was her date for the senior prom and the main suspect in her murder."

A finger of dread slid down Jazzi's spine. "Was his name cleared once the cops found her killer?"

"They never did, but they couldn't prove Damian was guilty. Trouble was, he couldn't prove he was innocent either. It ruined his life."

Ansel glowered even more.

Jazzi wasn't sure what to say. "I'm so sorry. That had to be awful for the entire family."

"It was terrible for the whole town. People took sides. Brett always stood up for his brother and lost some good friends because of it."

"Then they weren't real friends," Ansel said, joining the conversation for the first time.

"That's what I told him. Anyway, can you two come tomorrow? We'd really appreciate it."

Jazzi looked at Ansel. He grimaced, but nodded.

"We'll be there," Jazzi said.

"Good, let's make it six thirty. Does that work?"

"See you then." When Jazzi closed the conversation, she turned to Ansel.

He hunched his shoulders, looking more like a Viking than ever. Big and intimidating. "I knew it. I just knew it. You brought home the hope chest, and now we're involved in another murder."

"The hope chest didn't have anything to do with it." Jazzi squared her shoulders, too. "You're blaming me, and it's not fair. Merlot must have a hot gossip line. Brett would have known we were working on that house no matter what I did."

"Supper tomorrow night is going to be awful." Ansel stalked to the refrigerator for a beer. He poured Jazzi a glass of wine and brought it to the kitchen island. They huddled over their drinks there, their knees touching as they faced each other.

"I don't see how we could have turned Leesa down," Jazzi said. "She and Brett are our friends."

"That's what worries me. Brett must have something in mind. He probably wants us to look for clues hidden deep in closets or under floorboards." He tossed a dirty look at the hope chest in the living room.

"Maybe I should look through it before we go."

He shook his head. "Not yet. If we don't know anything, we can't share anything. I don't want to play a game of a hundred questions."

She didn't push it. He'd been through enough questions and answers when they worked with Detective Gaff.

Ansel quirked a brow at her. "You're not going to disagree with me?"

"No."

He blinked, caught off guard. "You're okay with that? With not looking through the chest yet?"

She smiled at him. He didn't like to make her angry. And it was mutual. Ansel's parents had such a dysfunctional marriage and family, Ansel craved a loving home. Her parents still enjoyed spending time together. She'd grown up in a happy family and meant to have one of her own. So she and Ansel were careful of each other's feelings. "I don't want to get involved in another murder any more than you do," she told him. "Gaff's in the River Bluffs police force. He couldn't help us in Merlot."

"Then we're on the same page." He looked relieved. He finally believed her.

She finished her wine and took her glass to the sink. "Let's hit the couches and watch some TV. Nothing serious. I'm ready to relax."

She didn't have to ask twice. He and George followed her into the living room. She didn't even glance at the hope chest against the wall. Jessica's secrets had waited this long. They could wait for another day.

Chapter 4

As they reached the Merlot house for work the next day, Jerod pulled in behind them. He got out and hurried toward them to help carry things in. When Jazzi opened the back of the van and grabbed the cooler, Jerod frowned at it.

"What did you bring today?"

"It's going up to the midseventies this afternoon—pretty warm—so I thought a big tossed salad and plenty of cans of soda might work best."

His whole face sagged with disappointment until he saw Ansel reach for the slow cooker Jazzi brought to keep things warm. Ansel motioned for Jerod to take it so he could carry George.

Jerod grinned at her. "And soup?"

She laughed. "Minestrone. I made plenty so you can take some home as leftovers."

He tossed the tool belts in the back of the van over an arm. "I know what you're doing, and I appreciate it, but you don't have to feed us. I can grill while Franny takes care of the kids."

She shrugged that off. "I know, but isn't it nice to have something different sometimes?"

"You know it. The kids are so tired of hamburgers and hot dogs, they cheer when I bring home pizza."

She tossed him a smug smile while they walked to the house. "When Ansel and I get around to having babies, you can grill for us. For now, we'll make one-pot meals for you."

"Deal."

After they stashed the food in the kitchen, they set up ladders to start work on the roof. Shake shingles took longer to install than regular shingles.

They'd probably be at it for the rest of the week. The house had two different levels—the main part with the entrance and a wing off it. But before they could start on the shakes, they had to tear off the old shingles.

Tugging on work gloves and knee pads, they got to work, starting at the top of the peak and working their way down. They'd rented a dumpster and put down drop cloths to toss the old shingles in, but it was easy to miss and have stray nails fall in flower beds close to the foundation or on the patio. And even in October, when the air was cooler, they got hot and sweaty.

By the time the sun was directly overhead, their T-shirts stuck to their skin and their arms and faces were smeared with grime. Jazzi glanced at George, lying in the grass under a shade tree in the backyard, and grumbled. Ansel's dog had it made.

They started down the ladder to the back patio, Jazzi first, the guys following. She always took that opportunity to turn to stare at Ansel's butt. It was worth a moment of homage. Her husband caught her and grinned. When Jerod joined them, they trudged inside, Ansel holding the door for George, then they went to wash up.

She knew the men would have big appetites after roofing, so she'd brought rounds of crusty bread to have with the soup and salad. A good thing, or Jerod might not have had any leftovers to take home. As it was, each man had two brimming bowls, and there was only enough left for one supper for Jerod, Franny, and the three kids.

Once they cleaned up after lunch, they headed back outside. George went back to his soft grass, and they took a few minutes to rake nails out of the beds and sweep them into a dustbin to throw away. Before they could climb the ladder again, the woman who lived next door came to peek over the short stone wall that separated the two yards.

"Hello?" she called. "Are you the new people who bought the Hodgkill house?"

The men hurried up the ladder, leaving Jazzi to answer her. Jazzi walked closer so they wouldn't have to yell back and forth. "Hi, I'm Jazzi. My cousin, husband, and I bought the house as a fixer-upper."

The woman bit her bottom lip, disappointed. She wore her graying hair short, curled, and sprayed until it looked lacquered. She wore gardening gloves and a crisp cotton shirt and creased capri pants. To *work* in. "You're not moving in?"

"Sorry, no. We're renovating it to sell."

"I hope someone nice buys it." She gave the back kitchen door a sad glance. "I'm Ruth Goggins. Madeline used to invite my husband and me over for lots of dinner parties. I suppose the next owners won't entertain the way she did."

"This house was made for big parties," Jazzi said. "Just like ours. And it has the same English cottage feel."

Her mother complained when she used that term. "Cottage makes me think of something small. Your house is bigger than ours."

But its rolled roof and eyebrow over the front window made Jazzi think of something she'd see in an Agatha Christie TV movie. The kitchen, combined with the dining room and sitting area, gave them plenty of space for lots of guests. And they needed it. Their Sunday family meals had grown to include twenty people most weeks. But they didn't regret that. It was their way of keeping in touch with everyone. This house would accommodate lots of people, too.

She returned her attention to the neighbor. "Madeline entertained a lot, didn't she?"

Ruth sighed, nodding. "She was such a nice person. Not like that awful girl, Jessica Hodgkill. Do you know, she had the nerve to break up with my nephew just before their senior prom? They'd been dating most of that year, and then, just like that, she was done with him. Went to the prom with the Dunlap boy, the older brother. He did the world a favor when he pushed her off the balcony."

Jazzi couldn't hide her shock. "You don't mean that."

Ruth arched an eyebrow. "Don't I? You didn't know the girl. Always so pretty, so perfect. I got pretty sick of hearing her mother brag about her."

Jazzi tried to steer the conversation to something happier. "Most mothers do that, don't they?"

"They're partial, of course," Ruth admitted. "But Jessica just had to beat everyone at everything she did. She had to be the best. Even her own father got tired of it."

Jazzi figured most fathers would brag more than their wives, but everyone was different.

Ruth covered her eyes with her hand to block the sun and studied the men on the roof. "You three are taking on a big job. We had a new roof put on our house three years ago, and it took the work crew two and a half days."

"It will take us longer," Jazzi said. "We plan to put up fake shake shingles."

The arched eyebrow rose again. "I see. Regular shingles aren't good enough for you?"

Jazzi wasn't about to be intimidated. "No. This house is special, so we wanted something special for the roof."

"And our house *isn't* special?"

Jazzi studied it. "Your house is lovely, as is."

Slightly mollified, Ruth sniffed. "This is Merlot's premium neighborhood. Doctors and professors live here. We keep up our yards and houses."

Jazzi glanced at Ruth's gardening gloves. "Your yard is lovely, too. I'd better scramble up the ladder now to help the guys work. It was nice meeting you."

"You're not going to sell the house cheap, are you, like the Hodgkills did to get rid of it fast? Or like Madeline? Who knows who'd move in if the price was too low."

Jazzi forced a smile. If she had to spend much time with this woman, she'd have problems. "We try to buy low and sell higher to make money."

"Good. Maybe we'll get decent neighbors." Ruth turned to start work on her yard, and Jazzi escaped to climb the ladder and get away from her.

When she told the guys about their conversation, Jerod snorted. "Maybe we should invite all the neighbors over when we finish the house to give them a walk-through. You could cook up some of your fancy party stuff. Maybe that would make her happy."

Ansel grunted and laid down his crowbar. "I don't care if she's happy or not."

"Neither do I." Jazzi scooted down on the roof to start work on a new row of shingles. "She sure didn't have anything nice to say about Jessica."

"Sounds like sour grapes to me." Ansel scooted down next to her. One more row of shingles gone. "She must have had a kid who Jessica left in her dust."

Jazzi's thoughts exactly. Ruth Goggins didn't like to come in second.

Chapter 5

When they finished for the day and drove home, Jazzi and Ansel spent more time than usual playing with the pets because they'd be leaving again soon. They weren't excited about going to Leesa and Brett's for supper. Usually, Ansel took George everywhere with him, but Brett was allergic to dogs. Finally, they had to hurry upstairs for quick showers before changing into nicer clothes.

"George isn't going to like this," Ansel complained.

Jazzi rolled her eyes. "Some dogs stay in crates all day while their owners are at work. And they still feel loved and survive."

Ansel frowned, but didn't comment.

Jazzi wore casual black slacks and a lightweight, red sweater that hugged her curves. Ansel gave a low, appreciative whistle when he saw her. He wore dress casual, too—Dockers with a button-down, royal-blue shirt. The color brought out the sky blue of his eyes. Brett must wear jeans around the house, but they'd never seen him in them. But then, they hardly ever went to their house for supper. They usually met them to eat out.

When they pulled into their drive, a black SUV with tinted windows was already parked by the three-car garage. Leesa's saltbox house was in a subdivision on the northeast side of River Bluffs, with all the central houses built around a man-made lake. The lake wasn't for swimming, with its steep drop-offs at the edges, but it made for a pretty view. The inside and outside of the house were very formal.

Leesa called to them from the garage. Four months pregnant, she was just beginning to show. As usual, she'd pulled her mahogany-colored hair into a bun at the back of her head, and tonight, she was wearing a long skirt and a loose top. "Come in this way. It's easier." She led them into a kitchen and family room combination. "Brett's brother's already here. I'll introduce you."

Damian was taller than his brother, but they shared the same sharp features and dark coloring. His wife, Kelsey, was shorter than Jazzi and on the plump side. She had streaked blond hair and a round, open face. The term "cute as a button" came to mind.

In slacks and a Polo shirt like his brother, Brett motioned for everyone to move to the dining room. "Can I get you something to drink?"

He served wine and beer all around, and water for Leesa, then went to help his wife carry two mustard-glazed pork tenderloins with roasted vegetables and a tossed salad to the table. Ansel gave Jazzi a glance at the simple, straightforward food. She half smiled. The man was definitely spoiled.

Brett steered the conversation to small talk as they ate.

Jazzi speared a baby potato. "What does Riley think about being a big brother? Is he excited?"

"Where is he anyway?" Ansel asked, glancing around the room.

"My parents are keeping him tonight," Brett said. "We didn't want him to overhear anything."

That was a bit of a downer. Neither Ansel nor she were looking forward to what was coming, but Jazzi returned to her original question. "Is he excited about the new baby?"

Leesa's eyes sparkled with pride. "He's going through his toy box to find things he's outgrown that he thinks his new sister might like."

"Sister?" Leesa was going to have a girl?

Leesa's whole face lit up. "I'm going to have a daughter."

"I get to go shopping with you to buy baby things," Jazzi said. "They have such cute clothes for girls."

Ansel shook his head. "We guys get a bum deal."

"Oh, please, most boys don't care about clothes until they want to impress someone," Jazzi said. "And usually it's a girl. But once you're very old, the toys you want are expensive—video games, stereo systems, and sports crap."

Damian laughed. "She has a point. We like our gadgets."

"All kids are expensive," Kelsey said. "My sister and her husband are always investing in something for theirs, and they have one of each, too."

Ansel glanced at Damian. "Do you have any kids?"

"Not yet, but we're going to start trying. We've let our jobs take up too much time. We need to find more balance in our lives."

Ansel reached for a second helping of the pork. "I know Brett's a financial analyst. Do you work with finances, too?"

"In a way. I'm an accountant for a big manufacturing company. Kelsey's a nurse."

They spent some time talking about their careers until Leesa and Brett cleared the table and Leesa carried a store-bought cake in for dessert. Ansel grinned. Her Viking liked almost any dessert.

When Brett cleared the table for the last time, he refilled their drinks, and then he turned to his brother. "Do you want to explain about Jessica and the aftermath?"

"Jessica's death was a nightmare." Damian scrubbed a hand through his thick, black hair. "I took her to the senior prom, then a few days later, she went out with some other guy. That got the whole school buzzing. People thought I'd be devastated, but Jessica did it to be nice to me. She didn't want me to look like a cad. I only went to the prom with her because Kelsey and I had had a fight, and Kelsey broke up with me. She and a girlfriend who didn't have a date decided to go together. I wanted to show her I didn't care, so when Jessica broke up with RJ Goggins, which nobody saw coming, I asked her out. But I was miserable. I wanted to be with Kelsey, and Jessica could tell. She told me to make up with Kelsey or I'd regret it. And she said she'd make it easy for me. But neither of us thought it would be such a big deal."

Brett listened to his brother and grimaced. "Our friends knew the whole story, but Lila Mattock spread the word that Damian was a horrible date and a worse kisser, so Jessica got rid of him as fast as she could, and then Damian had to crawl back to Kelsey."

Jazzi pursed her lips. "Did this Lila have a grudge against Damian?"

"She had a crush on him for years," Kelsey said, "but she's a mean, little viper. Damian didn't want anything to do with her."

"So she was jealous," Jazzi said.

"Itching for a smear campaign," Kelsey agreed. "But Lila hated Jessica just as much. They'd competed against each other from grade school on. Lila did all she could to make better grades and bag hotter boyfriends than Jessica, but it usually backfired."

"Did the police suspect her when Jessica was pushed?" Jazzi asked.

Damian nodded. "Her name was on the list, along with mine. So was Kelsey's. There was a girl on the tennis team they suspected, too. Nadia Ashton was trying for a sports scholarship but lost it when Jessica beat her in a match and won the tournament instead."

Ansel gave a grunt of surprise. "It's not Jessica's fault she played better than Nadia."

"Nadia didn't see it that way." Damian leaned forward, resting his elbows on the table. "She thought Jessica should have thrown the match because she needed the scholarship to attend college and Jessica had all the money she'd ever needed."

Leesa shook her head, a sad expression on her face. "It sounds like Nadia was desperate. It's easy to blame the haves when you're a have-not."

"But would Nadia kill someone for winning in tennis? None of you sound like you had strong enough motives to me." Jazzi wasn't buying it.

Damian shrugged. "The detective didn't seem to think anyone *planned* to kill her. He made it sound like someone argued with her at the party, got mad, and pushed her. I have to agree. I can't believe someone killed her on purpose."

"Accidental death." Brett had been ticking off suspects on his fingers. Now, he said, "They questioned RJ's aunt, too. She was Jessica's neighbor. She couldn't get over Jessica dumping her nephew to go to the prom with Damian. She spread rumors all over town, even making up stuff when she had to."

Damian put his head in his hands a moment, looking overcome, before rallying. "I finally couldn't take it anymore. The police couldn't prove I was guilty, but I couldn't prove I was innocent. I'd planned on going to college in town and living at home, but everywhere I went, people gawked at me and whispered. Some even pointed and said, 'There's the guy who got away with murder.' I applied for a scholarship in Illinois just to get away from the rumors. To this day, when I return home, the gossip mill starts up again."

Kelsey nodded. "I went to school in River Bluffs, then moved to Illinois when I got my nursing degree. I got a job there, and we got married in Damian's third year of college."

Damian glanced at his brother. "Brett always stood up for me, and it cost him some friends. But the pressure got to him, too, and he moved here after he graduated."

Brett let out a sigh of frustration and turned to Jazzi and Ansel. "I know you're close to Detective Gaff. This is an old case, but could you look in to it? See if you can find anything to prove Damian didn't do it? Maybe then we could visit our parents and family in peace."

Jazzi didn't answer. She looked at Ansel. She'd pledged no more dead bodies when she'd found the hope chest.

He took a long breath, then nodded. "We'll do our best, but don't get your hopes up. We don't know anyone involved, and Gaff has no authority in Merlot."

Damian, Brett, and Kelsey glanced at one another, evidently relieved. "That's all we can ask," Brett said. "Thank you."

Chapter 6

They didn't stay long after agreeing to help Damian and Kelsey. On the ride home, Jazzi reached across the gear console to squeeze Ansel's thigh. "That was nice of you. I know you're tired of thinking about murders."

He pressed his lips together, frustrated. "I know how hard it is on everyone involved when a brother's accused of murder."

And then she got it. She'd worked with Gaff to prove Ansel's brother, Bain, hadn't killed Donovan. They'd lived the stress Brett and Damian were suffering, only their case had been resolved much more quickly. She sighed. "I don't see how we can be of much help this time."

Ansel shrugged. "All we can do is try. But those brothers have been through enough."

Jazzi had to agree. Maybe that experience was why Brett was as aggressive as he was. She'd blamed it on his being so competitive in business, but if he'd stuck up for his brother over and over again, it had forced him to push back against unfair rumors. A lot of anger must be brewing deep inside him.

When they got home, they were both too keyed up to go right to sleep, so they sat up and watched TV longer than usual to relax. When the morning alarm rang, neither of them bounced out of bed, looking forward to a new day, but there was no choice. They had a fixer-upper to work on.

Jazzi called Gaff before leaving the house. He didn't pick up, so she left a message on his machine. It felt odd asking him for help with a case outside his jurisdiction and with something they weren't personally connected with. Once she thought about it, Gaff usually invited *her* to ride along with *him*. It had started when she and Jerod found her aunt's skeleton in a trunk in their house's attic. Gaff thought it would help her family members if she went with him to talk to them, that they might take the news better and remember more, especially because the murder had happened years ago.

When she'd finished her call, Ansel scooped up George, and she grabbed the cooler to load in their van. Ansel headed south on I-69 until he reached the turn for 114 to Merlot. Jazzi didn't pay attention to the scenery until houses grew farther apart and the terrain grew hilly. The leaves were beginning to change, splashing the trees with reds and golds. They passed a stand that sold pumpkins, and Ansel pointed in their direction.

"We should give a Halloween party this year."

Last October, they'd been getting ready for their wedding on November 10. They'd known each other much longer, of course, and lived together for a while before deciding to make it permanent. She glanced at her ring. It was exactly what she wanted—no big diamond to snag on things while she hammered and plastered. "Can you believe we've been married almost a year?"

"Best year of my life," he said.

She shook her head at him. He meant it. But he was right. "Mine too."

He grinned. "We'll make it a combination Halloween and anniversary party."

"I could go as the Bride of Frankenstein and you can be …"

"The monster?" He laughed. "I guess I'm tall enough." They'd almost reached the house when he said, "This would be the perfect time to finish the basement and add a playroom. Jerod and Walker's kids could bob for apples down there."

She turned to stare at him. "Why can't we just set that up on the back patio?"

"It might be too cold. You never know what the weather will be like by the end of October."

Right. "You just want a room in the basement."

His eyes twinkled. "That too."

It had just been a matter of time. They'd already agreed they could use the extra room when Ansel's family came to visit. "Ever since we helped Jerod build a playroom for his kids, you've wanted one, too."

He didn't even try to deny it. His voice turned to coaxing. "We could compromise. We wouldn't divide the big bedroom upstairs, but add daybeds down there. Then we'd only have one project to finish."

She liked compromises. She stopped to think about that. "Can we even get the room finished by Halloween? We're going to lose a weekend when we drive to Wisconsin for your brother's wedding." Bain had finally asked his Greta to marry him. They'd insisted they wanted a simple ceremony, just a justice of the peace and a family dinner. Nothing else.

"We don't want to be fussed over," Bain told them. "We only want it to be legal."

So she and Ansel were driving Radley and Elspeth to the family farm, then driving home the same day.

"We'll only lose one day," Ansel said. "I'll work on it in the evenings and weekends. The ceiling's high enough; all we need to do is frame out what we want and put up drywall."

That wasn't all that needed to be done, but it was the biggest part. "You're going to be working double-time for the rest of the month," she warned.

"I'm young. I can handle it. And you'll help me get started, won't you?"

"I suppose."

He smiled. "So, what do you say?"

"Why not? If your family comes for Christmas, we'll have somewhere to put them."

He slapped the steering wheel, happy. "It's going to be great. I was thinking we should put a pool table down there, too."

"Ah, the truth comes out." She smirked to let him know she was teasing. "If you plan on inviting Thane, Walker, and Radley over on Thursday nights, you're going to have to carry food in because I'm not cooking for you."

"We'll manage." He sounded awfully pleased with himself. When they reached the house and carted everything inside, he couldn't wait to tell Jerod their plans.

"A pool table? I loved playing pool when I was young and single." Jerod sounded as excited as Ansel. "We can disappear down there after the Sunday meal while the girls visit."

She could see it already. People were going to come more often and stay longer, but that was fine with her. As long as they helped with the cleanup.

They all headed up the ladders to the roof while George found the perfect spot of grass from which to supervise. They took shorter breaks than usual, and by the end of the day, they'd finished the shakes on the main part of the house. Tomorrow, they could start work on the wing. Its roof wasn't as high and might go faster. They stood back to admire the finished product. The shake shingles really did add a lot to the house's charm.

There was more traffic than usual on the drive home, and Ansel drummed his fingers on the steering wheel every time they had to slow down. "I want to measure everything in the basement tonight," he complained.

"I'll help you. We'll have plenty of time."

He was so impatient that when they got home and finished feeding the pets, Jazzi started to the basement stairs. "Let's measure for the room; then we can shower and start supper."

A good decision, because once he had all his numbers carefully written down, Gaff called.

"I'm not sure what I can do, but I have a friend who works on the Merlot force. I'll give him a call to see if he can tell me anything."

"Thanks, Gaff, we appreciate it."

"I'll get back to you when I hear something." And he hung up. Detectives didn't waste time with frivolous chatter.

She and Ansel took the rest of the evening at a leisurely pace, and by the time Ansel stretched out on his favorite sofa to watch TV, she pulled a kitchen chair over to Jessica's hope chest to start looking through it. Ansel was in such a good mood, he didn't even make a fuss.

Anticipation stirred when she dug through the contents and found Jessica's journals. The oldest one was written in round, childish handwriting. The first page read *Jessica Hodgkill, Sixth Grade*. Jazzi flipped through it. Jessica told about getting better grades on tests than Lila Mattock. *I don't try to get higher grades, but spelling and arithmetic are so easy. It makes Lila mad, though. She cut the safety chain on my bicycle and rolled it into the middle of Main Street. A nice driver stopped, though, and walked it to the sidewalk.*

Jazzi reread that. Did Lila have an emotional problem? She didn't think normal kids did things like that.

On the next page, Jessica wrote, *I told my dad what Lila did. He told me that no one likes a show-off. Mom said I wasn't showing off and not to listen to him, but Dad doesn't much like me. He wouldn't care if Lila ruined my bike.*

Jazzi reread that again, too. She'd never met Jessica, but she was beginning to feel sorry for her. "Listen to this!" she called to Ansel. She read him the two entries. "Sounds like both Lila and Jessica's dad had issues."

Ansel grimaced. "My dad wasn't very protective, but he'd have hunted Lila down for trying to ruin a bicycle. Property costs money, and he cared about that." He frowned, lost in thought. "There was a kid in some of my classes, though, who no one liked. He had more money than the rest of us and always rubbed it in how rich he was, looked down on the rest of us."

"I don't get that feeling about Jessica. She sounds more like the class brain."

"And she was good at sports? And pretty?" Ansel gave a quick nod. "Someone like Lila would despise her."

"But her dad?"

"Her dad sounds like a jerk. At least her mom tried to stick up for her."

It did sound that way. Ansel went back to his TV, and she went back to the journals. She read from grade six to grade ten, and Lila's pranks grew more vicious every year.

Her heart went out to Jessica when she wrote about her dream of becoming a photojournalist and traveling the globe, reporting on poverty and corruption. The girl was an idealist. Jazzi got the sense that she spent a lot of time alone. In ninth grade, she spent half a year talking about a boy she obviously had a crush on. Sadly, it wasn't mutual. She talked about spending summers on the swim team and swimming forty laps a day. And taking tennis lessons, and how much she loved them.

When Jazzi reached the journal for her sophomore year in high school, Jessica wrote, *I think my father hates me. He's always disliked me, but I've done it now. I beat Alwin's score on our IQ tests. My brother didn't care. He said the tests were stupid anyway. But Dad grounded me for a week and wouldn't speak to me.* The farther Jazzi read, the more Jessica worried that her father might disown her. But she added, *I cannot help but be myself. I refuse to play dumb just to please him. He can feed me bread and water, and I will not do any less than my best.*

Her entries disturbed Jazzi so much, she decided she'd read enough for the night. She put the journals away and closed the hope chest. Ansel could tell she was upset when she went to lay on the couch opposite his. Inky and Marmalade immediately jumped up to press against her when she stretched out.

"What is it?" Ansel asked. When she explained, he said, "Some fathers are like that. At our house, Bain was the favored son. Radley came in a distant second. I was better than Adda, because she was a girl. But we all knew that the dairy farm would go to Bain and Radley."

She realized Ansel understood exactly what Jessica had gone through. He'd lived it pretty much himself. She'd had a happy childhood. "I got lucky. My dad ended up with two girls. But it wouldn't have made a difference. My parents don't play favorites."

Ansel sat up to see her better, propping his elbows on his knees. "How did Jessica's father make all his money?"

"He owned a company, and everyone knew he was grooming Alwin to take over its reins when he retired."

"How much older was Alwin than his sister?"

"Two years."

"Did Alwin feel threatened by Jessica?"

Jazzi frowned, considering the question. "I don't think so. His dad's attention was always focused on him. He could do no wrong." That made her wonder. How much did Jessica's dad resent her? Would he push her off a balcony to clear the field for Alwin? She felt a little sick and pressed a hand to her stomach.

Ansel glanced at the clock. "It's getting late. We didn't get that much sleep last night. If we go up to bed, will you be able to shut off your brain and go to sleep?"

She stroked her cats' smooth fur and listened to them purr, then yawned.

Ansel smiled. "Come on, babe. I'll give you a hand." He walked to her couch and helped her to her feet. Once settled under the covers, he spooned his body against hers, laying his arm over her waist. She felt herself relax, wrapped in the safety of Ansel. And the next thing she knew, it was morning.

Chapter 7

Jazzi rushed around more than usual to get ready for work. Today was Thursday, which meant girls' night out. She was meeting her sister, Olivia, Walker's wife, Didi, and Radley's girlfriend, Elspeth, at the 07Pub for drinks and supper.

"Where are you and the guys meeting tonight?" she asked Ansel on their drive to Merlot.

"At our place. I'm carrying in wings, and they're going to help me start work on the basement."

She shook her head. "Let me guess. They're all excited about the pool table, too."

He laughed. "We're even thinking about an arcade game."

"You're building a man cave."

"The space is big enough for everything—games, a sitting area, and a kids' space. We might as well make it cover all our needs."

She hadn't known they had so many needs when they'd first talked about the project. But if it meant that someday down the road, she could ban the men *and* the kids to the basement, she was on board with the idea.

Jerod's truck was already in the driveway when they reached the fixer-upper. When he saw Jazzi carry in the slow cooker and Ansel tote the cooler in one hand while carrying George, he grinned. "What did you make for us?"

"All the fixings for taco salad and sweet tea."

He pressed a hand to his stomach. "This is going to be a good day. Franny asked me to stop to pick up fried chicken on the way home. She's hungry for it. She tried to cook it a few times, but it either turns out greasy or so dry, I have to drink a gallon of water to swallow it."

"It's a lot of work," Jazzi said. "I'd rather buy it."

"But yours is better," Ansel told her. "I'll help the next time you make it."

That wouldn't be anytime soon. She plugged in the slow cooker, and they headed outside. The weather was in the low seventies with a soft breeze—a perfect day for roofing. They hauled shingles up the ladder and got started.

They usually didn't talk much while they worked, but Jerod said, "Gunther brought home his first book from the school library last night. And he can read it. My boy's a genius."

Jazzi laughed. Jerod thought everything his kids did was pretty wonderful. "I take it he likes first grade."

Jerod couldn't keep the pride out of his voice. "He loves his teacher, and Lizzie loves all-day preschool. It's made life really nice for Franny. She can spend more time with Pete and still get some furniture refinished while he takes naps. She's been working on the antique chest of drawers from Jessica's bedroom. You should see it. It's gorgeous."

The man was crazy about his family. She and Ansel had started having Gunther and Lizzie spend the night at their house once in a while, and she had to admit, kids were a lot of fun.

Chitchat stopped, and they settled into work, trying hard to get the front half of the roof done before they left. They were installing the next-to-the-last row of shingles when a red convertible pulled into the driveway. A tall, thin woman with straight red hair that fell to her shoulders got out of the car and stalked toward them.

"Go see what she wants," Jerod said. "We'll keep working. If you stall her long enough, we can finish up."

Jazzi thought about pointing out that she'd never been named the official liaison person for their crew, but it would be pointless. Even if Jerod stopped working to talk to the woman, he'd only yell down, *We're busy right now. Go away.*

She made her way down the ladder. The woman came too close, invading her personal space, before putting her hands on her hips.

"Is it true that no one ever touched Jessica's room, and the three of you threw away all of her things?"

Jazzi raised an eyebrow. "Who wants to know?"

The girl flipped her hair. "I'm Lila Mattock. I was close friends with Jessica. I loaned her a few of my journals before she died, and I'd like to have them back."

Jazzi stared. Lila Mattock. A close friend? Hardly. "Sorry. We gave most of Jessica's things away and burned the rest. I have Jessica's journals at home, and I'm reading through them, but I didn't find any of yours."

Lila's eyes narrowed. "You're reading them?"

"I'm up to her sophomore year."

"What right did you have to do that?"

"What right do you have, calling yourself a friend?" Jazzi waved her argument away before she could make it. "We bought the house and its contents. I called Jessica's mother and she didn't want them. When I learned that Jessica was pushed off the house's balcony, I was curious."

"Nosy, you mean." Lila squared her shoulders. "Jessica was the world's biggest liar, you know. She hated me and did terrible things to make me look bad in high school."

"I've heard you hated each other, that it was mutual. Were you at the graduation party when she died?"

Lila's lips turned down. She whirled on her heel. "I don't have to talk to you. I don't like gossip, so if you say one bad thing about me, I'll sue. Just think about that."

Jazzi didn't like to be threatened. "I'm petrified."

Lila slammed her car door, then sent Jazzi a final glare before screeching out of the drive.

Jerod applauded from his perch on the roof. "Good job, cuz! I'm glad I never met that girl in high school."

"She hasn't improved with age, has she?" Ansel finished the last of the shingles, and the guys climbed down and headed into the house. They'd finished half the roof with twenty minutes to spare.

"Let's call it," Jerod said.

Music to her ears. It was Thursday. She could take a little more time getting ready to go out. They locked the house and drove away.

While Jazzi showered and got ready, Ansel took her pickup to the lumber yard and came home with all the materials he needed for framing. There was no reason for him to clean up when he was going to work in the basement and get dirty again.

He returned home when she was walking out the door to meet her friends. He stopped to look her up and down. "You look great in dresses and heels. Flash your wedding ring a lot, so everyone knows you're taken."

She rolled her eyes. If she were any more married, she'd need a big red M tattooed on her forehead. The pets looked surprised when she walked toward the van and Ansel stayed home on a Thursday night. The dog and cats knew the house's usual rhythms, and they knew something had changed.

When Jazzi parked behind the 07Pub and entered through its back door, she saw Elspeth waiting at a table. The four of them used to cram into a booth, but Didi was eight months pregnant with Walker's baby, so a booth was too crowded these days.

Jazzi smiled and slid onto the chair next to hers. "Hi. You got here early."

"I was hoping I'd get to talk to you before all the gossip starts." Elspeth smiled. She loved gossip as much as the rest of them.

"What's up?"

"I'm asking for a favor." Elspeth hesitated. She didn't feel comfortable with this, Jazzi could tell. She took a deep breath and forged on. "The lease for my apartment is up soon, and Radley's asked me to move in with him."

"I'm so happy for you!" Ansel's brother had found the perfect girl for him. They made such a sweet couple. She and Ansel got a kick out of watching them together.

Elspeth's smile lit up her face. "Thanks."

"His apartment's a lot smaller than yours. You realize how crowded you're going to be, right?"

Elspeth nodded. "But he only has four more months on his lease, too. And then we want to find a house together."

"Even better!" Jazzi would have clapped her hands, but people would stare.

A blush crept up Elspeth's cheeks to her hairline. "The thing is, I have a lot more stuff than I thought I did. We could use help moving this Saturday. We were wondering…"

"We'd love to help," Jazzi interrupted.

"Thank you!" Elspeth squirmed. "And since you and Ansel flip houses, we thought maybe we could talk you into looking at any we like to see if they're okay."

"No problem." The waitress came, and they ordered their drinks. Just then, Olivia and Didi walked in. Olivia laughed when Didi had to push her chair farther from the table to make room for her baby bump.

Once everyone had settled and the waitress left, Elspeth reached for a plastic bag near her chair. "I made you all something." She passed out aprons with frilly ruffles. Jazzi loved hers. Elspeth handed her another one—cobalt blue and plain. "For Ansel, because he likes to cook, too."

Didi's apron had extra-long strings, and she grinned. "It might fit. I hope I don't get much bigger by my due date."

The baby was due in the middle of December, and Jazzi was throwing her a shower the second Sunday in November. When it was closer to her friend Leesa's due date, she was throwing a baby shower for her, too. It seemed like all of a sudden, their world was going to be filled with diapers and bottles. Jazzi wondered if Leesa and Brett could go out to meet them at restaurants on the occasional Friday like they did now, or if that would change with a baby.

Jazzi smiled when Didi rested a hand on the top of her stomach. Leesa rubbed her stomach a lot these days, too. "My friend Leesa's going to have a little girl, and she's as happy about it as you are."

"Walker's so excited, he's going to need someone to hold his hand when I go into labor. River's glad I'm having a girl, too."

"He won't have to share his Tonka trucks," Olivia teased. River was six, the same age as Jerod's Gunther. The two boys loved seeing each other on Sundays, and Lizzie was happy to tag along after them.

The waitress came with their drinks, and the talk turned to gossip. Jazzi told them about the house they were working on, and about finding Jessica's hope chest. Olivia went on about a new hair product she'd started using at the salon.

"Does Mom like it, too?" Jazzi asked. Olivia worked with her mother at her salon, and Mom had finally made her a partner. She'd worried that Jazzi would feel left out, but she waved that concern away. "I have no interest in hair or manicures. You two do your thing."

The next hour and a half flew by, and soon, Jazzi was on her way home again. Tonight had been more fun than usual. When she walked into the house, all the other guys were gone, and Ansel grabbed her hand to pull her into the basement.

"What do you think?"

She blinked. "You need to spend more Thursdays at home." The entire frame was up. But she should have guessed that. When you had four big men going full steam at a job, a lot got done.

"Do you like it?" Her Viking sounded nervous.

"I love it. It's going to be perfect."

His smile dazzled, but then, everything about him did. Who knew a playroom would make him so happy? And then she remembered how few extras he had growing up. Everything on the dairy farm revolved around work. But he was making his own little piece of heaven here. They'd refinished the house to make it exactly what they wanted. And then he'd dug his pond. And now, the basement. She could only think of one more thing to make his happiness complete. And she loved making Ansel happy. Frowning, she scanned the size of the room.

"What is it?" The nerves were back.

"I don't think a regular TV is going to look right down here. I think we're going to have to go for something really big."

He picked her off her feet and whirled her in a circle. The cats ran beneath her, ready to play a new game. George lifted his head, then dropped it back on his doggy bed. He'd had enough excitement for one day.

When Ansel finally calmed down, they went upstairs to the kitchen, grabbed drinks, and sank onto their favorite couches in the living room. "Tell me about your night," he said.

"We volunteered to help Elspeth move her things into Radley's apartment on Saturday."

"Good for them!"

"And they're going to start looking for a house to fix up. They want us to look it over when they find one."

"We can do that."

She tried to look alluring. "It's been a nice night. I think we should end it on a high note."

His blue eyes sparkled. "I can do that, too." He walked to her couch to scoop her up. As he carried her up the stairs, George started to follow him, but he said, "Later."

The dog and cats settled at the base of the steps. They knew the routine.

Chapter 8

They finished the roof on Friday with enough time left over to start making a list of the projects they wanted to do inside the house, and the order in which they wanted to do them. They decided to finish the entire first floor before moving upstairs.

"That way, if anyone's interested in it and wants to see it, the first floor will look good," Jerod said.

Jazzi nodded in agreement. "But I'd like to wait to gut the kitchen until we refinish the wood floors and paint down here. That way, I can use the refrigerator and sink while we work."

The kitchen had a worn linoleum floor and the wood under it was in such bad shape, they couldn't save it. They planned on installing old-fashioned white ceramic tiles with cobalt-blue diamonds at each corner. They'd ordered white cabinets and butcher-block countertops and stainless-steel appliances. The island would have a midnight-blue base and a granite top.

"All of the rooms are big enough as is," Ansel said.

The kitchen was twenty by twenty, more than enough space for an eating area, and the dining room was a good size, too. The living room was twenty by thirty with a massive fireplace.

"I'd like to make the study into a library/reading room/office. It's doable, because it's twelve by sixteen. I brought a picture." He dug it out of his back jeans pocket.

Ansel smoothed out the folded paper for them to study. Three walls were lined with dark, wooden bookcases. A green-velvet love seat, a huge ottoman, and two easy chairs were arranged in its center, with a desk at the far end.

Jerod was reaching for it to see it better when Jazzi's cell phone buzzed. Gaff.

"Hello?"

Gaff, as usual, skipped the small talk. "Another girl died around the same time Jessica did, still in high school, too."

"Do you think the deaths are connected? Maybe Jessica's murder was just a random victim instead of a personal vendetta. Maybe no one killed her because of some grudge."

"Oh, Jessica's death was personal. There's more…" He stopped, and Jazzi heard a voice in the background. 'I have to go. I'll call you some other time."

She wanted to hear the whole story. She hurried to say, "Why don't you and Ann come for supper tonight? You can tell us then."

There was a slight pause. His voice muffled, he said, "Give me a minute and I'll be there." Then, he was back. "What are you cooking?"

She knew how to bribe Gaff. "Steaks. Ansel's grilling them." She didn't have any, but they'd stop to buy some on the way home.

"We'll be there. Ann was going to heat up leftovers. Your offer sounds better."

"We'll see you at six."

"Gotta go." Gaff clicked off, and she told the guys what she'd learned.

Jerod shook his head. "You're not thinking there was a serial killer, are you? They don't push girls off balconies. Besides, everyone would have noticed him."

"Unless one of the high school kids at the party *was* a serial killer," Jazzi said.

He looked skeptical. So did Ansel. But then Jerod passed Ansel's magazine picture back to him, returning their attention to work. "I like that. It fits the time period of the house's style. Let's do it. We can spend a little extra this time to play up what a great place this is."

They quickly mapped out the rest of their plans. Once they finished the downstairs, they'd move upstairs to the bedrooms, three baths, and the hallway leading to the balcony. They'd spend the majority of their time removing wallpaper. With everything decided, they packed up to head home.

"If you guys want to sleep in a little and come late Monday morning, it's fine with me," Jerod told them on their way out. He gestured to Ansel. "But I think you told your brother to plan his wedding for Sunday just so Jazzi didn't have to bother with the family meal."

It was the first one she'd canceled in years, but after their friends and family met Ansel's dad at their wedding, they knew how difficult Dalmar could be. If he could make something inconvenient, he would. Bain hadn't even told them about the wedding until a month ago. The whole thing was a rushed affair.

Ansel grimaced and shook his head. "Not hardly. It's going to be a five-hour drive to Wisconsin to watch Bain and Greta say I do before heading to a restaurant for a celebration meal, and then getting in the pickup for a five-hour drive home."

"Why the rush?" Jerod stopped at his truck to hear the answer. "Why not take the time to plan something special?"

"Because Bain probably didn't want to hear Dad complain about him getting married and spending money any longer than he had to. This way, it will be a done deal, and Dad will just have to make the best of it."

"Your dad's a pain," Jerod told him.

Ansel huffed his annoyance. "You're preaching to the choir. Just be glad you didn't have to live with him."

"Well, remember, if you're late on Monday, I won't storm to your house to knock on your door."

"Thanks." Ansel laid George on the back seat while Jazzi loaded their cooler and slow cooker. Then they headed to the butcher shop on West Jefferson and Jazzi chose four thick rib eyes for him to grill. Gaff's favorite was rib eye. At Fresh Market, they bought everything to make a chopped salad with blue cheese vinaigrette. Jazzi was putting romaine in the cart when she turned to look for Ansel. He'd disappeared. She found him in front of the dessert glass at the back of the store.

She should have known, but she didn't have time to make anything, so she said, "Pick one."

They went home with a fruit tart with a cream cheese filling.

The cats came to greet them at the kitchen door before padding to their food bowl. George joined them. Ansel fed the pets while Jazzi zipped upstairs to shower and change. Then he took his turn while she seasoned the steaks and left them out to reach room temperature. They wouldn't have a full hour, but it would be close enough. She was chopping ingredients for the salad when Ansel came to help. It would have enough different vegetables; it just took some time to make.

By the time Gaff and Ann gave a quick knock and entered the kitchen, Ansel had the steaks on the grill and Jazzi had set the table. She brought Gaff a beer and Ann a glass of wine. She'd already poured one for herself, and Ansel rarely manned the grill without a Michelob.

They made small talk over their steaks and salads, but once Ansel sliced and served the dessert, Gaff glanced at his wife.

"I know," Ann said with a smile. "Time to talk business. Let's hear about this new case."

That was what Jazzi liked about Gaff's Ann. Five three and thirty pounds overweight, with gray hair and laugh lines, she radiated warmth and vitality. And she understood what went with marrying a cop. How Gaff could have found a more perfect partner, she didn't know.

Gaff swallowed a bite of tart and got started. "As I told you, another girl was killed in the same year Jessica died, so I'm guessing the murders are related. So did my friend who helped with the investigations, but he couldn't prove anything."

Jazzi pinched her lips together. Two girls were dead and no one had ever been charged. "You said the second girl was in high school, too?"

Gaff nodded. "She was a cheerleader for a basketball team that Merlot High played that year—Wendy Roeback. It was an out-of-town game, and no one found her body until the bus for Merlot's team had already left. No one saw anything."

"Were the basketball players and coaches the only people from Merlot there that night?" Could they get that lucky and narrow down the suspects?

Gaff shook his head. "Two buses of fans and a bunch of parents and relatives drove to see the game."

Jazzi pursed her lips. "Did Ruth Goggins watch RJ every time he played?"

He grinned, obviously expecting the question. "She attended every school function he was in. Neighbor Ruth made quite an impression on you, didn't she?"

Jazzi grimaced in reply. "Was Jessica there?"

"No, she went to at-home games but didn't always drive out of town to see Merlot play. Alwin's dad was there, though. He supported everything Alwin did."

"He would." Jazzi made a face.

"The cops looked into everything," Gaff said. "The only tips they got were from RJ's aunt. She kept reporting fake information about Damian Dunlap. They mostly considered her a crank."

Too bad people in town didn't take her that way. She was a major reason Damian had had to move away.

"The killer had to be a guy," Ansel said. "No jealous girlfriend would kill *two* girls she thought were competition."

"Don't bet on it. But it's unlikely." Gaff pushed away his empty plate and reached for the coffeepot. He poured a second cup for himself and for Ann. "One more interesting thing," he said. "The girl who died had long blond hair, like Jessica's and was tall and willowy, also like she was."

A chill ran down Jazzi's spine. "That's what serial killers do, isn't it? They pick a certain look or type."

Ansel frowned. "Either that, or someone wanted to kill Jessica for a long time and couldn't, so he killed a surrogate instead."

"Where did Wendy Roeback die?" Jazzi asked. "In the high school?"

"Outside. She'd pulled on a heavy coat and snuck out behind the building for a cigarette break."

"Alone?" Jazzi shook her head. But why was she surprised? Kids did all kinds of things at that age. If she remembered right, Jerod had been known to sneak a puff or two between classes. Thankfully, he gave up smoking pretty fast.

"Was the lighting good behind the building?" Ansel asked.

Jazzi looked at him, surprised. "You think someone might have killed her thinking she was Jessica?"

He nodded. "If she had the same build and hair color..."

"She was in the shadows," Gaff said. "That's why it took a while before anyone found her."

"Poor girl." It was bad enough that she died, but to die for no reason? That made it even worse. "How did she die?"

Gaff sent an apologetic glance to Ann. "Someone picked up a heavy stone that kids used to prop open the door and bashed her in the back of the head."

Ansel blinked, surprised. "Either a man or a woman would be strong enough to do that, wouldn't they?"

"All they'd need is a good swing before they connected," Gaff said.

Ansel nodded. "I bet someone was really surprised when they saw Jessica alive and well the next day."

Chapter 9

On Saturday morning, Ansel carried George to Jazzi's pickup and put him on the seat in the back cab. Then he and Jazzi drove to Elspeth's apartment. Radley was already there, helping Elspeth pack up a few last-minute things.

Elspeth had her long, light-brown hair pulled back in a knot to keep it out of her face. She wasn't exactly pretty, but her gray, sparkling eyes and sweet smile made her attractive. As usual, she wore a loose-fitting top and baggy jeans. She never showed off her figure. Radley, tall and fair like everyone in his family, had fallen for her the minute he met her.

Neat piles of boxes were lined up by the door. Elspeth was nothing if not organized.

"Looks like you're ready." Ansel reached for a box. "I'll start loading these."

"The heavy things are on this side," Elspeth said, "so you can place them on the bottom if you need to. And the lighter boxes are over here."

A smart plan. Jazzi helped Ansel carry things to the pickup, and Radley and Elspeth carried more boxes to his work van. Once everything was loaded, Elspeth went back to the apartment for one last look-through. She walked from room to room while they waited and finally returned with a sigh. "It looks so different when it's empty."

Jazzi knew the feeling. She'd loved her first-floor apartment in West Central before she and Jerod bought Cal's house to renovate. She could hardly bear the thought of someone moving in after her who didn't care about the place. So she was overjoyed when Reuben and Isabelle bought the old Victorian to turn it back into a single-family home. Reuben was a decorator, so they'd restored it into the beautiful home it once was. Elspeth obviously had fond memories in this place, too.

"Do you have to paint the walls and make them white again?" Ansel asked.

She shook her head. "There's already a renter who wants it. He likes the colors I chose, so the landlord said I didn't need to worry about painting."

Good news. With one last look, Elspeth went to the door and locked up behind her for the last time. Then she dropped the key in the landlord's mail slot on the first floor. She rode with Radley to his apartment, and Jazzi and Ansel followed them. Once there, they carried everything to the third floor. Radley's not-so-gently used furniture was gone to make room for Elspeth's, which was in much better shape. Still, the apartment was cramped.

Elspeth nodded to the beat-up coffee table. "We're keeping that to remind us of Donovan. In time, we're going to ask Franny to refinish it."

It wasn't the most attractive table Jazzi had ever seen, but she understood the sentiment. Elspeth had been serious about Donovan before he died, and Donovan had been Radley's supervisor at work and a good friend. When he was shot, they'd both lost someone they cared about.

Ansel scowled at it but wisely didn't comment. Radley grinned at him. "We'll make it look better eventually." Then he went to the refrigerator and took out two beers. "When are you picking us up tomorrow morning? Bain's wedding's in the early afternoon."

"Seven a.m.," Elspeth told him. "Ansel told you that last Sunday at the family meal."

"Oh, right." Since Radley met Elspeth, he depended on her to keep him on track.

"Are we going out for pizza after the justice of the peace makes them legal?" Radley asked.

"Jazzi and I reserved a room at the Vine and Sea for a wedding supper," Ansel said. He'd volunteered to have the reception at their house, but Dalmar had refused to pay someone to milk the dairy herd while he was gone, so Bain had decided to have the wedding at the ranch-style house he and Radley had once shared and then go to a nice restaurant afterward. Dalmar even grumbled about that, so Ansel paid for the room and meal as Bain's wedding present.

Radley pinched his lips together. "The Vine and Sea is supposed to serve decent food. I never went there; too pricey. I hope it's as good as Jazzi's cooking."

Ansel rolled his eyes. "It's Bain's wedding. We're trying to help him celebrate. Bain and Greta chose salmon, so you shouldn't suffer too much. Adda and Henry paid for the wedding cake. Dad had a fit when Bain was going to order one. Said the money was…"

Radley finished for him. "…better used on the farm. Greta must be a good woman or she'd have told Bain to stuff Dad in the manure pile and be done with him."

The two brothers laughed. Jazzi pictured Dalmar buried in cow dung so that only his head stuck out. It was an appealing fantasy.

Ansel caught her expression and grinned. "We're only staying for the meal and then driving home. You won't have to be around Dad very long."

Three minutes was too long, but he was Ansel's father, so she'd try to bite her tongue and behave.

Elspeth glanced at Radley, alarmed. "You said your father was a hard man, but you're starting to scare me. Is he going to like me?"

"Not a chance. He's still not happy I stayed in River Bluffs and didn't return to the farm to help with the milking. He tolerates Jazzi because he kicked Ansel out of the house when he graduated from high school, and he knows it's his own fault Ansel doesn't want anything to do with him."

Elspeth turned to Jazzi. "Is he rude to you?"

"He's rude to everybody, even his wife. Don't worry about him. He's a lost cause."

Radley put his arm around Elspeth's shoulders. "Stay close to me and we'll get through this thing in good shape."

The poor girl looked doubtful, so Jazzi changed the subject. "Can we help you guys with anything else? Do you need us to move any furniture?"

"We can take it from here," Radley said, "and thanks for everything."

They took off and headed to the store for their weekly grocery shopping. It didn't take long because they weren't cooking for anyone the next day. Then they drove home to unload everything they'd bought.

George pouted when they put the groceries away before tearing off little pieces of the deli ham they'd bought, but when they made sandwiches for lunch, he came to the kitchen island to beg. So did the cats. The house was clean enough that Jazzi helped Ansel outside all afternoon, raking leaves and cleaning the yard while George watched from the back patio.

She put a chicken in the oven to roast for supper while they went upstairs to shower and change into their pajamas. A box of Stove Top and a bag of salad later made for a quick and easy meal. Ansel kept slipping the pets pieces of chicken while they ate, but there were still enough leftovers for sandwiches if her Norseman was starving when they got home late tomorrow night.

After that, they relaxed in front of the TV, ready to call it an early night. They'd have to get up before the sun the next morning to get ready for their trip and Bain's wedding. Ansel was taking George with him, but the cats would be left on their own for the entire day. She shouldn't have bought a bouquet of flowers at the store. When they got back, Inky would probably have chewed off the blooms from every stem to let her know how unhappy he was. She loved the furry brat, but he knew how to express his opinions.

The pug and her cats were happy when she and Ansel headed upstairs at ten, but when the alarm rang at six, Inky opened one yellow eye to glare at her. Yup, she was coming home to dead flowers.

Chapter 10

There was no small talk all the way to Chicago. Everyone was still half asleep. Jazzi and Ansel usually slept in on Sundays, but getting an early start made traveling easier. Traffic was light, and making the exits to Wisconsin was a breeze.

Once they were on their way to the green hills of their farm, Radley gazed out the window and sighed. "It's hard to beat how beautiful Wisconsin is. River Bluffs felt so flat when I first saw it."

"And now?" Jazzi asked.

"It's still flat, but once you get farther out in the country, the land rolls more. And I like everything you can do there. So many restaurants and shops. We hardly ever left the farm except to drive half an hour to town once or twice a month, and that was nothing to brag about."

Ansel had driven his brother to see the house they were working on, he was so proud of it. Radley had been suitably impressed, but he'd commented that Merlot was no bigger than their farm's hometown.

Jazzi's parents had taken a family trip every summer, visiting both coasts and a lot of places in between, but there was no place she'd rather call home than River Bluffs.

"You were never tempted to move away?" Radley asked.

She shook her head. "I'd miss my family."

"Me too," Elspeth said. "I can't imagine moving so far away I'd rarely get to see them."

"It's too easy to lose touch." Jazzi turned in her seat to see Radley and Elspeth better. George lay between them, his head on Radley's lap. "That's why I invite everyone to the Sunday meal, so that we stay close."

Radley snorted. "Your families are nice. They're fun to be with. Ansel and I left to get away from ours."

"I would have run from Dalmar, too." That made her think about Jessica. "The girl whose journals I'm reading wanted to be a photojournalist and travel the world. Probably to get away from her father. He treated her worse than your dad treated you guys."

"What did he do to her?" Radley tsked. "If he was worse than our dad, I have to feel for her."

"He punished her every time she did anything well. He didn't want her to show up her older brother."

Radley chuckled. "Well, that would have left me out. I didn't bother to excel at much."

Elspeth turned to him. "You're so smart. You weren't a good student?"

"What do you consider good? Passing?" He smirked. "High grades would have involved doing homework. That never happened. I was good at shop class, though."

Jazzi looked at Ansel. He shrugged. "I got Bs and Cs. We were so tired after working on the farm after school, the last thing I cared about was getting As. You?"

"Olivia and I both got As and Bs. Mom wasn't strict about it, but Dad was. He was in college when he met Mom. He wanted us to keep our options open, so we could go if we wanted to."

Ansel tilted his head, thinking. "I can see that. Your dad's a smart businessman. He has to be to run successful hardware stores."

Jazzi bit her bottom lip, remembering. "He was a little disappointed that I was more interested in the tools he sold than getting a degree, but college isn't for everyone."

"Did Jessica's dad expect her to go to college?" Elspeth asked.

"Oh, yeah. It was a status thing. He just didn't want her to get better grades than Alwin."

Elspeth's voice had an edge to it. "Then he was a stupid man."

"No argument there," Jazzi agreed.

Two hours later, they pulled into the drive of Bain's ranch house. They'd never met Greta, and Jazzi was curious about her. The woman who opened the door to greet them was an inch shorter than she was, and thin to the point of being skinny. She had drab brown hair and a ruddy complexion, but a beautiful smile.

"I finally get to meet all of you!" She threw open her arms for a group hug, and they all circled her, putting their arms around her.

Bain pushed outside to be part of it. When they separated and he led them into the house's living room, Radley looked around, eyes wide.

"It looks homey in here." He couldn't hide his surprise.

Bain nodded toward Greta. "All her doing. She has a way of making everything nice." He motioned for them to take seats. "Hon, let me introduce you."

Ansel's eyebrows rose, and Jazzi exchanged a quick glance with him. She never thought she'd hear the word "hon" roll off Bain's tongue.

Bain started with Radley. "Radley's four years younger than I am, and this must be his new girlfriend, Elspeth." He pointed to Ansel. "Ansel's the baby of the family, only twenty-six now, and that's his wife, Jazzi."

He'd just finished when a gray cat with no tail streaked into the room from the kitchen and leaped on his lap. Bain reached out to pet him.

Jazzi smiled. "Stubs! He's doing all right." Bain, a suspect in Donovan's murder, had adopted the stray while he stayed at their house. He'd started feeding it by the side of their garage. They'd taken the cat inside after a coyote bit off his tail.

Greta gave him an indulgent look. "He loves that cat." Then she beamed a welcome to them. "I've heard so much about all of you. Bain wants to travel to River Bluffs to show me where you live when the weather gets cooler and the farm work slows down."

"We'd love to have you as guests." Ansel included his brother in the invitation. "We're building a family room in our basement, so there'll be plenty of space for everyone."

Bain surprised them by saying, "Let's hope Dad doesn't want to come."

What an about-face! At their wedding, Bain was just as unhappy as Dalmar about having to make the trip for her and Ansel's marriage ceremony. He wouldn't have come at all if Ansel's mom hadn't threatened to drive to River Bluffs with Radley. Back then, in Bain's mind, Dalmar could do no wrong.

A sympathetic smile tugged at Greta's lips. "Dalmar isn't any happier about our wedding than yours, and he won't even miss one milking. But the man's always had to work hard. The only thing he focuses on is the farm." She didn't sound one bit bothered by that. Jazzi got the feeling that she'd met a lot of irascible people with her job caring for people in their homes. She seemed to take them in stride.

Radley glanced at his watch. "Will Mom and Dad be here soon? Should we get changed for your ceremony?"

"Might as well," Bain told them. "Everyone will be here in half an hour. Dad will probably come a little late, just to make us wait."

The men grabbed suitcases and each couple disappeared into a different bedroom. Ten minutes later, they emerged, dressed for the wedding. Jazzi wore a midcalf, wraparound, rust-colored dress, and Elspeth had chosen a long, navy-blue skirt and a matching blouse. The guys wore black dress slacks and white shirts. Greta had changed, too, into an ivory dress that skimmed her knees, and Bain was dressed like his brothers—in black slacks and a white shirt. Appropriate for the occasion.

A few minutes later, Adda and her husband, Henry, arrived. Ansel was partial to his sister, and his eyes lit up at the sight of her. She'd chosen a midcalf, periwinkle-blue dress that matched her eyes, and Henry had gotten the memo for black and white. They were all visiting and catching up with one another when the justice of the peace arrived. And just as Bain had predicted, ten minutes later, Dalmar led Britt into the room. Their mother looked lovely in a below-the-knee, rose dress. Dalmar wore work jeans and a flannel shirt.

Jazzi had to bite her bottom lip to keep from commenting, but Greta's smile blossomed as she said, "We're so glad you're here. We can start now."

The ceremony took less than ten minutes; then Bain paid the man and he left. Ansel grinned and went to their pickup to bring in two bottles of champagne they'd kept cold in their cooler. He and Radley popped the corks, and Bain returned with plastic water glasses. Ansel poured the bubbly, then lifted his glass in a toast. "Congratulations!"

Greta laughed and took a sip, then gave Bain a surprise smack on the lips. He looked delighted and kissed her back.

Dalmar grumbled, "Britt didn't make lunch. Are we going out to eat?"

Britt's cheeks reddened with embarrassment, but Greta's laugh tinkled again. "Ansel and Jazzi are providing us with a wedding feast. Does everyone know how to get to the Vine and Sea? We can lead the way. Dalmar and Britt, you can ride with us if you want to."

"We'll drive them," Henry volunteered. "This is your big day. Enjoy it."

They filed out to their cars and followed Bain to the restaurant. When the hostess led them to the private room, Greta blinked in surprise and tears filled her eyes. "It's beautiful."

Adda clapped her hands, happy. "Henry and I decorated it this morning. We left your present from us and Radley on your place at the table."

Bain went and handed Greta the envelope to open. She sucked in her breath. "A gift card for a two-night stay in the Concourse Hotel in Madison."

Dalmar frowned. "I can't milk the herd alone for three days."

Bain waved him off. "We'll figure something out. Thanks to all of you. You've made our wedding better than we dreamed it could be."

"Then let's eat!" Radley found a seat at the table. A waiter came with more champagne, and then the salads were served. Dalmar silently ate while everyone else laughed and talked, but Jazzi noticed that he cleaned every morsel from his plate.

Greta put a hand to her throat and blinked back tears again when the waiter carried in the wedding cake. Jazzi had learned that Greta collected baskets, so the sides of the cake were decorated in a basket weave pattern, with the top covered with frosting flowers.

The cake didn't just look pretty. It was delicious, and Ansel ate three pieces before he was satisfied. The bottom layer was still intact, and Bain gladly boxed it up to take home. When the meal was over, Ansel discreetly left the room to pay for everything, including a nice tip. Then everyone got ready to load into their vehicles to return home. Henry and Adda drove her parents back to the farm, and Ansel, Jazzi, Radley, and Elspeth got into Jazzi's pickup to drive back to River Bluffs.

"First, we have to stop at your place to pick up George," Ansel told Bain. "And maybe we'll change back into our comfortable clothes for the ride home."

"Good, we'll get to see you a little bit more." Greta sounded happy about that. Jazzi sure liked Bain's new wife.

They didn't stay long, because it was a long drive home, and when they got up to leave, Bain grabbed both of his brothers for rough hugs. "Thanks for making this day so special."

"Keep in touch," Ansel told him. "Remember, we have extra room if you want to come to visit."

Bain glanced at Jazzi. "Could you stand seeing me again?"

"You're always welcome." And this time, she meant it. Bain was a changed man since he met his Greta.

The drive home was filled with talk about the wedding and how much Bain had changed. It was after ten when they dropped off Radley and Elspeth, and close to eleven by the time they got home. The cats ran to greet them, Inky meowing loudly and stalking to his food dish. They fed and petted the pets, then dragged themselves up the stairs to bed. Even though Jerod had told them he didn't mind if they came to work late, they wanted to put in a full day. They could crash after that.

As Jazzi drifted to sleep, she pictured Jessica in a long, periwinkle-blue wedding dress. Ansel's sister, Adda, with her silky, blond hair and gorgeous blue eyes, reminded Jazzi of the young girl. Probably because of their similar coloring. But thinking of Jessica made her sad. There was no college for her, no career, no marriage. Someone had stolen that from her.

Chapter 11

Monday morning came too early. While Jazzi packed sandwiches for their lunch at work, she noticed the blinking light on their message machine. Not many people called their home phone—mostly clients—so she listened to it. Gaff informed them that he planned on dropping in to see them when they got home from Merlot, if that worked for them. He had more information about Jessica's case.

Jazzi gave him a quick call and left a message on his phone that they'd be home and hopefully awake that night if he didn't wait too long. Then she packed food and chips in the cooler, Ansel grabbed George, and they drove to their fixer-upper.

When they got there, Jerod was lugging two more rented sanders into the house. They already had one of their own.

"A brilliant idea." Jazzi smiled at him. "We each have a sander, so we should be able to sand every floor before lunch. Then, after we eat, we can stain them and let them dry overnight." The floors were all good except in the kitchen. They had to put a new one in there, but that meant they could walk on it today. "How was your weekend, cuz?"

"We packed up the kids and drove to Salamonie Dam. On the way, I stopped in Huntington to grab food for a picnic. After we ate, I carried Pete in a baby backpack on one of the trails. He liked being outdoors. So did Gunther and Lizzie. We let them wade at the beach. It was all fun, but not the same as coming to your place. The kids like seeing River there. Plus, the food's a whole lot better."

He sounded so grumpy, Jazzi grinned. "Glad you missed us. Bain and Greta had a nice wedding, though."

"Good, but next time, I might pack a picnic and bring the kids to your place and let them play in your pond when you're gone."

She shrugged. It was a little cold for that, but they could wade out a long way. The drop-off was so gradual, the water was shallow for quite a while. "Feel free. Eat in the gazebo if you want to."

Ansel grabbed a sander and headed to the dining room. "Our basement should be done by the time the weather's bad. Then they can play down there."

"Only if you're home."

Jazzi and Ansel exchanged a glance. Her cousin's Sunday must have been a bummer. He was nuts about his wife and kids and usually enjoyed spending time with them. "I take it everyone fussed more than usual," she guessed.

Jerod shook his head. "I should just have stayed home. The kids' legs got tired halfway through the trail. Pete got cranky and wouldn't take a nap. Franny started snapping at everyone." He stalked to the living room to sand, and Jazzi carted her machine upstairs to start on the bedrooms. She and Ansel were tired today, but at least they'd had a good time the day before.

She had three rooms sanded by lunchtime. The floors were in such good shape, they didn't need much. When she walked into the kitchen, though, and saw George in his doggy bed, sound asleep, she had to shake her head. The trip yesterday had worn him out. Still, when she opened the cooler, the pug perked up his head and trotted to the worktable to beg for scraps.

"Did you get your rooms done?" she asked the guys as she finished the first half of her ham and cheese sandwich.

They both nodded. "And you?" Jerod asked.

"One more bedroom to go."

Ansel reached for a second sandwich and Jerod grabbed more chips. "Jerod and I will come up with you after lunch and clean the floors that are done. Then we can start staining them and shut the doors to let them dry. We thought we could work from the upstairs down, then stain the study, then the dining room and living room, so we end up in the kitchen. That way, we can finish all the staining in one day."

She nodded. A good plan. When they finished eating, they trudged upstairs and George returned to his nap. With all three of them working together, they finished it all before five thirty. By then, her knees were tired, and she'd stained more oak than she wanted to. She was ready to go home. They all were, so they packed up, locked everything tight, and took off.

"We'd better feed the pets and hurry through our showers," Ansel said on the way. "We stayed on the job longer than usual, and Gaff's stopping by earlier than he normally does. After supper, I might slip down to the basement to work a little."

She rolled her eyes. "We didn't work hard enough on the floors today?"

"I'll do easy stuff."

"Like drywall?"

He grinned. "It's heavy, but easy." The man *really* wanted his basement playroom.

Once home, they hustled through their usual routine. A good thing. Gaff arrived while they were coming down the steps after cleaning up and changing. Ansel would have plenty of time to nail up drywall tonight. If she wasn't too tired to move, she'd help him.

Jazzi led Gaff to the kitchen island to talk. Ansel got beer and wine, and Jazzi started throwing the ingredients for a quick tortellini soup in the Dutch oven. "Can you stay and eat with us?" she asked Gaff.

"I wouldn't mind. Ann has card club tonight, so I'm on my own."

"It's soup, salad, and a round of crusty bread. You've been warned."

He grinned. "I'm partial to soup. Can I help with anything?"

"No, this is easy. We can talk while I cook." She threw a pound of ground beef in the pot to brown, then sliced Italian sausages to add.

While those seared, Gaff said, "I told you Wendy Roeback was killed close to the same time as Jessica, and we suspected the two had to be connected, but I wanted to make sure. I talked to the detective who worked that case, and he said her boyfriend played center for the other team and was with his fellow players and coach all that night. He couldn't find anyone who might have slipped off to bash her, so her case was never solved either."

She nodded and added chopped onions, celery, and carrots with minced garlic.

"Brett's brother, Damian, was one of the top players on the team. Jessica's brother, Alwin, was a senior when Damian was a sophomore, and he was on the team, too."

She noticed Gaff didn't say Alwin was a top player. Poor Alwin must not have excelled at anything. "I thought he'd graduated by the time the murders took place."

"He had," Gaff explained, "but he went to college at Tri-States, close to home. He didn't have the grades to get into the school he wanted. He lived so close, though, he drove home and worked as an assistant coach for the team until Jessica died and the family moved away."

Jazzi turned down the heat under the pan and added a big can of diced tomatoes, a box of beef stock, and a can of cannellini beans. "What about some of the other people on my list? RJ, his aunt…"

Gaff cut her off. "I checked, and every single one of them was either watching the game or at the party when Jessica and Wendy were murdered. Any of them could have killed both girls."

Jazzi shook her head as she added Napa cabbage, zucchini, and fresh spinach to the pot. "That means we haven't narrowed down the suspect list at all."

"At least we didn't add anyone from the other town to it." Gaff watched her throw in a bag of frozen tortellini and seasonings. "The soup looks good."

"Thanks. But the list?"

He drained his beer, and Ansel went to get each of them another one. "Nothing's changed," Gaff said.

"Bummer." She gave the soup a final stir, then went to grab a bag of salad from the fridge. The bread was already on the island, along with butter.

"Better too many suspects than none at all," Gaff told her.

Maybe. She turned off the heat and stuck a ladle in the pot. "Soup's on," she said. Then the men got quiet while they dished up food and ate. Jazzi knew they liked it when they both went back for seconds. She didn't bother with desserts during the week.

When they finished their meal, Gaff left and Jazzi volunteered to do cleanup. "There's not that much, and you can start work on the drywall."

Ansel dropped a kiss on her forehead and headed for the basement. "You're the best."

Yeah, right. She couldn't have kept her Norseman upstairs with her if she nailed the basement door shut. When it was just her, the cats, and George in the kitchen, she gave a small laugh. If he thought she was the best, why fight it? It was easy to please him, and food was at the top of the list.

There was enough soup left to take for lunch tomorrow. That would make Jerod happy. When she finished putting everything away, she'd gotten a second wind and went downstairs to help Ansel. He did all the heavy work, and she manned the nail gun. At eight, she declared, "Enough for tonight."

He didn't argue, just held a hand to his back. Her Norseman might have overdone it. "We got two walls done. I'm happy with that."

"Good, 'cause it's quitting time. Another shower, pajamas, and TV."

The TV didn't happen. They were both asleep by nine.

Chapter 12

The floors were dry when they reached the fixer-upper. Dry and beautiful. Jazzi took a second to admire them, then glanced at the job sheet. When she groaned, Jerod laughed at her. "Thought you loved removing wallpaper, cuz."

"Yeah, as much as I love having cavities filled by my dentist."

He motioned to three steamers. "I rented one for each of us."

"Be still my heart." She grimaced and went to grab one. The men followed her. Maybe with three steamers going at the same time, the wallpaper would give up and sag to the floor. But whoever put up the darn stuff must have used superglue. It took forever to scrape each wall. They'd spread drop cloths around the edges of each room to catch them, but progress was slow going.

Luckily, the master bedroom only had wallpaper on one wall as an accent piece. It took two hours to remove it, though. The second bedroom was smaller, but every wall was covered with drums, horns, and violins on a blue background. Someone must have loved music. By the time they finished steaming and scraping, Jazzi didn't want to see another musical instrument for a long time.

They broke for lunch, and as Jazzi expected, when Jerod saw the soup *and* sandwiches, a smile stretched from ear to ear. George hadn't been happy about having soup for supper the night before, so he was glad to see deli meat, too. After lunch, they bundled the wallpaper they'd removed into a garbage bin, and Jazzi scooted it down the stairs and out the kitchen door to throw away. She was on her way back into the house when Ruth Goggins called to her from over the stone wall.

Jazzi reluctantly went to see what she wanted.

"I told my nephew, RJ, that you were flipping the Hodgkill house, and he got excited about it. He's coming into town later this week and asked if I could let you know he'd like to see what you're doing to it."

It didn't sound like a request. Ruth Goggins expected to get what she wanted. Jazzi considered turning her down, but she'd love to meet RJ and get to ask him about Jessica, so she smiled instead. "Sure, why not?"

Ruth's lips turned down. "The silly boy still thinks the world of Jessica. Can you imagine? After the way she treated him? But RJ's such a nice boy, he doesn't think ill of anyone."

Jazzi wondered how he felt about his aunt. Maybe he'd moved from Merlot to get away from her.

Ruth went on. "Do you still have a lot to do to the house? I thought it was lovely when Madeline lived there and invited us over for parties."

"It *is* a lovely home, but we still want to gut the kitchen and update it."

Ruth shrugged. "If you must. Most people don't spend much time there."

"That's where everyone congregates at our place," Jazzi told her.

Ruth sniffed. "I guess if you like that kind of thing. We prefer cocktail parties and spending time in the dining and living room."

She would. But Jazzi forced another smile and motioned toward the empty garbage bin. "We're stripping wallpaper. The guys are going to need that."

Ruth turned to go, saying over her shoulder, "Remember that RJ's coming soon."

When Jazzi dragged the bin back up the steps, Ansel was on his cell phone and Jerod was running his steamer over burgundy wallpaper decorated with sports equipment—basketballs, bats, football helmets, and golf clubs. "Ugly, isn't it?" he asked.

"It was probably popular when they put it up." Trends changed. What people paid extra for in the sixties was considered hideous today. She got her steamer and started on the strip next to his, wrinkling her nose. The room smelled like wet paste.

Ansel closed out his call. "Radley and Elspeth found a house they're interested in. It's close to the ball diamond downtown. I told him we'd stop and go through it with them tonight; then we can grab Coney dogs and eat supper at Radley's apartment."

She nodded. They'd still be home at a decent time. Ansel started work on the next wall, while she and Jerod each worked on theirs. Hers must have been used as a focal point, because it had another layer under the first to steam off. Three hours later, they'd finished that bedroom. She sent up prayers of thanks that Jessica had wanted a pink room. No wallpaper. They only had to remove it from one small bathroom and they were finally done.

This time, Ansel carried the garbage bin outside, and she and Jerod started mopping down walls to clean them to prime. They'd do that tomorrow.

Finished for the day, she and Ansel loaded everything into their van and drove to meet Radley and Elspeth. Jazzi's arms ached. Moving the steamer up and down the walls made them feel too heavy to lift. As Ansel pulled to the curb in front of a tall two-story with peeling paint, she shook her head at the sagging porch.

George opened his eyes when the van stopped, glanced out the window at an unknown destination, and closed them again. Ansel cracked the windows for him. "It's cool enough, he can stay in the van. He doesn't like looking at houses."

Jazzi zipped up her hoodie. It was borderline chilly outside. It was the second week of October, though. Temperatures bounced back and forth. This day had started out brisk and never warmed up.

When Radley's work van pulled in behind them, Ansel's brother and Elspeth came to meet them. He gestured to the house. "It could be great, couldn't it?"

Ansel looked doubtful. "Looks like it needs some structural work done."

"The porch?" Radley shrugged. "You've fixed those before."

A dark, shiny car parked behind Radley, and a man in a suit got out to walk toward them. He held out a hand and gave a confident smile. "I'm the Realtor. Glad you could make it. I don't think this place will be on the market long. This has become a desirable neighborhood since more people are moving close to downtown."

Radley gave a quick nod at Ansel and Jazzi. "My brother and his wife are house flippers. They've come to help us make a good decision."

The man's smile faded. "Well, then, let's take a look inside, shall we?"

The rooms had all been freshly painted. There was new linoleum on the kitchen floor. The cabinets had been painted, too. When Ansel opened one, he raised an eyebrow at crooked shelving. "What happened here?"

The Realtor spread his hands. "My client started to renovate, but his job got too busy, so he's decided to sell it as is."

"As is?" That was never a good sign. Jazzi looked at the way the floor sank on the far side. She squatted and took a marble out of her pocket. They kept it in the glove compartment of the van. When she put it down, it rolled to the far corner.

The Realtor shrugged. "It's an old house. It's settled a little. Let me show you the bedrooms upstairs."

Ansel shook his head. "Right now, I'd rather see the basement."

"You know how old houses are," the man said. "Basements are only used to do laundry and store things."

Ansel headed to the steps. They followed him. Then they stared at the cracks in the cement walls and the damp floor. It hadn't rained for a while. Ansel shook his head. "I know you love this place, Radley, but I'd pass. The house has issues that are going to cost a lot of money to fix."

The Realtor nodded toward the house next door. "Those people jacked up a corner of the house and poured new cement. Pronto. Problem fixed."

Ansel gave him a cold stare. "The whole side wall of this house would have to be replaced. Cement's not cheap. The floors upstairs would have to be stripped to the joists and completely relaid. It can be done, but it will cost a lot of money." He looked at Radley. "Do you have that much?"

Radley sadly shook his head. He looked at the Realtor. "We're going to have to pass."

The man gave a tight smile. "If you say so, but in a few years, this place is going to be double what it's worth now."

Elspeth spoke for the first time. "We understand that, but we can't afford to invest in it. Thanks for your time. We appreciate your showing this to us."

With a curt nod, the Realtor led them back upstairs and outside, then locked up behind them. "If you see another house you're interested in, give me a call."

They watched him drive away, then Ansel said, "You can't trust that man. I'd find someone else."

Radley's shoulders stooped in disappointment. Elspeth wrapped her arm through his. "There'll be more houses. We'll find one we like." Then she turned to them. "Thanks for saving us from a money pit. Let's grab some Coneys and stop at our place to eat."

They didn't stay long. Radley tried to be good company, but he looked totally deflated. Ansel had bought a plain hot dog for George, and as soon as they finished eating, they made excuses and headed for home.

That night, after they'd showered and changed into pajamas, Ansel hit the couch, and Jazzi sat next to Jessica's hope chest to look through more of her things. She'd meant to read through most of them by now, but life had been busy. Jessica remained in the back of her mind, though. She dug until she found Jessica's journal for her senior year of high school. And as she read, she loved Jessica even more.

People keep telling me that I'm lucky. I'm pretty, they say, and smart. Boys stare at me, but I haven't found one who really cares about me. RJ asked me to go steady with him, but every time Tilly enters a room, he can't help watching her. He knows I notice, and he knows it makes me feel second best, but he can't help it. He got more agitated the closer it got to prom. He wants his Tilly, so I broke up with him. And he asked her to go with him the next day. I'm happy for them. Then Kelsey broke up with Damian, and he asked me to the prom. Damian's tall and good-looking, genuinely nice, but all he did was watch Kelsey while we danced. So I broke up with him, too. What's wrong with me? Why doesn't someone look at me that way?

Her next entry tugged at Jazzi's heart even more. *RJ, Damian, and I are great friends now, but their girlfriends resent me. If they only knew. My best friends tell me not to worry about it, that people don't realize how nice I am, but I wish I was more popular, that more people liked me. I'm so awkward. I don't make friends easily.*

Jazzi flipped through more pages.

Lila started a rumor about me, that I broke up with Damian because I was pregnant with RJ's baby, but RJ's so popular that it backfired on her. Now she hates me more than ever. Three pages later, she wrote, *I won our region's tennis tournament and made an enemy for life. Nadia was trying for a sports scholarship. I didn't know. But I wouldn't have lost on purpose anyway. Why do more people hate me than like me?*

Her last entry read, *My mother's giving a party for my graduation. I'm going to be glad to leave Merlot. My friends are all going off to school, and I wouldn't see them anyway. My father's furious at me, as usual. Ruth Goggins can't say enough bad things about me. Neither can Nadia and Lila. It might be nice to start over, to find people who are interested in the same things I am. Maybe life will be better after high school.*

Jazzi bit her bottom lip. Jessica never found her better life. And she'd deserved it.

Chapter 13

When they walked up to the Merlot house, Jerod was standing at the front door, staring at the staircase, his hands on his hips. Always a bad sign. They stopped beside him.

"Well?" Ansel asked.

"We need to refinish the stairs and railings. The floors look so good, it makes them look shabby."

Jazzi frowned. "I thought we were going to prime and paint today."

Her cousin looked at her. She knew that look. "Would you mind working on the bedrooms while Ansel and I work on this?"

She could live with that. She agreed with a shrug. "Six of one, half a dozen of the other."

He grinned. "Good. I already took the paint, rollers, and brushes up there, along with the drop cloths."

"Let me put the cooler in the kitchen and I'll get started."

Jerod glanced at the cooler, at the way she was carrying it. "You're being careful with that. What's for lunch?"

The man didn't miss anything. "I had frozen pasties in the freezer, thawed them last night, and brought them to pop in the oven for a few minutes. Thought I'd bring a salad, too."

"You're a good woman, cuz."

"Tell me about it." But she did love to spoil her cousin. She put the food in the refrigerator and closed the cooler, leaving the cans of soda on ice. While she did that, Ansel moved George's dog bed to the living room, where he could watch the men work. Jazzi watched the pug settle and close his eyes. He'd open them on occasion to supervise. Then she headed upstairs.

Taping around windows and woodwork took what felt like forever, but once she had that done, the priming went fast. She decided to stop for lunch while the primer dried; then she could start painting. They'd decided on neutral colors: Martha Stewart's sharkey gray for the master bedroom and honeysuckle—a soft, soothing yellow—for the four others.

Jerod and Ansel were sanding the handrail when she zipped down to the kitchen to put the pasties in the oven. "Will you be finished with that soon?" she asked.

Jerod nodded. "We can wipe it down before we eat, then stain it after lunch. Do you want to paint down here while we stain? We don't need to prime these walls, and then the ground floor would look pretty good if someone knocks on the door and wants to see it."

"You keep changing your mind. I thought you wanted me to paint *upstairs*."

"I did, but I was thinking about Ruth's nephew coming. If the rooms look good, maybe he'll spread the word about how the place is coming along."

They'd sold houses before they were finished a few times, the market was so tight. He might have a point. She groaned. "I'll have to tape everything again." Not one of her favorite jobs.

"I'll help with that," Ansel said. "You and I can paint while Jerod works on the staircase. Two people can't really stain together anyway; not enough room."

Jerod nodded. "I'm okay with that. You?"

"Sure, if Ansel helps. Between the two of us, we might even finish all the rooms but the kitchen."

"We're gutting that anyway." Jerod put down his sander and reached for a rag. "And we'll help you paint upstairs after we finish down here."

Ansel's gaze swept the area. "Can we bring the card table out here to eat? Then we can study the rooms over lunch and maybe come up with a few more ideas."

Her Norseman loved renovating and coming up with new suggestions for the spaces they worked on. Jerod was always mindful of the bottom line—how much profit they'd make on each project—but Ansel enjoyed making each room special almost as much as she did, so she carted the card table and chairs into the living room. They filled their plates in the kitchen and ate where they could see what they were talking about.

"I still can't think of anything to do with the fireplace, the opening's so big," Jerod complained. "The stones are a great feature, but no one needs that big a fire."

"I saw a magazine where owners put a black, cast-iron stove inside the opening and still had room to put a basket filled with wood on one side of it and a tall vase with fake flowers on the other. It looked really cool."

Ansel narrowed his eyes, trying to picture it. "Can you find the magazine?"

She got up to get her purse. "I think I tore out the page to show you but forgot." She returned with it, and both men smiled.

"Okay, we still haven't decided on the backsplash for the kitchen," Ansel said.

Jerod waved that away. "We can do that later. None of us can agree on anything yet. Maybe we'll know if we can up the budget for it by then."

Ansel liked that idea. "Spending a little more would be nice."

They'd agreed on a rich cream color for the downstairs walls—not a white and not a yellow—but luxurious, so after cleaning up and putting the card table and chairs away, they got busy. Jerod stained the stairs while Ansel and Jazzi climbed ladders to start taping. Once they finished that, they used long rollers to paint the ceilings white. With only one color for every room, they got the study, dining room, living room, and hallway finished before Ruth Goggins rang the front doorbell at four thirty.

Jazzi glanced at the clock and pressed her lips together. Her shirt was speckled with sprays of paint and a bandanna covered her head. What did the woman want now? But when she went to answer the door, a tall, young man stood next to her. Of course he'd be tall, probably six feet. He'd been on the basketball team. He must be RJ.

He grinned when he saw her. "That color looks good on you."

Jazzi wrinkled her nose. Right. Nothing brought out a woman's earthy beauty like splatters of paint. RJ wasn't especially good-looking, but when he smiled, his whole face lit up. She bet he had lots of personality. She opened the door wider. "You must be Ruth's nephew, RJ. Come in. We've opened up the house, but the paint fumes are still strong."

He and Ruth stepped inside. She put a hand over her nose, but RJ let out a low whistle. "I like what you've done."

Always happy to talk about one of their fixer-uppers, Jerod came to greet them. "Hi, I'm Jerod." They shook hands. "We're going to gut the kitchen next." Stepping back, he motioned to the staircase. "Just refinished it. It makes all the difference."

Ruth stepped farther inside and pursed her lips. "Good, you haven't done anything too outrageous."

Jazzi rolled her eyes. Was that the best compliment the woman could come up with? It would probably choke her to say anything too nice.

RJ had no such trouble. "The old place needed a little sprucing up. You're making it look great."

A car drove into Ruth's driveway next door, and she grimaced. "I have to go. I'll be back as soon as I can." She rushed to meet her guest.

RJ smiled. "I give her two minutes. She won't be able to stand missing anything we talk about."

And he was right. Two minutes later, Ruth was back. Ansel went to the door to let her in. Ruth glanced up at him. "I told Marigold I'd call her later. I want to be able to spend time with RJ."

The boy's eyes sparkled with mischief. "I was telling them what a nice girl Jessica was."

Ruth's shoulders stiffened. "I don't know what you ever saw in her."

"I liked her almost as much as I love my Tilly."

Ruth glared. "I don't know what you saw in that girl either. Her father works in a factory and her mother's a school librarian. We all know that job doesn't amount to much."

"All of us kids loved her," RJ said. "She picked the best stories to read us."

Ruth puckered her lips in a sour expression.

"How long have you and Tilly been married?" Jazzi asked.

"Six years now, and for picking the wrong girl, we've been awfully happy. We went to River Bluffs to culinary school before moving to Ohio. Now we own and run a food truck together."

He'd caught her interest.

His grin grew broader. "The kind you take to fairs and festivals. We travel a lot. We're known for our pork tenderloin sandwiches and fried vegetable baskets."

"Love both," Ansel said. Jerod nodded agreement.

Ruth's lips turned down. "He hardly ever comes to visit me these days."

"Summer and fall are our busiest times. But, boy, being in this house sure brings back memories."

Jazzi studied him. "May I ask why you broke up with Tilly in your senior year?"

He laughed. "Because I was a dimwit. We'd gone steady since our freshman year, and I was afraid I might be missing out on something better. I was never so miserable as when I got what I thought I wanted— Jessica Hodgkill. Tilly never forgave Jessica for that, but I'm the one she should blame."

"If you liked Jessica so much, why go back to Tilly?"

"Because Tilly was more my speed. Jessica had big, lofty dreams. Not my style. And every other guy in my class was hitting on Tilly the minute I broke up with her. I kept thinking I was going to lose her, and that drove me crazy."

Because he was in the mood to reminisce, Jazzi asked, "Do you remember anything about the party when Jessica died?"

"Like it was seared in my brain." He took a deep breath. "She screamed all the way down."

"Where were you when it happened? Do you remember who was with you?"

He glanced at his aunt and squirmed. "I was in the kitchen with Felicity, hiding from Aunt Ruth."

Ruth's jaw dropped and she turned to glare at him.

He grimaced. "Love ya, Ruth, but I liked Jessica and you didn't, and when I saw you looking for me, I didn't want a lecture."

Jazzi frowned. "Tilly wasn't with you?"

"No, I left her in the backyard, near the buffet line. The brats, burgers, and hot dogs were on a table near the grill. People were loading their plates."

Jazzi made a mental note of that. Ruth gave her a hard look. "I think we'd better go now. We've wasted enough of your time."

On their way out the door, Jazzi heard her say, "How stupid are you? She was checking for alibis, and now you don't have one."

"Sure I do. I was with Felicity—she'll remember. And I'm glad someone cares about Jessica being murdered." She could hear RJ's grumble. "I didn't kill Jessica, so I don't have to worry."

"But what about Tilly?"

"She was in line for food, and Jessica's dad was working the grill. People can vouch for her, too."

They'd gone far enough, Jazzi couldn't hear the rest, but she was glad she could rule out RJ and Tilly as suspects. She kept Ruth's name on her list, though. RJ had just said that Ruth was at the graduation party when Jessica fell. She'd wondered about that.

Jerod's blue eyes twinkled when he looked at her. "That woman's going to like you less and less."

Big deal. "Then it's mutual."

With a laugh, Jerod started picking up his sander and rags. She and Ansel began cleaning up, too. Half an hour later, they grabbed George, locked up, and drove away.

Chapter 14

They didn't shower when they got home, just fed the pets, played with them awhile, then went to the basement and put up the last two walls of drywall. The cats loved it, chasing each other through the room and around the sawhorses they'd set up; George—not so much. He found a faraway corner, out of the way, to stay in. Jazzi had meant to make another pot of soup for lunch tomorrow, but that would have to wait for some other day. Instead, she boiled a dozen eggs to make egg salad in the morning—Jerod and Ansel were both partial to it—while she made pork chops and rice for a quick supper.

George was a fan of pork and begged more than usual. Then they cleaned the kitchen, showered, and relaxed for an hour before bed. Even with an early night, the alarm rang too soon the next morning. Working double shifts was getting to Jazzi. She dragged herself downstairs to make the egg salad, ate the two slices of pumpernickel toast Ansel pushed in front of her, and tried to wake herself up on the drive to Merlot.

Ansel glanced her way, looking guilty. "You're going to sell me pretty soon, aren't you? I'm pushing you too hard."

"You want the basement done before Halloween."

"But I still want a wife who likes me."

She laughed. "Invite your buddies to our house again tonight and put them to work. Splurge. We're on the home stretch. Buy them each a meat lover's pizza, whatever it takes."

"I'm ahead of you. They're coming at six. You'll be eating and drinking with the girls by then."

She smiled. "You're a good man. What do you want to get done?"

"I warned them to wear junk clothes. Taping and mudding the drywall."

She wouldn't miss having to do that. When they reached the Merlot house and went inside, Jerod didn't look any perkier than she did.

"What happened?" Ansel asked.

"Pete's cutting teeth. He's grumpy and has diaper rash and diarrhea. He's kept Franny up the past two nights, so it was my turn last night."

Trying to cheer him, Ansel said, "Jazzi brought egg salad today."

Jerod turned to her. "I'd hug you, but my work clothes are so dirty, you might not appreciate it."

She looked him up and down. "It's the thought that counts."

He laughed. "Today's going to be fun and games. Thought we'd tape heavy plastic over the kitchen archway, then gut it. If we have time, we can paint it before we lay flooring."

They'd have time. The kitchen cabinets were so old, they were going to bust them apart and toss them in the dumpster. Lots easier than trying to keep them intact to save.

Ansel strapped on his tool belt and picked up his sledgehammer. He looked like a marauding Viking. "Might as well get to it."

They left George's dog bed in the living room because the kitchen was going to be such a mess. Soon, they were smashing top and bottom cupboards apart. The walls behind them were in such good shape, all they had to do was scrub them down before painting them. They'd agreed on sky-blue to offset the new white cupboards they'd ordered. Those were being delivered on Monday, along with the appliances.

While they ate lunch, Ansel looked at the boxes of tiles they'd splurged on for the floor. "You know, a backsplash with this same white and blue pattern, only smaller, would look great in here."

It would. Jazzi looked at Jerod for his reaction. Her cousin sighed. "You're right. Why not? Kitchens help sell a house." He reached for another sandwich, then roused himself enough to ask, "What are you guys up to tonight? It's Thursday. You always go out."

"I'm meeting Olivia, Didi, and Elspeth at the Gas House," Jazzi said.

"Nice." Jerod turned to Ansel.

"Walker, Thane, and Radley are coming to our place to help me work on the basement. We're not going out, so Walker's bringing River with him."

Jerod rubbed a hand across his forehead. "I feel bad. You guys helped me build my kids' playroom, and I haven't come through for you."

Jazzi stared at him. "You have a baby! You don't have time."

Ansel grinned. "Another reason I wanted to build ours now, before Walker and Didi are losing sleep over their future baby girl."

"That's fair," Jerod told him. "You guys helped all of us with our projects."

Jazzi reached across the table to slap his shoulder. "We're family. That's what we do. We're there for one another."

"Well, once Pete's a little older, if you guys need anything..."

Jazzi cut him off. "We know. Now quit fussing. Let's finish up here so we can go home."

By the time they left at four thirty, the kitchen was gutted and painted.

Once home, Jazzi hurried to shower and do her hair and makeup. Her sister, Olivia, came straight from the salon on Thursdays, and she always looked glamorous. Elspeth came from her job, too, and looked professional. So Jazzi and Didi tried harder than usual to be presentable.

As Jazzi pulled into the Gas House's parking lot, she thought about Reuben and Isabelle. She and Ansel often met her former upstairs neighbor and his wife here for supper, but it had been a while. She'd have to call Reuben to set something up. When she'd moved out of the bottom floor of the old Victorian in West Central, they'd sworn they wouldn't lose track of each other, but life got busy.

Didi was already in the restaurant when Jazzi got there. And Olivia and Elspeth walked in a minute after Jazzi got seated. The waitress came to get their drink order, and then they settled in to talk.

Didi reached for her water glass and winced. Putting a hand to her stomach, she said, "This baby loves to kick. My insides must be bruised by now."

Jazzi, Olivia, and Elspeth looked at one another. None of them had experienced the joys of pregnancy and childbirth yet, and at the moment, watching Didi, they all looked glad of that.

Then Didi beamed. "Walker and I have started decorating the nursery. He'd have pink everything if I let him. He's so excited about having a girl."

Olivia snorted. "That kid is going to have him wrapped around her little finger. Our dad was a sucker for girls, too," she said, glancing at Jazzi.

A lot of dads and daughters had special relationships. Not poor Jessica, though. Her father was her biggest detractor.

Olivia watched her and shook her head. "You're thinking of Jessica. Stop that. Not tonight. Tonight is about girl power and gossip, having fun."

Jazzi forced a smile. Her sister was right. She pushed Jessica out of her mind. Their wine came, and Jazzi took a sip of hers. "Mom balanced Dad out. She was the disciplinarian."

"So was my mom," Elspeth said. "But if she told Dad that we'd driven her nuts that day, he always took Mom's side. Whatever she said, went."

"You've waited a while to do the nursery, haven't you?" Olivia asked Didi.

With a sigh, Didi nodded. "I'm a little superstitious. I didn't want to jinx anything, so we waited until the doctor told us the baby would be fine, even if she came early."

"Have you picked out a name?" Elspeth asked.

"Not yet. Same reason. I didn't want to rush things."

The waitress came to take their orders. Once she left, Elspeth turned to Olivia. "Radley and Thane are installing a heating/cooling system together at some factory. Thane told him that you guys are doing another house project."

Olivia's brown eyes lit up. "We're having a gazebo built in our backyard. Thane likes to grill, so we're making an entertaining area outside. Thane's wanted one ever since he saw Jazzi and Ansel's by their pond."

"You're going to love it," Jazzi said. "We use ours a lot." Ansel had a charcoal grill by theirs, along with a picnic table.

Didi rested her hands on her stomach. She did that a lot these days. "Talking about entertaining, River was excited about going with Walker tonight to work on your basement. He can hardly wait until your Halloween party."

A party. That's how Jessica…Jazzi pushed the thought away.

Olivia gave her a look, then said, "Neither can I. It's going to be fun. I love parties." Her eyes lit up. "I've got it! Why don't we all dress up? Every single one of us should wear a costume."

Jazzi groaned, but Elspeth leaned forward, grinning. "I can sew outfits for Radley and me."

Sew? Jazzi could hardly thread a needle. "How complicated are you thinking about?"

"We can rent costumes from Stoner's downtown," Olivia said. "Maybe I could come as Cleopatra."

Eww! Did that mean Thane would come as Julius Caesar? Jazzi couldn't imagine him in a toga. "I don't like dressing up."

"You can make an exception for Halloween." Her sister ignored her whining.

Didi looked down at her protruding belly. "Do they rent costumes for pregnant women?"

Olivia waved her off. "You'll think of something. This will be fun!"

Their food came, and Jazzi stewed while she ate her crab cakes. It was one thing finishing the basement for the party, another to make food for it, but costumes? Ugh!

Olivia's face crumpled, and she sighed. "I know that look. It's your party. If you don't want to bother with costumes, that's fine."

Elspeth looked disappointed, too. Jazzi rolled her eyes. Olivia was using one of her little sister ploys on her and she knew it, but Olivia looked so disappointed—another thing she'd perfected—that Jazzi sighed and gave in to the inevitable. "Just don't expect ours to be anything wonderful."

Olivia smiled, completely unrepentant and happy to have gotten her way. "Whatever you say."

Yeah, right. Jazzi had been had by a pro. She and Ansel would have to think up some kind of costumes or they'd look like poor sports. Her sister had outmaneuvered her and she had to admit it.

When she got home that night, the cats ran to meet her. She stooped to pet them both, then went to find her husband. He was in the basement with George. The walls were taped and mudded, and he was holding up paint chips, putting most in a throwaway pile but keeping a few.

When he saw her, he smiled. "What do you think?"

"Olivia's decided we all have to wear costumes to the Halloween party."

"Great! That'll be fun."

Of course he'd think that. Jazzi glanced at the three paint chips he'd taped to the wall. "I like the soft, sandy color."

He nodded. "I do, too."

They made their way upstairs and sat at the kitchen island. Ansel drank one last beer and she had another glass of wine, and they shared any news they'd learned. Ansel was excited that Thane was building a gazebo, and he got sentimental about Walker wanting an all-pink room for his baby girl. Jazzi watched his expression and smiled. When they decided to have kids, he'd make a wonderful father.

Finally, they headed upstairs. The cats jumped on the bed and begged for attention while they changed into their pajamas, and even George wanted extra petting before he settled in his dog bed. Then Inky curled next to her, and Marmalade pressed herself against Ansel.

As she drifted to sleep, Jazzi thought about Jessica. She'd written about how happy she was the day of her graduation party, how proud her mother was of her. Her friends were all coming to celebrate with her. She must have been happy until the moment someone gave her a hard push and sent her over the balcony railing. Jazzi bit her bottom lip, more determined than ever to find Jessica's four best friends to talk to them. Friends were the ones she shared secrets with. And Jazzi wanted to know what some of those secrets might be. Over the weekend, she was going to scan through Jessica's journals again and write down the girls' names, then look them up.

Chapter 15

On Friday, Jazzi, Jerod, and Ansel spent the entire day on their hands and knees, installing the new kitchen floor. They'd picked a pattern that took more time than usual—a stone tile with the look of marble, a white lantern pattern with blue dots connecting the lantern shapes. By lunch, they'd only covered half the space needed, and Jazzi was beginning to hate everything about it. Once it was finished, she'd love it again, but at the moment, her eyes saw swirls everywhere she looked.

They were sitting in the living room at the card table, eating roast beef sandwiches, not talking much, when Leesa called. Jazzi was glad for the distraction, but she didn't have much news for her friend.

"I know this is short notice," Leesa began, "but Damian and Kelsey are coming in this weekend, and we wondered if we could meet you guys for supper at Dicky's Wild Hare tonight."

Jazzi glanced at Ansel. "Supper with Leesa and Brett?" she asked. When he gave a quick nod, she said, "We're on." They both liked the restaurant, and it was on the north side of River Bluffs, so it wouldn't take long to reach it. Traffic on Friday nights was always busier than usual, but not impossible.

"Good, see you at six. And thanks." Leesa clicked off.

"This is a good night to eat out," Jerod said, wadding up his paper plate and napkin to pitch in the trash bin. "I'm not going to have much energy after fussing with this floor all day. I'm grabbing takeout on the way home."

"I'm glad we don't lay this pattern very often," Ansel agreed. "It's fine for a small space, like a bathroom, but this kitchen's huge. Let's get back at it. I don't want to face it again on Monday."

They pushed harder than before, and they were all relieved when they laid the last tile. The cabinets and appliances were being delivered on Monday. The floor would have the entire weekend to set.

Ansel carried George to their work van, and Jerod waved as he walked to his truck. "See you on Sunday. I might have energy by then."

Jazzi wasn't worried. Her cousin always had enough energy for the family meal. On the drive home, Ansel let out a long breath. "Maybe we'll skip working on the basement tomorrow."

Jazzi stifled a cheer. Her Norseman was losing steam, too. She wasn't the only one. It was never fun to sand drywall, but it needed doing. She sighed. "It won't take us long to sand the walls and clean the dust. Then we can relax the rest of the day."

"No, we can't. We'll have to go to the store and fix something for the family meal on Sunday." Ansel rarely grumbled. He was raised on a dairy farm and was used to getting up to work every day.

She shrugged. "We like cooking together. We'll turn on music and make something easy."

"That's what you always say."

She turned to look at him. "Do you want to cancel everything and have a quiet weekend?"

"No. Sorry." He ran a hand through his blond hair. "I like having your family over. It's my fault we've tried to do too much in too little time. I should have held off on the Halloween party."

"Everyone's excited," she said. "It's like the kitchen floor. It took more time than we expected, but we'll love it once it's done."

He gave her a grateful smile. "Thanks, Jaz. River's sure excited about it."

"So is everyone else. We'll just have to get up to speed."

He laughed. "You're right. The big stuff's almost done. Then we can do the fun stuff, like decorate and install the pool table and arcade."

"Don't forget your big-screen TV."

He grinned. "Yeah, I have to keep the end goal in mind."

Once they'd sanded and painted, he'd be excited again. They were close. When they reached the pumpkin patch on the highway, she motioned for him to pull in. "Let's buy enough for the kids to decorate our back patio when they come on Sunday."

He liked the idea and loaded a bunch of them in the back of the van.

When they reached the house, they hurried through their normal routine. Inky and Marmalade were used to them going out on Friday nights, but George, as usual, pouted. Ansel snuck all of them a few extra treats. Then they got ready and drove to the restaurant.

They got lucky and found the last parking space in the main lot. Dicky's did a mean barbecue and had a brewery, too. It was a popular spot. When they walked into the lobby, Leesa was waiting for them.

"The guys and Kelsey are saving a table for us. Come on."

While they ordered drinks and food, they made small talk, catching up with one another. But once the niceties were out of the way, Brett said, "Have you learned anything? What's going on?"

Jazzi told them what she knew. "It isn't much, but the case is old. It's been slow going."

Damian rubbed his chin, thinking. "You know, RJ was right when he told you he could remember exactly where he was and who he was with when Jessica fell. We all heard her scream. I'll never forget it. I was with Jillian. When the detective asked about it, he wouldn't use her as an alibi."

"They wanted you to be guilty that much?"

"Lila did. She swore she saw me going upstairs right before Jessica fell. But the detective didn't believe much of what she said either. She was too determined to throw me under the bus."

Jazzi turned to Kelsey. "Were you with someone who gave you an alibi?"

She shook her head. "I was in the bathroom. I'd drunk too much punch, but I could still hear Jessica's scream. It gave me goose bumps."

"But no alibi?"

"Everyone else was standing in line for food or hanging out."

"Do you know where Lila was when Jessica fell?" Jazzi asked.

Just then, the waitress returned with their drinks and the appetizers they'd ordered. Ansel had gone with Shaggy Snacks—fried potato wedges with a dipping sauce. He reached for one. The man loved anything potato.

Damian took a sip of his beer before answering. He shook his head. "Jillian and I were in the kitchen at the punch bowl. We wanted to get away from the noise for a minute. I didn't keep track of Lila."

"What about RJ's aunt?"

"Can't help you," he said. "Whenever I saw her coming, I ran."

Jazzi laughed. "So did RJ." She bit into one of the potato wedges. "Wow, this is good. What were Jessica's friends like?"

Damian's face lit up, smiling. "The Fantastic Five? That's what RJ dubbed them. Jessica and her four buddies made a neat group. All attractive. All supersmart. And all different from one another."

That caught Ansel's interest. "How different?"

"Darcie Winters was a nature girl, always preaching about the environment. Jillian Hendricks was the artist of the group. She made most of the drama settings and painted all the murals around the school.

Felicity Kellman was in Future Teachers of America and went on and on about child development, and Molly Kroft loved antiques and was forever rearranging things. They were all in to biking and hiking. Not one of them was shy about expressing their views."

Kelsey grinned. "They were a force to be reckoned with. Not a snob among them, and they all came from money. All down-to-earth and idealists."

Damian looked at her, surprised. "I thought you hated Jessica."

"I was jealous of her, but I admired her. She was light-years ahead of all of us. I wish we could have seen what she'd do with her life. She's the type who'd have made a difference."

He pressed his lips together in a tight line, suddenly serious. "Such a waste. For all of us."

Their meals came, and they dug in. Ansel started with the ribs on his combination plate. Jazzi had ordered the fish tacos. The moans around the table attested to how good everything tasted.

Once they'd slowed a bit, Jazzi said, "I've been reading some of Jessica's journals, but I can't figure out how she and Alwin got along. Was her brother nicer to her than their dad was?"

Damian and Kelsey glanced at each, frowning. Finally, Damian said, "They had sort of an odd relationship. It's hard to explain."

Kelsey nodded. "Alwin was proud of her, you could tell, and was even a little protective of her, but never around their dad. They never did anything together. If they were at the same school dance, they never talked to each other or hung out. He didn't even tease her, like most brothers do."

Some shredded cabbage slipped out of Jazzi's taco, and she leaned over her plate to avoid a mess. "Their dad must have made it hard for them to get along."

Damian blotted barbecue sauce off his lips. His pulled pork sandwich looked delicious. "Jessica was always extra-kind to him. It was almost like she tried to bolster his confidence."

Kelsey tilted her head, looking thoughtful. "It had to be hard on Alwin, having her for a sister. He couldn't compete. And even when he did things well, it didn't make him more popular. He was a good, solid player on the basketball team, but everyone knew Damian was the star, and RJ was a close second. Plus, there was just something about Alwin. He was sort of reserved, and you were never sure if he actually liked you. He'd bottle things up and then just explode. Jessica was beautiful, but he was sort of drab. He was easy to overlook."

Jazzi almost felt sorry for him. She wondered if he'd blossomed once he was out of Jessica's shadow. "Do most of Jessica's friends still live in Merlot?"

Damian glanced at Brett for an answer.

"All four girls returned after college," Brett said. "Darcie became a master gardener and owns a landscaping business. Jillian owns a craft shop in town. Felicity teaches grade school, and Molly's an interior decorator who lives in Merlot but travels to take care of important clients."

"All successful." Jazzi finished her last taco and took a sip of wine.

Damian grinned. "They had success written all over them from first grade on."

"And nothing ever changed that, made people worry?" Ansel asked. When Brett stared at him, he shrugged. "Our high school quarterback was on the fast track until he got one of the cheerleaders pregnant. Now he's a car salesman in my dad's small town."

"Is he happy?" Jazzi hated to hear about dashed dreams.

Ansel smiled. "He has a serious paunch and five kids, and he's still married to the girl."

That made her feel better. "Could someone have shoved Jessica over the railing to protect a secret?"

Damian pushed away his empty plate, shaking his head. "I don't think so. Those four girls would have just squared their shoulders and faced whatever it was head-on."

"Even if one got pregnant?" Ansel asked.

"Even that," Kelsey said.

Jazzi shrugged. "I'm out of ideas. But when I go back to Merlot, I'd like to track down Jessica's friends and ask them about her."

"Good luck." Brett tossed down his napkin. "It's beginning to look like we're not going to get any more answers this time than the last."

"Hey, Jazzi's doing her best!" Leesa said, defending her.

Brett cringed. "I'm not saying that. I really appreciate what you're doing for us, Jazzi. It's just not looking good, is it?"

Damian shrugged. "At least we tried."

They had to leave it at that. Even with the journals and Gaff's help, they weren't making much progress.

Chapter 16

They slept in on Saturday, and it felt good. When they finally tumbled out of bed, the cats raced to the kitchen to their food bowls. Ansel chuckled. "One extra hour and you'd think they were starving."

Jazzi watched him pick up his pug to carry down the steps. "The same cannot be said about George."

He laughed. "He's too weak to walk. He might perish if we don't feed him soon."

"Right." While she fed the furry beasts, he poured coffee for them and toasted four slices of pumpernickel. They sat next to each other at the kitchen island, enjoying the slow start of their day.

"What's first up for us to do?" he asked.

"Sanding the basement. Then we can give the house a quick clean and head to the store after lunch."

He agreed with a nod. They'd both dressed in their work clothes, so half an hour later, they turned on their sanders and got busy. He wore his baseball cap, and she'd covered her hair with a scarf. By the time they finished, though, they were both plenty dusty. A good time to clean the house. Inky chased her dust rag as she worked, and Marmalade helped Ansel scrub the sinks and tub. The cat enjoyed smacking the running water with her paw, tossing it everywhere. George supervised. They showered before lunch so her hair would dry while she ate.

"Did you already make a list for groceries?" Ansel asked, finishing his sandwich.

She was ahead of him. She pointed to the sheet of paper stuck on the fridge with a magnet.

"What did you decide on for tomorrow?" He didn't sound hopeful. She'd promised something quick and easy, but they'd had too many fast lunches and suppers lately. Sundays were usually special.

"Sauerbraten and potatoes."

His eyes lit up. "I like German food."

"I know." She smiled. "I was thinking about making apple strudel for dessert, but that might be too much bother."

"I can help you." She knew he'd volunteer if she picked the right dessert. "Is the dough hard to make?"

"Not for me. I cheat and use puff pastry."

"Even better. I'll buy vanilla ice cream to go with it."

"It's already on the grocery list." She knew what Ansel liked.

He pushed to his feet. "Then let's go. The sooner we shop, the sooner we can cook. And then we can rent a movie to watch."

"No horror." He'd picked their last movie, and it was her turn.

He grinned. "But when you get scared, you cuddle close to me and..."

She put a hand on his hard chest, interrupting him. "But when I watch romance, I feel all girlie and mushy."

He wrinkled his nose at the thought of a romance, then pulled her in for a quick kiss. "I like girlie and mushy, but when you watch a chick flick, you get a little spunky."

"You like spunky?"

"I like anything you throw at me." This time, the kiss lingered. Finally, he straightened and shook his head. "For later. Right now, grocery store."

When the cats saw her grab the list to walk out the door, they knew where she was going. The felines didn't miss a thing. They knew when she came home, she'd throw brown grocery bags on the floor for them to play in. They left George home, too. He didn't like it, but he'd live.

They'd shopped together so often, they knew every aisle in the store by heart. A half hour later, they were checking out. When they got home, they were just as efficient at putting groceries away. Then Jazzi started the chuck roasts for the sauerbraten. She'd remembered to buy gingersnaps to grind in later.

Ansel peeled apples while she cooked, and they had three strudels in the oven in no time. The number of people who came for the Sunday meal had grown. It had started with Jerod and his family, Jerod's parents, her parents, Gran and Samantha, and Olivia and Thane. Now, it included Walker and Didi with River and Radley and Elspeth. Twenty people in all, including them, if you counted baby Pete. People threw money in the Mason jar on the counter to help pay for the ingredients, but the meal was more work than it used to be. Elspeth and Didi talked about helping out, and Jazzi was to the point where it sounded like a good idea.

When they finished, they still had time to relax before ordering a pizza for supper. Ansel went to flip through TV stations to find a sports program, and she settled next to Jessica's hope chest. She'd skipped the beginning of her journal for her senior year, going to the end months for the prom and her graduation party instead. Now, she turned to the beginning, and she wished she'd read it earlier.

Alwin's getting more and more upset with me every time he comes home from college. Dad encourages it and joins in. Mom keeps telling me it's a normal part of sibling rivalry, but something's changed between us. I don't know what.

A week later, she wrote, *I heard Mom and Dad arguing about me last night. I'm surprised they're still together. Mom says he's going to regret the way he treats me when I leave for university, but he says Mom always takes my side in everything. Mom told him it's because he always sticks up for Alwin. Sometimes, I think they hate each other, but Dad says that no Hodgkill ever got a divorce, and he won't be the first one. Why Mom stays, I don't know.*

Inky jumped on her lap for attention, and she stopped to pet him. Marmalade bumped her leg, and she bent to pet her, too. Then she returned to the journal.

Alwin keeps pressuring me to live at home and go to Merlot University, or drive to Tri-States with him. He doesn't realize how much I want to escape Dad. I don't want to stay in Indiana. I want to explore the world. But that only makes him angrier. I tried to explain that I wasn't trying to make him look bad. His grades are better now. I told him to follow me to a new school, but he won't hear of it.

A month before her prom, Jessica wrote, *Alwin keeps telling me the dangers of being a woman alone in the world. He'd swaddle me in cotton and keep me at home if he could. I don't know what he's thinking. Lots of women go off to college on their own. Then he told me about the girl who'd been killed in our area, that the police questioned the entire basketball team about her. The murder's rattled him. He doesn't want me to ever be a victim. He's afraid for me. That's sweet of him, but I won't let fear hold me back from my dreams. I'm going to pick a college and be done with it.*

The week before her graduation party, she wrote, *I wish Alwin would find some wonderful girl who'd clamp on to him and make him her own. A few have tried, but he never dates them for very long. If he had a girlfriend, he'd pay less attention to me. A win-win. He'd be happier, and so would*

I. The more upset Alwin gets, the more Dad hates me. I can't leave Merlot fast enough.

The buzzer on the stove rang, jerking Jazzi from her thoughts. She went to take the strudels out of the oven, and Ansel came to join her.

"Ready for pizza?"

"I'm hungry." They'd had a small lunch.

He called in their order, and Jazzi put the finishing touches on the sauerbraten. The potatoes had cooked along with the roasts, and they'd have lots of flavor. All they'd have to do tomorrow was make a salad and a vegetable. She pinched her lips together. She was out of reading time for tonight and wished she'd gotten further.

Half an hour later, the deliveryman came and supper was served. Ansel clicked on the movie they wanted to rent, and they settled in front of the TV to eat while they watched. She'd chosen a thriller romance, a woman in jeopardy with a hunky detective trying to keep her alive. She thought that way, she and Ansel would both enjoy it. What she hadn't counted on was the movie making her think of Jessica. In the movie, a serial killer was targeting girls with long blond hair and willowy builds. At the end, the detective caught the killer and saved the heroine at the last minute. Jessica hadn't been that lucky, and no one ever caught her killer. He was still out there.

Chapter 17

On Sunday, Jazzi started making the salad sooner than usual, impatient to finish everything and see her family. They'd only missed one week for Bain's wedding, but somehow, it felt like she hadn't seen her parents or Gran and Samantha or the others for a long time.

As usual, Jerod and his family walked through the kitchen door first, and Jerod hovered around the cheese ball and crackers. Franny brought her usual vegetable tray and dip, and as people entered, they gathered at the island to sip their drinks and eat their snack. The minute Walker and Didi arrived, Gunther and Lizzie ran to River, excited to start playing.

"Not so fast. I have a job for you first," Ansel told them.

They stared up at him, stunned.

"Jerod and Walker can help me show you what needs to be done." He motioned for them to follow him to the garage. Once inside, he threw open the back doors to his van, full of pumpkins. Lizzie squealed. "The back patio needs to be decorated for the party," he told them. "Can you handle that?"

Lizzie spied the felt-tip pens on the patio table. "Can we make faces on them?"

"Don't make them too scary. I have to pass them every day."

River laughed up at him as the men helped the kids carry the first load of pumpkins behind the house, then they left them to it and came in to visit. When Jazzi glanced out the French doors, she watched the kids carefully pick spots for the pumpkins they'd chosen.

"That reminds me," Jerod said. "I haven't seen your basement for a while."

The three men started downstairs, and when Jazzi's dad and mom arrived, Doogie went down to join them. So did Jerod's dad, Eli, when he came.

Jerod's mom, however, headed straight to baby Pete. Eleanore couldn't keep her hands off an infant. When Didi had her little girl, Eleanore would want baby time with her, too. Radley and Elspeth came next. As usual, Olivia and Thane were last. When they finally walked in, Jazzi started loading food on the kitchen island. The men tramped upstairs, and everyone got in line to dish up.

Jazzi poured Gran a glass of red wine while they waited their turns. Her housemate, Samantha, decided on lemon water for lunch, because she was driving. Gran frowned at Jazzi and shook her head. "Your mom told me that you've found another body."

"Not a body." Jazzi explained about Jessica's hope chest.

Gran pursed her lips. "I remember reading about that poor girl. Her picture was on the front page. A beautiful child. There was another one, too, wasn't there?"

"A cheerleader," Jazzi said.

Gran cocked her head to the side, as though listening to something. "This time, you'll find what you need to catch the killer. Look in his secret pocket." She frowned. "It won't be there yet."

"Whose pocket?" Jazzi had learned never to doubt Gran's sight.

Gran sighed and shrugged, as if returning to her from a long distance. "I don't know. That's all I got. It just came to me."

They'd reached the kitchen island, and they stopped talking to fill their plates. When they took their places at the long farmhouse table, Gran was near the end on one side and Jazzi near the end on the other. No way to talk.

Elspeth took a bite of her sauerbraten and licked her lips. "This is wonderful, Jazzi. Radley and I have been talking. When we find a house and make it presentable, we want to take turns with you, having people over for the Sunday meal. We even thought about switching off who makes the main dish and who does side dishes and desserts."

Radley leaned forward. "We're not trying to intrude on your tradition, but you have to do a lot of work every week for this. We'd like to help."

"Me too," Didi said, "but I don't want to offend you."

"No offense taken. I'd love it." The meal had grown into something bigger than she'd anticipated, and eventually, it would grow larger.

Didi blinked. "You'd be okay with that?"

"Better than okay. I'd like it."

Elspeth smiled. "Until then, what if you and I take turns switching back and forth on who makes the main dish and the dessert?"

"Works for me."

"I'll make a side dish if you let me know what you're having that week to make sure it works," Didi said.

"We can decide each Thursday at girls' night out," Jazzi said.

She was surprised when Olivia added, "Mom and I will be glad to bring drinks. Neither of us intends to cook, but we can handle buying soda, wine, and beer."

"Sounds like a plan." Jazzi glanced at Ansel. "Is that okay with you?"

"I'm all for it."

That decided, they went back to catching up with each other.

"Is the lake cottage all closed up for the year?" Ansel asked Eli. Jerod's dad let him and Jazzi use it over Labor Day weekends, when he and Eleanore liked to travel.

Eli nodded. "The boats are in storage and the pier's put away. We still go up once in a while in the winter just to get out of town, but we usually don't go out on the ice. A few friends of ours icefish in front of the cabin, though."

Ansel's blue eyes lit up, and he glanced her way.

Jazzi shook her head. "You can go, but Eli talked me into trying it once, and I just sat on the ice and froze half to death until he let me go back to the cabin."

"Do you icefish?" Ansel asked Jerod.

"Not me. I catch enough fish during the summer."

Ansel glanced at Walker and Thane. They both nodded, and he grinned. "Maybe the three of us will try it sometime."

"Knock yourselves out. Let me know, and I'll give you a key to the cabin. You can go in there to get warm," Eli told him.

Once they'd finished eating, Ansel helped Jazzi clear the table, and they carried the strudel and ice cream to the kitchen island. There were so many drips and spills on it, Jazzi was glad they'd installed a butcher-block countertop. Easy to clean.

More small talk flowed over dessert and coffee, then the men all disappeared in the basement again, and the women headed to the living room. Half an hour later, the men joined them, and a short time later, people started heading home. Everyone liked to call it quits earlier on Sunday nights to relax before work on Monday.

Once everyone left, Ansel turned to her while they finished cleaning the kitchen. "What was your gran telling you about Jessica?"

"To look in his secret pocket, but it wouldn't be there yet."

He frowned.

"I know. Elusive as always. Gran has the sight, but the sight doesn't make it easy. Most of the time, I have no idea what she means."

"Maybe when the time's right, you will."

She smiled at him. "You have a knack for saying the right thing."

He hugged her. "'Happy wife, happy life.' I believe that." He did. So did Radley and the rest of their friends, but he sure didn't learn it from his father. Dalmar let Britt know he needed her to put meals on the table and care for the house, but that was about as far as his affections went.

Ansel hung up his dish towel. "I'm going upstairs to change into my pajamas; then I'm going to look for a sports channel. What about you?"

"PJs sound good, but I think I'll look up Jessica's four friends to see where I can find them. I'd like to hear their take on Jessica and the graduation party."

"Easy enough." He climbed the stairs with her. "Merlot's not that big. They can't live that far out of our way when we work there."

"Three of them have shops," she said. "We can stop by and check them out, talk to them there."

"And the fourth?"

"Is a teacher. I'll have to give her a call, make an appointment to see her."

"We could visit one every night after work," he said. "We'd still be home at a decent time."

A good plan. She was looking forward to it. Maybe Jessica's best friends would know more about Jessica's dad and brother, anyone who might have held a grudge against her. It was time to dig deeper.

Chapter 18

The white kitchen cabinets and stainless-steel appliances arrived on Monday. They'd ordered a six-burner stove and a deep farmhouse sink like Jazzi and Ansel had at their house. Once everything was delivered, they got busy hanging the cupboards and installing the bottom cabinets. They had to break for lunch, and George came to beg, happy they were having deli ham sandwiches and chips, his favorite.

During lunch, Jerod glared at the cupboards, glowering.

"What?" Jazzi asked. "What did those cupboards ever do to you?"

He snorted. "I held up the knobs we bought for them, and I don't like them. I should have gone with your idea: plain blue ones instead of the metal."

She refrained from saying *I told you so*. He wasn't in the mood. Instead, she shrugged. "We can use the metals ones on some other job. Leave early today and buy the ones you want."

He arched an eyebrow. "I have a better idea. We'll send you to the hardware store in town, and if they have them, get them. I don't want to bother with them tonight."

He wasn't usually so impatient, but why not? "I'll take off now if we're finished with lunch."

He waved her off. "Go already. I want to see what they look like."

Someone was in a mood. Pete must still be keeping them awake nights. Jazzi went to the work van and made the short drive into town. When she walked into the store, a man whose name tag had the same last name as the shop's sign came to greet her. Must be the owner.

"You're new here. Are you one of those flippers working on the Hodgkill place?" he asked. When she nodded, he shook his head. "Lila Mattock's been spreading rumors all over town about how rude you were to her. She even called the Hodgkill family in Carolina to complain about you."

Jazzi laughed. "I didn't make a good first impression. I wouldn't give her Jessica Hodgkill's journals."

He shook his head. "She'd only burn them. She hated Jessica with a passion. Are you keeping them?"

"It doesn't feel right, throwing them away. We called her family, but they didn't want them, so I took her hope chest home, and I'm reading through her things. I didn't realize she'd been murdered when I started."

"You're stirring up old memories. People are beginning to gossip about what happened again. Some folks, like Ruth Goggins, are hoping you find something to pin her death on Damian Dunlap. Others, like Damian's parents, are hoping you find something to prove him innocent."

She frowned. "Why the focus on Damian?"

He gave a wry smile. "That would be because of Lila and Ruth. Pot stirrers. They wouldn't leave it alone."

"They drove Damian out of town, made his life miserable. I've met him. He's hoping I find something in those journals, too."

He grimaced. "I'm none too proud of the way Merlot handled that boy. Some people made themselves judge and jury, decided he was guilty when there was no evidence."

Jazzi shook her head. "I'd love to find something. I really would, but I'm not having any luck. Maybe after all this time, someone will remember some small thing in a different light from back then."

"You're hoping to find Jessica's killer, too, aren't you?"

She nodded. "That girl had so much potential and was genuinely nice. According to her journals, too many people gave her grief."

"That would be her dad and Lila's fault. Neither of them ever had anything good to say about her. Lila was just jealous, but I never understood how a dad could be so cruel to his own daughter. He was a haughty person, so I thought he'd boast about Jessica's achievements. Instead, he insulted her for them."

"Did he influence other people to dislike her?"

"No, no one liked him much, but people listened to Lila back then. She had a way of insinuating things that made you believe her. Not so much now. After her divorce, we heard the same horror stories about the nice boy who married her. He won custody of their kids. That says something."

"It says a lot." Jazzi hesitated. "I've heard that Jessica's four good friends are still in town."

He grinned. "Part of the Fantastic Five? One of them was in here yesterday—Darcie Winters. She wants to get together with the other three and rehash memories they have about Jessica. They'd like you to find out who killed her as much as Damian and his family would."

Excitement buzzed through her veins. "Maybe they'll remember something."

"Maybe. I hope so. I always liked Jessica. My daughter was a year behind her in school, and Jessica tutored her once when she got behind in chemistry. Helped her pass her next test." The bell over the door rang, and another customer walked in. He shook himself, getting back to business. "But you probably came in here to look for something. How can I help you?"

Jazzi described the blue knobs she needed, and he nodded.

"Got 'em. I'll show you where they are."

When she walked to the counter to pay, he came to ring her up. "Good luck with everything. You've sure made the house look good."

"Thank you, and nice meeting you."

She meant it. As she walked to the van, she thought about what a nice man he was. And she'd learned a little more about Jessica and Merlot. A double win. Maybe this time, the town was ready to look for the truth, not just chase rumors.

Chapter 19

When she and Ansel got home that night, they worked in the basement. They used sprayers to paint the ceiling black, which meant Jazzi's face was speckled with black spatters of flat paint. She and Ansel had both covered their heads and worn long sleeves, and that was a good thing. It protected most of their skin. Then they grabbed rollers for the walls. The soft, khaki satin finish made the room feel bigger without being too stark.

When they finished, Ansel smiled, admiring their work. "I like it."

"So do I." Jazzi narrowed her eyes at the floor. "You were thinking about indoor/outdoor carpeting once, but what about plank tiles that look like wood instead? We can add lots of throw rugs for color and warmth."

He scowled. "That's a lot more work and more expensive."

"But if someone spills something, we wipe it up. No big deal. I think this room is going to get a lot of use."

"Are you up for laying tiles down here?"

"If you like the idea, we should buy what we need tonight, so we can get them done before Halloween."

He swatted her fanny. The man had a thing about her booty. Actually, he liked all of her curves. "Race you to the truck."

Rolling her eyes, she jogged up the steps after him. George came to the door to go with them, but Ansel patted his head. "Not this time, buddy. We'll bring something back for you."

The pug knew those words and understood them. He trotted to his dog bed to wait for his treat.

They both liked oak flooring, but they decided on a darker look to make the khaki walls pop. Area rugs were on sale, so they threw in five of those, too. Their next stop was a drive-through to buy burgers and fries to take home. Ansel bought one for George, and when they walked through their back door and George saw the bag, he hurried to the kitchen island. Jazzi tossed fries on the floor, and Inky and Marmalade batted them back and forth.

It had been a long day. Supper was so late, when they finished, they showered and changed into their pajamas before settling on their favorite couches just as Jazzi's cell phone rang. She frowned at the number. No one she recognized, but she picked it up.

As soon as she said hello, a man started yelling at her. "My wife asked you to stay out of our personal lives. She's suffered enough. You don't have any business reading Jessica's journals!"

"You must be Mr. Hodgkill." Jazzi pushed the Speaker button so that Ansel could hear. Keeping her voice calm, she said, "I called and asked your wife if she'd like us to send her any of Jessica's things. She didn't want them."

His voice only grew angrier. "That doesn't mean she wanted you to take them home and poke your nose into our lives. Lila said you wouldn't even let her look at them."

"Lila was never nice to your daughter. She doesn't deserve to see them."

"That's for us to decide! If you don't give them to her, I'm calling my lawyer. Do you understand that? If you want to cause trouble, we'll give you trouble."

Jessica's dad must be used to getting his own way, but yelling and threats didn't affect her. She was about to tell him that when Ansel took the phone from her.

"Look at the contract you signed when you sold the house. It's the same one Madeline signed when she sold it to us. We bought the house and all of its contents. The journals are ours. Stop yelling at my wife or we'll talk to *our* lawyer. Don't call here again." And he hung up.

Jazzi stared at him. "I was going to explain about the contract."

He pressed his lips together. Her Norseman got protective once in a while. "It wouldn't matter what you told that idiot. He's not the type to listen. He's a yeller, like my dad."

He was right. And Dalmar dismissed anything said by a woman. After reading Jessica's journals, she knew Mr. Hodgkill had little respect for anything female either. She settled back on her sofa, putting the call behind her. She had no respect for bullies.

Chapter 20

On Tuesday, the butcher-block countertops came, and they looked perfect with the white cabinets. The only thing they still needed to do was install the backsplash. The tiles they'd chosen would take most of the day because the countertops on the back and side walls were so long.

Jerod was in a better mood, so he must have gotten more sleep. "The last tooth came through," he told them. "Pete's back on schedule. Life will be good until he cuts his molars."

Gunther and Lizzie must have gone through the same thing when they cut teeth, but Jazzi didn't remember it. Raising kids wasn't all baking cookies and playing peekaboo. When it was their turn, she hoped she'd survive it.

Jerod scraped another layer of mortar on the wall, then reached for a tile. "I'm buying pork steaks to throw on the grill for supper tonight to celebrate."

"My mom used to fry those," Ansel said.

That didn't surprise Jazzi. Dalmar watched every penny his wife spent. With three kids, Jerod budgeted, too. No one-inch chops for him, but whatever he made was good. The man was a solid cook. He just didn't bother with fancy.

"I don't know about other people, but the kids changed what we cook and eat," he told them. "Franny read the articles that said if you start your kids on broccoli and spinach, they'll love them. Not ours. They eat carrots, corn, and green beans without suffering, but the only broccoli they'll touch is yours, and only if you drown it in cheese sauce."

Jazzi laughed, applying the next row of mortar. "Didi says the same thing about River. She has to hide vegetables in soups or sauces to get him to eat them."

"I'm not above that either." Jerod grinned. "I bought an immersion blender, and Gunther and Lizzie don't even know some of the vegetables I sneak into their food."

Ansel scowled. "We ate whatever Mom put on our plates. No one cared if we liked it or not."

His childhood was so different from hers. She shook her head, remembering. "I went through a phase when I only ate bologna, hot dogs, or peanut butter sandwiches. I remember Mom lecturing me about it."

"But she still let you?" Ansel asked.

"Olivia and I were spoiled. What can I say?"

"You forgot pizza." Jerod opened a new box of tiles. "Kids inhale that, especially pepperoni."

"Kids change your life, that's for sure. I've watched it happen with every one of my friends who started a family." She turned to Ansel. "Have any of your old friends had kids yet?"

"I only stayed in contact with Ethan. And yeah, he's struggling. He got married right out of high school, has two boys—four and one. His wife isn't working right now, and money's tight."

They reached the last row at the top of the backsplash. Jazzi grimaced. "We're going to have to start cutting the tiles to fit."

They had a special saw for that. Jerod measured and Ansel cut while Jazzi mortared. Ansel pressed the last piece of tile into place, finishing the back wall, and they started on the side one with the refrigerator and more counters. It was nearly four when they finally finished. They were cleaning the tiles' surface when someone knocked on the front door.

"Oh, no. Not Ruth again." But when Jazzi went to greet her, it was a woman with short brown curls and a deep tan who peered through the screen at her.

"Hello? I'm Darcie Winters, a friend of Jessica's when she was alive. Joe, from the hardware store, called me and said you were looking into Jessica's death. Can we talk?"

Jazzi held the door open wider for her to come in. Darcie wore old jeans with stains at the knees. She was of medium height and looked fit and strong. She stopped to stare. "You've made the house beautiful. I hope someone buys it who'll love it as much as Jessica did."

"She loved it?" Jazzi hadn't read that in her journals.

"She was so attached to it, it made her sad when she talked about leaving. But she had to, to get away from her dad."

Jazzi motioned for her to take a seat at the card table in the front room. "Sorry. We carried everything out to work. This is the only place to sit."

Darcie chuckled. "No problem. When I'm in the middle of a landscaping project, I usually end up sitting on a log or the grass."

The men finished in the kitchen and came into the room to meet her. Jazzi made the introductions.

"Everything's done for the day," Jerod said. "I'm going to take off and head home. Nice meeting you, Darcie."

Jazzi noticed her check out Jerod's ring finger. Her cousin was a good-looking guy, and he had a mischievous gleam in his eyes. That gleam had attracted many a woman.

When he left, Darcie pinched her lips together. "Married?"

"With three kids."

"Just checking. I couldn't think about another man after my divorce a year ago, but then I decided I just needed to pick someone better the next time." She quirked a brow at Ansel. "You're too handsome. Besides, you can't keep your eyes off your wife." She grew somber. "But that's not why I came. I heard that you were reading Jessica's journals and were interested in her murder."

"I don't like the idea that her killer's never been caught. I think Jessica got a bum deal all the way around."

Darcie nodded. "Her dad was a tyrant. All other mortals were beneath him and Alwin. Men ruled supreme, and Hodgkill men were at the top of the pinnacle."

Jazzi blurted out the question she really wanted an answer to. "Did her dad hate her enough to push her off the balcony?"

"It wouldn't surprise me at all, but he couldn't have done it. He was manning the grill all day." Darcie clasped her hands together, looking nervous and excited at the same time. "You've made me realize that we all took sides when Jessica died, but we never sat down and thought things out. I've asked a few friends to stop by my house on Friday night to figure out who was at the party and exactly where they were when Jessica fell. I'll question everyone in town if I have to. That way, we can rule out who *didn't* kill her." She straightened her shoulders. "This time, I'm going to find answers."

"A great idea." Jazzi glanced at Ansel as he settled at the table with them. He started to stretch his legs but stopped. They were too long. He'd cramp Darcie's space. But now that Darcie was here, Jazzi had another question for her. "Do you remember if anyone unusual was at the party? We have a friend who's a detective. He said another girl was murdered close to the same time Jessica died. Is it possible that girl was the main target and Jessica just reminded the killer of her?" Maybe she had events the wrong way around.

"I heard about that, and it made me wonder, too, but there were no strangers. Everyone there lived in Merlot. I was surprised to see Ruth Goggins. No adults were invited, only Jessica's class, but I got the idea she wasn't invited. She came to keep an eye on RJ."

Poor RJ. No wonder he'd hidden. Jazzi asked, "When you make your lists, will you let me know what you come up with?"

"That's why I stopped here. We'd like you to come, too." Darcie reached into her purse and handed Jazzi a business card. "We're meeting at my house on Friday night at six. Can you make it?"

Ansel gave her a quick nod.

"I'll be there," Jazzi said. "And thanks."

"You can bring tall, blond, and handsome, if you want." Darci's eyes sparkled, and she winked at him. "We don't mind gorgeous scenery."

Ansel shook his head. "I'll stay home and work on the basement. We're close to getting it finished."

"Can't say that I blame you for passing." She looked back to Jazzi. "See you on Friday."

After Darcie left, Jazzi tamped down hope that they'd finally make a new discovery. She knew the odds were against that, but the more people who helped, the better chance they had.

Ansel brooded on the drive home, wearing his glowering Viking look. Jazzi left him to it. When he was ready to tell her what was bothering him, he would. Finally, he said, "We just keep getting the same information over and over again with every person we talk to about Jessica."

"But we learn a little bit more each time. Just not enough to do us any good."

"I still think the other murdered woman and Jessica have to be connected." He stopped for a red light and turned to her with a frown. "Don't you?"

"They have to be. She looked like Jessica. It's too much of a coincidence."

Running a hand through his short blond hair, he made it spike in front. He looked good when it stood on end at his forehead. "This is the thing: A guy could lose his temper and give someone a push, sending her over the balcony by accident. But no one accidentally bashes a cheerleader with a rock behind a building. So the guy killed them both for some reason. But he stopped when Jessica died, which makes it look like she was his intended victim."

"Maybe he didn't stop with Jessica."

Ansel looked surprised. "There weren't any more bodies after that."

"Maybe there were." It was the first time she'd thought about it. "Maybe he moved away, and no one connected the new murders with the girls around Merlot." She should ask Gaff about that.

Their turnoff was coming up, and he slowed for it. "When you bring up people who moved, that covers quite a few of them."

She nodded. "Brett, Damian, Jessica's entire family, RJ, his wife, and Damian's wife."

"I'd vote for RJ's aunt if it weren't for the other girl."

She grinned. "That's just wishful thinking."

"Maybe. I'd be happy with Lila, too."

"She'd have been at every event that the basketball team went to, at every place Jessica went."

His blue eyes glinted. "Then she's a possibility. I don't want it to be Brett, Damian, or RJ."

She didn't either, and she didn't think it was, but she couldn't prove it.

They pulled into their driveway and he stopped the van near the back patio to let her out before parking in the garage. When he joined her in the kitchen with George, he glanced at the basement door. "I'm too restless to relax right now. I think I'll head downstairs and start working on the floor."

"I'll help you."

"This was my idea. I'm not trying to work you to death. You can stay up here and play with the cats if you want to."

She followed him to the basement. "The cats have enough fun helping us work. I'm making pasta tonight with artichokes and mushrooms. Quick and easy. Let's see how much we can get done before then."

They surprised themselves when half the tiles were laid by seven. If they got gung ho again the next night, the floor would be finished. Ansel crossed his arms, running a critical eye over the finished product. "I'm glad we bought the rugs. The room needs some color."

"When you get furniture and a pool table down here, it's going to look good."

They went upstairs to cook together. This time, after supper, Ansel grabbed George, and when they went up the steps, they didn't make it back down. After showering and changing, they crawled into bed to read to relax—the last thing Jazzi remembered. She woke the next morning to find her paperback on the floor where she'd dropped it.

Chapter 21

The kitchen was done, and it looked gorgeous. The extra money and touches were worth it. They were gutting the half bath across from the library when they heard a car pull into the drive. Jazzi went to see who was there.

Gaff stalked up the sidewalk, scowling. Medium height and stocky, the detective reminded her of a tank—solid and heavy. She knew that look, that walk, and braced herself for bad news. She called, "Guys! It's Gaff!"

They came to the door, too.

She opened it for him and he moved inside. Without preamble, he barked, "My detective friend called. Darcie Winters was shot at around three this morning in her home in the country. I don't like it. He thinks it has something to do with people stirring up old news. And you're in the middle of it again."

Jazzi pressed a hand to her throat. Poor Darcie. Guilt washed over her. "She came here yesterday. She asked us about Jessica. She was going to get her friends together to figure out who was where at the graduation party. Do you think that's why someone shot her?"

Gaff marched into the kitchen to the coffee urn and poured himself a cup. "I hope not, but the timing's sure suspect. It can't be a coincidence this girl was murdered when she was digging into Jessica's death."

That word again. "Coincidence." Jazzi went to the card table and sagged onto one of the chairs. "It's my fault. I shouldn't have taken Jessica's journals home and gotten involved. The man who owns the hardware store told me everyone was getting riled up about the murder again. Jessica's father called to warn us off."

"When was that?" Gaff reached for the notepad he always carried in his shirt pocket.

"A couple of nights ago. He's an unpleasant person. He threatened to call his lawyer, to make me give her journals to Lila Mattock."

Gaff stopped writing to look up at her. "Why Lila?"

Ansel carried mugs of coffee to the table and passed one to Jazzi. Voice dry, he said, "Because Lila called him to complain about us."

"Does she keep in touch with them?" Gaff asked.

"I don't know. She's spreading rumors all over town, though, about how rude we were to her." Jazzi's hands shook. She had to use both of them to sip her coffee. Gaff's news was so unexpected, so out of the blue, it threw her.

Gaff went for more coffee. "Odd. Why does she care so much about old history? Makes you wonder, doesn't it?"

Jazzi stopped to consider that. "At first, I thought she knew Jessica's journals would be full of all the crap Lila did to her, that they wouldn't make her look good. But maybe it's more."

"Maybe she has something to hide." Gaff made more notes.

Jerod chimed in. "Maybe Darcie's death doesn't have anything to do with Jessica. She said she was divorced, didn't she? Does her ex still resent her leaving him? Is there a new boyfriend on the scene? And she was a master gardener, a landscape artist who traveled and worked with lots of clients. Did anything go wrong there?"

Ansel raised a brow, skeptical. "Do you really believe that?"

"No, but killing her doesn't make much sense either, does it?"

Ansel looked pensive. This case was getting to him as much as it was her. "She lived in the country, right? Did any neighbors see any cars drive past their houses they didn't recognize?"

"At three in the morning?" Gaff shook his head. "No one even heard anything."

She wouldn't either. She and Ansel were both sound sleepers. Unless a thunder clap boomed directly above their house, storms didn't even wake them.

Gaff stared at his notes. "I'd be relieved if an ex or a boyfriend got picked up for this, but my money's still on something to do with Jessica. Tell me everything you've learned and think so far."

Jazzi named the people who could possibly be suspects. "Brett's brother, Damian, and his wife, Kelsey, *could* be, but I don't think so."

"Because you like them?" Gaff nailed her with a look.

"I do like them, but mostly, they were trying to decide who was where during Jessica's graduation party, too, and both of them were with other people when Jessica fell."

Gaff nodded and put a big question mark after their names. "Anyone else?"

"Ruth Goggins next door."

"Is that because you *don't* like her?"

Jazzi raised an eyebrow at him. "No, it's because she hated Jessica almost as much as Lila Mattock did. She's on my list, too, but they're both iffy because even though I think they'd push Jessica if they could, I don't know if they'd kill a girl who looked like her."

"If those murders are related," Jerod said. "Maybe you're linking things that don't link."

"Maybe." She thought they were connected, though. "I guess you'd have to list Ruth's nephew, RJ, and his wife, Tilly, but RJ liked Jessica. I don't think he'd hurt her."

"And Tilly?"

She pursed her lips. "I've sort of overlooked her. Damian's wife, too. They were both really jealous of Jessica, but I think they were with other people when Jessica fell."

"Or so they said. Darcie was going to check on that, right?" Gaff put check marks beside their names. "Anyone else?"

"Jessica's dad and brother, Alwin. Her dad actively disliked her, and I can't quite decide about Alwin. People have said he was protective of her but couldn't show it because of their dad. They had an odd relationship."

"What about her mom?"

"Her mom did her best to stick up for her. She was proud of Jessica."

"Is that it, then?" Gaff put his pen in his pocket.

"That's all I can think of for now. Darcie invited Jessica's three other best friends to her house on Friday. Me too. I'd like to talk to each of them. To see if they had anyone else they wondered about."

Gaff closed his notepad. "This isn't just satisfying curiosity anymore. It's not just digging into the past. Someone killed Darcie. She'd been calling lots of people, asking them about the graduation party. My friend thinks she got too close to discovering something. If you get too close, you'll be on this guy's radar, too."

"I'm going with you if you talk to these women," Ansel said.

Jazzi didn't argue. Better safe than sorry. She glanced out the front window at the hydrangea and rhododendrons planted along the house's border, trying to concentrate. "If we call everyone on the list to see where they were at three this morning, we should be able to rule out some people, shouldn't we?"

Gaff grinned. "My friend's already ahead of you. He asked me to talk to you, to give him a list of names if you had one, to check on their alibis."

"Will you let us know what he finds out?"

"Will do." Gaff drained his coffee, then gave a grunt. "Guess we've gotten as far as we're going to for now. I have to get back to River Bluffs. I'm working a case. If you hear something, let me know. This isn't a past murder anymore. It's gone active."

Jazzi walked him to the door.

Before leaving, he gave her a stern look. "Be careful."

"I will." She watched his car pull away.

Ansel came to stand behind her, wrapping his strong arms around her shoulders. "It's not your fault someone killed Darcie."

"She wouldn't have been calling people, digging for clues, if I hadn't brought up old memories."

"Who could guess the killer would even care after all this time? No one could prove anything back then. Why think you'd find proof now?"

But she *had* thought that. She *had* wanted to find Jessica's killer. Just not at the price of another life. She sighed, and the guilt returned.

Ansel planted a kiss on top of her head. "You didn't ask Darcie to get involved. She took that on herself. You'd have warned her off if you thought it could get her in trouble. *But...*" He gave her a stern look. "If someone killed Darcie to keep secrets buried, he could look at you next. You're not going to talk to *anyone* without me. I'm going to stick so close to you, you're going to be sick of me before this case is finished, one way or another."

"You're right. I never expected poking around would be dangerous." There was no way she'd have encouraged Darcie if she thought the killer still lurked in the area. She frowned at that. Did that mean Jessica's murderer lived in or close to Merlot? She'd almost decided he must have moved away. Now she wasn't so sure. Having Ansel beside her sounded better and better.

Chapter 22

They finished gutting the half bath before lunch. When Jazzi took out deli sandwiches again, Jerod looked disappointed.

"Sorry," she said. "We've been working on the basement every night."

He nodded. "Hey, you feed me. I can't complain."

Ansel snorted. "When did that ever stop you?" He tossed a scrap of roast beef to George.

"Hey, I understand about working days and nights," Jerod said, defending himself. "You guys have been beating yourselves up to get the basement finished on time for the party. What still needs to get done?"

"We've painted and laid the tile," Ansel said. "Once we put up trim, we can start furnishing it."

"Does that mean a pool table might be down there for the Sunday family meal?"

Ansel sounded as excited as her cousin. "We've already picked it out. All I have to do is call for them to deliver it."

Jazzi half-listened to them go into raptures about a pinball machine and an enormous TV. She thought about installing the trim. They could do the baseboard tonight when they got home and the ceiling trim tomorrow, but she was quitting in time to make sloppy joes for lunch tomorrow. Jerod was right. She was getting really tired of deli sandwiches.

Ansel broke into her thoughts. "What do you think? Should I call and have everything delivered on Thursday? That way, the guys can help me set it up."

"Why not? Then you can test them out." Like she could keep them from it.

He caught the jibe and grinned. "Do you want me to decide where to put them?"

"We've already talked about it, but if I don't like it, you have to change it."

"Fair enough." Anything to get to his pool table early.

That meant that by Thursday night, the basement would be done. The heavens must be taking mercy on her. She could go home, put up her feet, and relax again.

They finished eating and decided to start measuring the study to build bookshelves. Lots of bookshelves. Jerod had found a retired carpenter with a barn full of beautiful boards he wanted to sell off. Jerod had made an appointment for them to drive there in the morning to choose what they wanted for Ansel's vision of the library.

"They won't be cheap," Jerod said, "but he wants to get rid of them. He'll give us a good price."

Ansel looked at the magazine page he'd taped to a wall. "Maybe he'll have cherry. I love how that looks."

So did she. Three walls of cherry bookcases would be impressive. It took two hours of serious planning to decide on measurements and how much wood they'd need. When they finished, Jerod said, "Let's call it an early night. If we start another project, we'll be staying late, and I promised Gunther and Lizzie that we'd go fishing in our pond tonight. We usually don't catch anything, so I'm stopping on the way home to buy fish sticks."

Jazzi blinked at him, surprised. "But you have a freezer full of fish."

"I know, but if I thaw them, it looks like I don't expect the kids to provide supper for us. I don't want to hurt their feelings."

"Isn't it too cold to fish?" Ansel asked.

"Nothing much is going to bite, but the kids have fun anyway."

She grinned. He was a good dad. "It's true love when you eat fish sticks instead of perch."

Besides fishing at his parents' lake cottage, Jerod and Franny rented a cabin in Michigan every summer. Jerod came home with whitefish from there. And once a year, he and Thane drove to a river in Michigan to spend a long weekend catching salmon when they ran.

"You should come with Thane and me the next time we go," Jerod told Ansel. "We have a great time."

Ansel glanced uncertainly at Jazzi. "It sounds like fun."

"Then go." He'd love it. "I can live without you for a weekend."

He frowned at that, and Jerod laughed at him. "Franny loves to see the backside of me. Her parents take the kids, and she has a weekend all to herself."

"You'd miss me, wouldn't you?" Ansel asked as the three of them grabbed their things to lock up.

"As much as you'll miss me," she told him.

When he scowled, Jerod laughed harder. "See you tomorrow!" he told them.

On the drive home, Ansel fretted. "You missed me when I went to Wisconsin to work on my dad's roofs."

"I felt sorry for you because you were so unhappy there."

"But if I went fishing, I'd be having a good time, and you wouldn't."

"I'd think of something."

"Like what?" He sounded worried.

"Olivia and I might go shopping and eat out together."

That satisfied him. They were almost to their turnoff for home when Ansel's cell phone buzzed. He glanced at the caller ID. "Didi." He pushed it to Speaker, and they both listened.

"I have a flat tire, and I'm stranded in a parking lot near the corner of Ardmore and Jefferson with River. Walker's pouring cement somewhere or I'd have called him."

"No problem," Ansel assured her. "We're almost home. I'll drop Jazzi off and come to help you."

"Thank you." She sounded frazzled.

"Is there somewhere you can go to sit and snack until I get there? It'll take me a while to cross town."

"There's a Chinese buffet."

Ansel slowed by the back patio to drop Jazzi off. "Go buy a couple of egg rolls and a cup of tea, and I'll be there as soon as I can."

Jazzi watched him pull away with George before going inside. Inky and Marmalade ran to greet her. She fed them and pulled a string around the kitchen island to play with them before going upstairs to shower and change. Ansel would be a while. She decided to call Leesa and tell her about Darcie. After that, she called Damian and Kelsey.

Kelsey answered. "Damian's not home from work yet. But you said Darcie was shot at three this morning? We were both home in bed. In Chicago."

Jazzi thought about nurses' hours. "When was your shift?"

"Three a.m. to three p.m., but I had last night and tonight off. Then I have three on."

Jazzi shook her head. She'd hate those hours, but she knew that was part of a nurse's life. "Is there any way to prove you were both there?"

"At three in the morning? We don't have company then. Do you?"

Jazzi sighed. "No, but most cops will think that because you're husband and wife, you're giving each other alibis."

Kelsey's voice sounded strained. "I know. We got that when Jessica died, but I can't do anything about it." She took a loud breath, then blurted out, "Why would anyone kill Darcie?"

"Were you friends?"

"I wasn't part of Jessica's group, but I always liked her. She didn't put on airs, shot straight from the hip. Most everyone liked her."

Jazzi explained their theories.

"You're right." Kelsey paused. "It's odd someone shot her right after she started digging into Jessica's death. How many people would know about that?"

"Probably all of Merlot. News seems to travel fast there."

"Especially if Ruth Goggins hears it. That woman can't keep her big mouth shut."

"And Lila calls the Hodgkill family in Carolina to tattle on everyone, so I'd guess they know, too."

"So the usual suspects," Kelsey said.

"Looks like it."

Another pause. Finally, "We can't drive to River Bluffs this weekend. Not when I work Wednesday, Thursday, and Friday. I'd be too tired. But we'll try to get there again. Maybe if we met with some of our old friends, we'd hear something new."

"That got Darcie killed."

Kelsey's sigh traveled over the phone. "Jessica's murder just won't go away, will it?"

"There's a new victim. Maybe the police will find something this time."

"Maybe. I hope." She didn't sound hopeful when they ended the call.

While she was at it, Jazzi called RJ next. He answered on the third ring. "Hey, nice to hear from you!" But his tone changed after he heard her news. "Tilly and I were in Indianapolis last night. Took today off so we could stay up late to attend a concert there. We might have been in our hotel by three a.m., but I'm not sure. We had a little too much fun."

She smiled. "Where was the concert held?"

"In a bar. It's one of Tilly's favorite groups. There were so many people there, though, I don't think anyone would have noticed or remembered us. I have my ticket stubs, but no one could swear when we left. The place was jammed."

Jazzi blew out a breath of frustration. Another couple who could only alibi each other.

After RJ, she called Gaff. "Have you talked to anyone for alibis yet?"

"Nadia Ashton, Lila, and the Hodgkill family. Jessica's mom and dad swore they were home together. Nadia said she was asleep—what did I think she'd be doing? Alwin, though, was in Brown County, Indiana, on a short vacation, alone, to visit the shops and the national park. He supposedly needed a break and went sightseeing all day, but Brown County closes up shop early, and he rented a cabin that's sort of secluded, so no one could see if he came or went. He says he never drove to Merlot, had no desire to."

Jazzi gave up after that. She wasn't learning anything worthwhile. Ansel still wasn't home, so she started a pot of sloppy joes for lunch tomorrow, then put together a one-sheet-pan meal and slid it in the oven. She was cleaning the kitchen when Ansel walked through the door.

"Did you change Didi's tire?" she asked.

He nodded. "She's driving on a donut now, but Walker can put on a new one tomorrow." He sniffed the air. "It smells wonderful in here. What are you making?"

"An oven one-pan, pork-chop meal."

"I like those."

As long as she didn't get too crazy, there wasn't much he didn't like. "Want to work on trim until it's ready?"

"You remembered. I thought you might want to skip it because I got back late."

"If we finish the baseboard, we can do the ceiling trim tomorrow. And then on Thursday…"

His eyes twinkled. "My toys arrive."

She laughed, and they headed to the basement. Inky and Marmalade raced ahead of them, and when they cut trim to size, they'd toss thin, extra pieces for the cats to bat and chase. They'd finished three walls before the oven buzzer rang. Then they stopped to eat and returned to finish the last wall before calling it a night.

Jazzi stretched out on her couch to read while Ansel went up to shower and change. She'd started a new (for her) J. D. Robb book that she was hooked on. She was only on book three, so she was *way* behind in the series, but that gave her plenty of good books to look forward to.

When Ansel took his place on the sofa opposite hers, he lifted George up to lay with him, then clicked on the TV. He happily flipped through channels while she hurried through another chapter.

Finally, at ten, he stood and yawned. "Ready to call it a night?"

With a nod, she followed him upstairs to bed. Maybe tomorrow Gaff would have talked to more people, and he'd have more news for her. But she meant to look up Jillian Hendricks at her craft shop in Merlot to see what she could learn herself.

Chapter 23

When Jerod saw a Crock-Pot full of sloppy joes come into the kitchen, he raised his arms to give her a mock bow. "You rule my lunch heart."

She rolled her eyes. "I was tired of sandwiches, too."

Laughing, he turned to George. "We're going to eat good today."

George lifted his head and looked straight at the slow cooker. The pug understood everything to do with food.

Jerod waited until Jazzi plugged in the pot, then, before they removed their heavy jackets, asked, "Are you ready to go look at the wood for the bookshelves?"

"Might as well." She zipped up her jacket again. Nights had gotten colder the longer the month went. By afternoon, the temperatures rose and were more comfortable, but mornings and evenings demanded warm jackets. Jazzi was hoping an Indian summer would heat things up for Halloween, but it didn't look promising.

"Are you driving?" Ansel asked.

"Sure, I know the way."

They followed Jerod to his truck and set off cross-country to Highway 14. The air was brisk. Trees flamed with color. They passed a farmhouse where the owner had raked a pile of leaves and stood watching over them as they burned. The scent of smoke filled the car. Ten minutes later, they were looking at a barn full of beautiful wood. And yes, there was cherry. They bought and loaded what they needed, and as they started to pull away, the carpenter called, "If you need more for anything else, give me a call. The walnut's gone. A contractor bought it all, but I still have plenty to look at."

She'd noticed a stack of maple boards that were especially appealing. "The maple would make great shelving in our basement."

Ansel turned in the front seat to ask, "For the entertainment area?"

"We could store CDs and movies on them, craft stuff for kids."

"I'll give the guy a call and arrange to pick them up after work." Jerod's truck wouldn't hold any more.

Once back at the Merlot house, they unloaded the boards and stored them in the three-car garage, locking it securely. They were walking back into the house when Gaff arrived. He walked in with them. Jerod looked at the kitchen clock.

"How do you end up here so often at lunchtime?"

Gaff smiled. "A cop's instinct. Besides, Jazzi told me you were fishing last night. I expected to have fish sandwiches for lunch. What's the matter? Didn't catch any?"

"I'm lucky I lived through it." Jerod shook his head. "Gunther got his hook caught in a tree twice. Lizzie cried when I put a worm on her hook, so I used lures on hers instead. She almost fell in the pond trying to cast her line."

Gaff laughed. "You didn't catch anything?"

"A headache." Jerod and Gaff loved to give each other a hard time. "You're here, though, so you might as well eat with us."

Gaff immediately took his place at the card table and managed to eat two sandwiches and his fair share of chips. "My friend called me. He said he checked Darcie's phone, and she'd called a lot of different people, asking them what room they were in and who they were with when Jessica fell. She must have called the wrong person and made him or her nervous."

"Did you find any notes she left?" Jazzi asked.

"He found a notebook, but three pages were torn out of it. No prints. He checked."

Jerod loaded another bun for his third helping. Jazzi chastised herself. She'd have to make something different more often for lunch. "Doesn't that make it seem like someone *could* have seen the killer where he shouldn't have been?"

Gaff nodded. "Could be, but it doesn't guarantee it. Maybe the killer's just worried about it." He went on. "Everyone my friend called said that Darcie had never gotten over Jessica's killer getting away with it. She wanted him caught."

"At the cost of her life," Ansel said.

Gaff leveled a look at Jazzi. "Keep that in mind. This killer doesn't intend to be punished for what he did."

"I get it. I'll be careful." She crossed her heart.

"I'm serious. You do that." Gaff carried his paper plate to the trash and headed to the door. "Gotta go, but you might want to back off for a while, let my friend take it from here."

When he left, Ansel narrowed his eyes to study her. "That's not going to happen, is it?"

"I can't sit it out now." She sighed, frustrated. "I feel too responsible. I got the whole thing started."

He nodded but didn't look happy. "Then we'll go to visit Jillian Hendricks after work, like you planned, before picking up the maple shelving."

Her shoulders relaxed. She hadn't realized how tense she'd been. "Thank you."

"But you only question people when I'm with you."

"Scout's honor."

He gave her a look. "Were you ever a Scout?"

Jerod laughed. "Not a chance. She wouldn't do crafty stuff like the other girls. She wanted to chop down saplings, build fires, and camp out with the guys."

"If she'd joined our town's Boy Scout group, I would have, too," Ansel told him.

"Not at that age. At ten, girls had cooties. I didn't even chase skirts back then."

"So not true." Jazzi called him on that one. "You kissed Tessa Parker on the bus in fourth grade."

Jerod grinned, remembering. "Oh, yeah, forgot about that."

Jazzi shook her head at both of them. "Lunch is over. Time to get back to work."

They finished the half bath, installing a new toilet, a sink, and a medicine cabinet. Then they started cutting the cherry boards to size for bookshelves. There was no way they could finish, so they knocked off work at their usual time. Jerod headed home, but the others drove the few blocks to downtown Merlot and parked at the curb outside Jillian Hendrick's craft shop.

The day was nippy enough, so they tugged their jackets closer as they left the van. "Stay," Ansel told George and walked through the door with Jazzi.

Chapter 24

Jillian's shop was long and narrow, with brick walls and a high ceiling. It was crammed full of hand-painted coasters, tiles, hand-tossed dishes and bowls, and one-of-a-kind throw pillows. Incense gave the space a spicy scent. Jillian sat in the front behind a long counter, working on a watercolor painting.

She looked up, saw Ansel, and her green eyes lit up. When he unbuttoned his jacket and let it hang open, showing off his snug T-shirt stretched over bulging muscles, she said, "I don't suppose you'd sit as an artist's model?"

He blinked. "I'm not good at sitting."

Her lips curled. "No, I suppose not. I can picture you in action."

Jazzi could imagine that kind of action would have to be censored. She raised an eyebrow in warning, and Jillian grinned.

The woman's brown hair was parted in the center and pulled up on each side into a knot with feathers decorating each. It was so unusual, Jazzi stared. Few people could get away with it, but she looked so artsy, it worked for her. Her smile was wide and cheerful.

"Welcome to my shop. If there's anything I can help you with, let me know."

Jazzi nodded, her attention caught by the colorful couch cushions. A few of them would be perfect as accessories for the Merlot house. Then she spotted a giant diamond and wedding band on Jillian's finger. Married. Just enjoying herself. Why not? Ansel was worth looking at.

Jillian's gaze rested on her. "Everyone's talking about the two blondes in town. You must be the people flipping Jessica's house." Her smile faded. "Have you come about Darcie?"

No more looking around. Jazzi focused. "She came to visit us, and invited me to a get-together at her house to try to remember exact details about Jessica's party."

Jillian came out from behind the counter to talk to them. She was probably five four and thin. She looked small standing next to Ansel. Voice gruff, she said, "The police have to find out who killed her. They can't come up empty like last time."

"They're working on it. People don't realize how much goes into an investigation. It's hard to find leads."

"There has to be something!" Jillian grimaced. "Sorry, but I've lost *two* of my best friends now. I want answers."

"A lot of people do, and not just accusations and gossip."

Jillian snorted. "This is a small town. There's no way to avoid that."

With a nod, Jazzi acknowledged the point. "Darcie was trying to determine who was at Jessica's party, what room they were in when Jessica fell, and who they were with, so that she could eliminate people who might have pushed her."

"Just like her. A solid plan. I vividly remember who was with me when Jessie fell. I bet we all do. It was so horrible, it's seared into my memory. Damian was in the dining room, where I was. We were at the punch bowl. He was getting drinks for Kelsey and him."

"Kelsey wasn't with him?" She'd told Jazzi that, that she'd been in the bathroom at the time.

"No."

"Was there anyone else with you to corroborate he was with you? Because Lila Mattock swears she saw him going up the stairs right before Jessica fell."

"Lila Mattock's a freak," Jillian spat. "No, it was just Damian and me. So it was my word against hers. The detective wrote off both of us."

"He'd have to. No one else could vouch for you and Damian?"

She shook her head. "But I know what I know. Damian was with me."

Jazzi nodded. "We'll mark him off our list. Do you know where anyone else was?"

Jillian shook her head.

Jazzi thanked her, and they headed toward the door. Ansel stopped her. "Did you want some of the pillows here?"

"Do you mind?" Jazzi asked Jillian.

The woman smiled. "No, a double win for me. I can help clear Damian's name and make a sale. A good day."

Jazzi chose several pillows, then they took their leave.

"Still in the mood to get the maple boards from the carpenter?" Ansel asked.

"If we want them, we'd better get them. They're going to go fast."

On the drive there, they were both quiet. Jazzi's thoughts spun, placing people at the party when Jessica died. Jessica's dad was at the grill. Damian was with Jillian. RJ was hiding from his aunt with another one of Jessica's friends—the schoolteacher, Felicity—and Tilly was in line for food at the grill. She'd have to substantiate both of those alibis, but she mentally put check marks next to their names. She'd have to write out a list and begin scratching people off. Kelsey wasn't with anyone.

Ansel pulled into the carpenter's drive and parked near the barn. She pulled her thoughts back to renovations and getting the basement done.

Chapter 25

When they got home, Jazzi helped Ansel unload the maple boards and carry them into the basement. He had a workshop against the far back wall, so he could saw the boards down there. It would make it a lot easier to build the shelves for his man cave. Before starting work on the baseboard, though, he said, "Let's take a break and sip a little wine and beer to relax."

He could tell she was still brooding, troubled by Darcie's murder. Even George sensed her mood. He left his doggy bed and came to rest his paw on her foot, looking up at her with a pained expression. Bless his little pug heart. He was trying to comfort her.

She reached down to pet and reassure him. The cats jumped on the kitchen island to rub against her. Normally, she'd shoo them off, but she was worrying the furry felines, too. She took a deep breath, trying to snap out of her mood. "I'm okay, guys. Really."

Ansel pushed a glass of wine in front of her. "I get it. Darcie's death hit you hard, but you're not responsible for it."

He'd told her that before. She even believed it, but somehow, that didn't erase all the guilt.

"I'm going to make a map of the house and write down where each person was when Jessica died. If I can *see* it, it might help."

"Not a bad idea. You can call and question everybody. I'll help you if you need it."

He was such a keeper. How lucky could a girl get, snagging a guy like him? She decided not to focus on what had happened, but what to do so that it didn't happen again. Not one more person should die because of this. She'd always believed if she messed up, it didn't help to wallow in what she did wrong, but to focus on how to fix it. She finished her wine and braced her shoulders. "I'm okay now. I've moped enough. It's time to do something about it."

He grinned. "Good, let's go finish the basement. That's something you can check off your to-do list when we're done."

She liked checking things off, so she pushed to her feet. The cats raced down the stairs in front of them, and two hours later, the basement was completely finished and cleaned. Just in time. The furniture, pool table, and pinball machine were being delivered the next day, and then it would be ready for the Halloween party—not this coming weekend but the one after that.

"We need to celebrate," Ansel said. "Let's order Chinese."

A wonderful idea. She wouldn't cook tomorrow night either, because it was girls' night out. Two nights of avoiding the kitchen. "And another glass of wine," she said.

Ansel grinned. "I'll call it in, and you can take your shower and change into your PJs while I go to pick up the food. I can shower after supper."

It sounded like a great trade-off to her, so after he called in what they wanted, she trudged up to their bedroom and he drove to their favorite Chinese takeout place.

The rest of the night, they avoided anything serious and just enjoyed themselves. When they went to bed, though, Ansel almost vibrated with excitement. Like a kid on the night before Christmas, he couldn't wait for the deliveries tomorrow.

He took so long to fall asleep, she thought he'd mutter at the alarm when it went off in the morning, but she should have known better. His hand patted her fanny at six fifteen.

She gave him the one-eyed glare. "You couldn't wait another fifteen minutes?"

He laughed. "Sorry, but I was thinking about where you wanted to put the sofa in the playroom. Do you think it would be better to put the two easy chairs across from the TV instead?"

It was illegal to maim or kill your husband, and it was a good thing. She took a deep breath. "We were going to put the couch there because you like to lie down when you watch TV. If you'd rather sit, then put the chairs there instead."

"Maybe we should have bought recliners."

Another long inhale. Patience was a virtue. She was growing virtuous. "I suggested that. You said that when we opened them up, they'd take up too much space and we'd have to put the coffee table too far from them."

"There are wall recliners, aren't there?"

Would she be arrested for hurting him? Bashing him over the head with a pain-in-the-fanny stick? "We looked at some. You didn't like the looks of any of them."

"Oh, yeah."

She swung her legs out of bed. She might as well get moving. He popped to his feet, too, too freaking cheerful for this early in the morning. "If we get an early start in Merlot, maybe we can head home early," he said.

The sooner to see his toys. But if that made him happy and helped him settle down, why not? After a quick breakfast, she packed sandwiches for lunch. If Jerod said one word, he'd be wearing his. But when they got to the job site, Jerod looked at her face. With sneaky strategy, he smiled instead. Her cousin had learned long ago to read women's moods.

In the magazine picture of the study, the room had a swirled-plaster ceiling. They climbed ladders to give the flat surface that kind of finish. Then they started building bookcases. They broke for lunch and then built more. It was after four when they nailed the last one together.

"We'll install them tomorrow," Jerod said, "and then I don't want to see another bookshelf for a long time."

She agreed. When they were up, they'd look great, but she'd never expected them to take this much time. They hurried to get ready to leave. Ansel scooped up George and she grabbed the cooler to carry to the van.

Ruth Goggins stalked to the stone wall and called to them on the way. "Are you happy now?" she asked with a sneer. "Another nice young girl is dead because you couldn't leave things alone."

Jazzi wasn't in the mood. She'd made her peace with that, and Ruth annoyed her. "If you hadn't lied and spread untrue gossip all over town when Jessica died, the case might have been solved. So I'd say there's more blame on you."

Ruth's jaw dropped. "How rude!"

"Tell me about it." Jazzi walked away from her and got in the van.

Ansel grinned. "Well done! That woman is a menace."

"I try not to be like that. I lost my temper."

"She asked for it." Ansel pulled out of the drive and headed for home.

It was a good thing they got there earlier than usual. They'd left the garage unlocked and spent a good half hour oohing and aahing over the deliveries that were left in it. Jazzi had parked her pickup on the turnoff so the heavy trucks that brought the furniture, pool table, and pinball machine could back into the drive and deliver them.

The two-car garage was nearly full. She admired the red, fake-suede couch with two matching easy chairs, chosen because they were durable and easy to clean. She even liked the poker table, which could easily be covered to serve as a dining table, too. When she offered to help Ansel carry some of the lightweight items to the basement, he shook his head. "Thane, Walker, and Radley will help me with all of it. Don't worry about it. You can see what you think when you get back later tonight."

Worked for her. She went in the house to get ready. She didn't bother to dress as glam as her sister this time. They were meeting at Trubble Brewing on Broadway, and it was a low-key, funky kind of place. She pulled on her favorite jeans and a V-necked red sweater with ankle boots. She'd still need her jacket when she left the house. The temperatures had dipped below sweater weather. She decided on a fitted, lightweight leather jacket. Ansel loved it. It showed off her curves.

When she came downstairs and Ansel saw her, he stopped and stared. "Do you have to wear that when I'm not with you?"

She crinkled her brow, surprised. "I thought you liked it."

"I do. So will every guy in River Bluffs."

She shook her head. "I'll be with Olivia, Didi, and Elspeth. No one will pay attention to me."

"Babe, you're the best-looking woman in the bunch, but thank heavens you don't believe that. If you flirted, I'd have to fight duels to kill off the competition."

She laughed. The man was prejudiced, and that was nice. She gave him a quick kiss goodbye and set off for the south side of the city.

When she and the others all got settled and their drinks came, Olivia reached in her purse and handed each of them an envelope. "This saves me some postage. I knew you'd all be here. Invitations for Didi's baby shower."

Elspeth ripped hers open. "I'm curious what Didi has on register. My little sister Hillary has been married a year and just told us that she's three months pregnant. I hope Radley and I find a house by then. I'd love to have my family here to give her a shower."

"Are you having any luck with the house search?" Jazzi asked.

"We've driven by a few, and they looked a lot better in the real estate book than they did in real life."

Olivia laughed. "Yeah, Thane and I noticed that, too. Where are you looking?"

"We'd like to stay close to downtown, and we both love old houses."

Olivia nodded. "I'll spread the word at the hair salon. We meet a lot of people. Maybe someone will know somebody who wants to sell. We found our house because a guy Thane works with told him it would be on the market soon."

"Thanks! We'd appreciate that."

Their food came, and they switched to small talk and catching up while they ate. No one lingered after they finished like they sometimes did. Everyone was in the mood to get home.

"I'm still working on the Halloween costumes for Radley and me," Elspeth said.

That made Jazzi remember she and Ansel hadn't bothered with costumes yet. Olivia raised an eyebrow at her. "Have you found anything?"

"Not yet. We will. But we did get the basement finished and ready to go."

Olivia grinned. "Thane's so excited about the new pool table, he might not be home when I get back. He might sleep over at your place."

"The daybeds haven't arrived yet," Jazzi told her, "but we can make do."

They left in high spirits, and Jazzi was still in a good mood when she got home. Ansel was even happier. He grabbed her hand and dragged her down to the basement.

She blinked. She had to admit, the room had turned out better than she'd ever expected. The TV on the far, side wall centered the sitting area with the couch and chairs. The big Oriental rug they'd bought made the sitting area cozier. The poker table was near the end of the room closest to the stairs, and the pool table and pinball machine were across from it. There was still room for two daybeds near the kids' play area.

"Walker suggested putting the kids' stuff on the far back so that people won't have to trip over toys to get to everything else. What do you think?" Ansel asked. "He said even with all the storage, the floor wouldn't be clear."

Walker would know. River loved his LEGOs and toy cars. "You done good. What did the guys think of it?"

He beamed. "It's everything any of us ever wanted. River loved it, too."

"We'll have to buy some toys and games for down here." They already had Yahtzee and a few card games for kids for when Gunther and Lizzie spent the night, and they'd set up Jazzi's old Atari with Donkey Kong, Frogger, and Yoshi's Island. Jerod's kids got a kick out of the old-school system.

He nodded, satisfied, and walked to the refrigerator they used to keep in the garage. When he returned, he had two flute glasses and a bottle of champagne.

She laughed. Time to celebrate! He popped the cork, and they enjoyed the entire rest of their night, carrying the champagne up to their room to finish it there. She set the mystery and worry of the murders away for tomorrow.

Chapter 26

On Friday morning, Jazzi spent more time in the kitchen than usual, making wraps for lunch. She spread tortillas with Boursin cheese before adding slices of deli turkey and ham, cucumber and red pepper strips, and shredded lettuce. She put some plain deli meat in a small baggie for George. Then they drove to Merlot to install the bookshelves on three walls of the study. Each unit had a wooden back so that none of the cream-colored walls showed through. Only the narrow end wall was left plain. That was where the oversize desk would sit. Once the shelves were attached, they worked on the crown molding, stained a shade darker than the shelves. They worked longer than usual, agreeing to eat a late lunch.

When noon rolled around, George came to stand beside Ansel and whine.

Jerod laughed at him. "Your pug's hungry. He might starve if we wait too long to eat."

They all looked at George. Starvation was a long, *long* way away, but Ansel bent to pet him and reassure him. "Later, bud."

Head drooping, he wandered back to his dog bed. He understood the word "later."

When they finished the room, Jerod shook his head. "I liked the magazine picture, but this looks even better. I feel like I should smoke a pipe and sip a glass of brandy."

Ansel chuckled. "It works, doesn't it?"

Jazzi loved it. "Now all we have to do is make the hallway off the back patio into a mudroom, and this floor is done. We can start work upstairs."

"Upstairs will be quick," Jerod said. "The floors are done. All we need to do is paint and gut the bathrooms."

Right. Working on five bedrooms and three baths was never quick. Just gutting bathrooms wasn't exactly a breeze, but she knew what he meant. If they were lucky, they could finish the second floor by the end of next week—maybe. After that, all that was left was the basement. With its crumbling cement, it would take longer.

They decided to stop for lunch, and when Jazzi pulled baggies out of the cooler, Jerod tried to hide his disappointment. Though when she passed him one, and he saw the tortilla, he grinned. "You went to a lot of bother. Thanks."

"Anything for you, cuz. Within reason," she added.

Ansel's cell phone buzzed while they were eating. "Radley." He put him on Speaker.

"Hey, Ansel." His brother sounded excited. "Olivia called, and one of her clients told her about a house on Wilt Street. Elspeth drove past it on her lunch break and really liked it. Would you mind going through it with us? The Realtor said he could show it tonight."

Ansel glanced her way, and Jazzi nodded. She'd meant to stop at Molly Kroft's shop for interior designs to ask her about memories of Jessica and the party, but that would have to wait. He quirked a brow at her. "You sure?" When she gave another nod, he said, "Works for us. Text me the address and we'll meet you there after work." They all got off at five, so it would be convenient for all four of them.

After they cleared their lunch things, they started work on the mudroom. They built a bench along one wall with room for boots and shoes underneath. Then they installed a long board with hooks above it for coats and jackets. It took the rest of the day to finish, but when they did, it was the perfect spot to come inside, sit down, and slip out of shoes and hang up a coat.

That night, when they locked up and left the Merlot house, the first floor was done. If anyone came to view it, it was ready. In high spirits, Ansel and Jazzi drove to meet Radley and Elspeth. Even George was perkier. He'd seen the bag of deli meat Jazzi had packed for his lunch and knew he'd gotten special treatment. When they reached the brick, two-story house on Wilt Street, the pug hopped out of the van and followed them up the shallow steps to the front porch.

Jazzi stared. "Do you think your dog's all right?"

Ansel laughed and knocked on the door. Radley and Elspeth were already there. A shiny car was parked behind theirs. It must be the Realtor's. "George knows our workload has eased up. There'll be more couch time to share. It's put him in a good mood."

Radley opened the door and motioned them inside. There was a narrow foyer that led to the steps going upstairs in front of them and the living room to the right. "Where do you want to start?"

"We'll look down here, then move upstairs, and end at the basement," Ansel decided.

The rooms had high ceilings and beautiful woodwork. The living room was a good size, the dining room, behind it, a little cramped, and the kitchen a disaster—dated and tiny. But there was a large room behind the kitchen that Jazzi had no idea what to make of, and a room off it behind the stairs. A half bath with a washer and dryer separated the two rooms. It was poorly arranged.

"There's nothing here that can't be fixed," Ansel said. "I'd knock out the wall between the dining room, kitchen, and back room and make one huge room for entertaining."

Elspeth smiled. "And the room off it?"

"Maybe a guest room and study?" Jazzi suggested. "I'd gut the half bath and redo it."

With a nod, Radley led them upstairs. George opted out of steps. There were three big bedrooms and two baths. Dirty, matted carpets covered the floors, and Jazzi knelt to lift a corner of one to peek under it. "Wood, in bad shape. Not sure we could refinish it."

"I like carpets in bedrooms," Elspeth said. "It makes them warmer and quieter."

"Then an easy fix," Ansel said.

Radley grimaced as he led them to the basement, but the Realtor smiled. "It's not as bad as most around here."

It was solid and dry. Those were the most important features. The furnace was old, with thick arms stretching from it.

"Furnaces can be replaced," Ansel said. "The basement's not pretty, but it's in good shape. The ceiling's too low to make a room down here."

Radley shrugged. "We'll just use it for storage. I like having a basement. I don't like crawl spaces."

"Then you're good to go." Ansel and Jazzi scanned the walls and ceilings for cracks. "I'd say this is a well-built house."

Jazzi pointed to the electrical box. "You'll have to update this. Some of the plumbing, too, I'd guess. Old lead pipes clog with time."

"All doable," Ansel repeated.

Radley smiled. He turned to Elspeth. "Well?"

"Let's make an offer, contingent on it passing a home inspection." Elspeth glanced at Jazzi. "You told me to still ask for that, right?"

"It never hurts. The roof looks good, but the inspector will get up on it to see if there are any dips or soft spots. He'll check the gutters, too."

"Okay, then," Radley said. He turned to the Realtor. "The asking price seems fair to us. What if we offer the full amount? With a home inspection."

The Realtor smiled. "I'll call the owners to let them know. You're getting a good house for a good price. The husband and wife who lived here moved to a retirement community. They priced it to sell. It just went on the market this morning."

"We know." Elspeth hugged herself, she was so happy. "Olivia called us the minute she heard about it. We owe her a big thanks."

Fifteen minutes later, Jazzi and Ansel left them to it and drove home. "I hope they hear back soon," Ansel said, stopping for a red light. "Or Radley's going to chew his nails to the quick."

Jazzi had left out two sirloin steaks to thaw, so when they stepped into their own cozy stone cottage, she patted them off and seasoned them for Ansel to grill later. Then they fed the pets and played with them before taking their showers and changing into PJs.

Radley called two hours later. They got the house. He'd be bursting to tell everyone at the Sunday meal.

Jazzi and Ansel settled in the living room for the evening. This Friday, they planned on taking it easy. No work. No journals. But she was going to draw a map of the Merlot house tomorrow and start putting people in the rooms where they'd been when Jessica fell to her death. And tomorrow night, she was going to read through as many of Jessica's journals as she could.

Chapter 27

They slept till nine on Saturday morning. There'd be no outdoor work today. Rain pummeled the house and yard. When Jazzi looked out their bedroom window, she could hardly see the woods at the back of their property. Turbulent, charcoal-gray clouds hunkered overhead, threatening a whole day of foul weather.

"I hope this lets up before we have to go to the store." Ansel came to stand behind her, watching the downpour. "Sometimes I wish we had an attached garage so we don't have to drown getting from the house to the van and back."

"Even with an umbrella, we'll get wet." The wind was whipping the rain sideways. Jazzi's mom and dad's trilevel house had a two-car garage connected to the house. She'd loved that convenience when she was growing up. When she'd bought this house, she'd taken theirs for granted, but since tramping through rain and snow here, she'd realized how nice it had been.

"Maybe we could build a walkway with a roof." She glanced at her reflection in the glass and winced. Her unruly hair looked like a rat had made a nest in it last night. "It wouldn't protect us from the cold, but at least we wouldn't get soaked."

"No easy way to make it look right." Ansel frowned, trying to picture it. "We'd have to get creative."

She grinned at him. "You're creative. You'll think of something."

Her praise didn't fool him. He gave her a look. It would be a pain in the fanny, and they both knew it. "It might be easier to build a new garage with a breezeway to the house."

"Another project, but it might be worth it."

When they started downstairs, the cats flew to their food bowls. George sat patiently at his. The cats wound around her ankles, begging for more, so she gave them each a little shredded cheese. They didn't like milk, wouldn't touch it, but they looked forward to cheese once in a while. Morning chores done, she and Ansel carried their coffee to the living room and settled in for a slow start.

"What are you making for the Sunday meal?" Ansel asked. "Stuff we need to start early? Or can we wait longer than usual to shop and hope the storm blows away?"

"My dad loves pork goulash with buttered noodles. It's gray and gloomy outside—the perfect weather for it. Olivia loves Greek salads, so I thought I'd make one of those, and a certain man I married has a fondness for Black Forest cake."

His eyes lit up. "I can help with all of those."

"What do you have planned for the day?"

His gaze slid away from hers. "I was thinking of buying a few Halloween decorations. I saw these three witches stirring a cauldron who cackled when a motion sensor went off."

"Almost life-size. I've seen it."

"Well?"

"I won't fuss about you buying that if you help me draw a plan of the Merlot house and start marking off which people were in which room when Jessica fell."

"A trade-off?" He grinned. "You know I'd have helped you anyway."

She laughed. "And I'd have let you buy your witches, but is it a deal?"

They linked pinkie fingers to make it official. He went to get more coffee for them, and she tore up a white shopping bag to give them a big surface to draw on. He did that while she sipped coffee and watched him. He was better at drawing things to scale than she was.

When he finished, she put two *x*s in the kitchen. "The only people I'm sure about are Damian and Jillian." She added a question mark in the backyard and wrote "Mr. Hodgkill." "Everyone so far has said he was at the grill, but he could have left for a few minutes once he'd made the burgers and brats." She put another question mark close by. "Tilly was supposedly in line for food. I need to ask if anyone can confirm that." Two more in the kitchen. "RJ said he was in the kitchen, hiding from his aunt, with Felicity. I need to check with her to corroborate that." Another *x* in the bathroom. "Kelsey doesn't have an alibi."

"What about Jessica's mother?" Ansel asked.

Jazzi stared. "She was Jessica's champion."

"Just saying, if you're going to list people, you should list her."

She nodded. He was right, but it would only be a formality. "I'll ask someone."

"Her brother?" Ansel asked. "Was he home?"

"I don't know. I'll put him down to check on, too."

"Who else is there?"

She counted them off on her fingers. "Nadia Ashton, the tennis player. Lila Mattock, the…" She let that go. "And RJ's aunt."

He grimaced. "You have a lot of people to account for."

"I know."

"We'll stop to talk to someone every night next week when we leave the Merlot house."

Staring at the drawing, she nodded. She'd feel a lot better when she could cross off more names. "And those are just the obvious people. There could be more."

Ansel glanced outside. "The rain's letting up a little. Want to make a run to the store now before it starts up again? It's supposed to rain harder later today."

She draped the drawing over Jessica's hope chest and went to get the grocery list. Sliding into her shoes, she shrugged on her heavy jacket. George trotted to the French doors and looked out. When he saw the light rain, he turned back to his dog bed.

"Smart boy," Ansel said. "Let us bring all the food to you."

There was something to be said for the pampered pet life. Jazzi put on a baseball cap to keep her head dry and made a run for the garage, Ansel close behind her.

They got lucky. They'd carried the last grocery bag into the house in a steady drizzle and put the pickup in the garage before the deluge started again. The idea of a new garage was looking better all the time. They had plenty of room to build one.

They turned on all the overhead kitchen lights while they unloaded the groceries. It was so gloomy outside, they needed to combat it. Inky and Marmalade, as usual, ran in and out of the empty, brown paper bags, pouncing on each other now and then. George came to inspect the groceries, hoping for small snacks, and when they finished and started cooking, he parked himself beside the kitchen island.

"The meat has to cook through before you get any," Jazzi told him. He understood those words but sat, staring eagerly, while she and Ansel cut pork loins into cubes to brown. Chopped onions and garlic went in next. Ansel fished out a few browned pieces of meat for George before they added the seasonings, ketchup, and water. Finally rewarded for his patience, George wandered to his dog bed, content.

"We can cook the noodles and make the salad tomorrow," Jazzi said. "That only leaves the cakes." They'd have to make two of them. Because it was one of his favorites, she went to the extra work to make them from scratch. She started by making four layers of chocolate genoise for each cake. While they baked, she made the filling, and Ansel made chocolate swiss meringue buttercream for the icing.

"I used to just make chocolate box cake mixes and use cherry pie filling," Jazzi said. "A lot fewer steps."

"But this is so good, and you have me to help you."

There was that. And it really was worth the extra work. It was such a miserable day outside, it was fun spending time together in the kitchen anyway. Inky jumped up to sit on the wide window ledge in the sitting area. He watched the rain pound the front lawn. Jazzi glanced out the window over the sink and saw the last of the leaves blown off the trees. Marmalade curled in front of the French doors.

Usually, when they spent most of the day cooking, they ordered in pizza for supper, but she didn't want to make some poor deliveryperson come out in this, so she started a big pot of soup for supper instead. She could take the leftovers to the Merlot house for lunch on Monday.

Ansel loved soup, and one of his favorites was white chili, so the whole thing went together quickly with them working together. By the time they ate and cleaned the kitchen, they were both ready to relax in the living room for the rest of the night. Ansel watched TV, and she settled in the chair beside Jessica's hope chest, determined to read as many journals as possible.

This time, she scanned through the earlier ones and made it up to sixth grade before the entries got really interesting. Jessica's mom let her and Alwin invite friends to their house for a Halloween party.

The party was for Alwin, too, so Dad rented a pony for our friends to ride in the backyard, Jessica wrote. *And Mom made all kinds of treats. She organized games for us to play, too.*

Jazzi paid closer attention because she had little idea of what kinds of games to have for kids. Maybe she could pick up some tips for Gunther, Lizzie, and River. Jessica painted a picture of a lovely family time until she and Darcie won at the sack races and Jessica hit the piñata hard enough to break it open. Alwin had wanted to do that, so he pushed his hand on the back of her head when she was bobbing for apples. He held her underwater until Darcie punched him so hard, she knocked him down. When Darcie told Jessica's mom that Alwin tried to drown his sister, Alwin only laughed and said he was only trying to scare her.

But I'm not so sure, Jessica wrote. *When I complained, Dad told me to get over it. It was only a joke.*

It wasn't a funny one, their mom snapped. *Alwin, go to your room and stay there until the party's over.*

No need for that, her dad ordered, canceling the order. *Boys will be boys.*

Jazzi shivered, rubbing her arms. The next time she saw Gaff, she was going to ask him to check on Alwin's whereabouts more carefully. Suddenly, he didn't look like the protective brother anymore.

Chapter 28

As usual, Jerod and his family were the first to walk into the kitchen for the Sunday meal. Instead of taking their position by the cheese ball and crackers, Jerod nodded toward the basement door. "We're excited about how the room turned out. Can we take a look at it?"

Ansel was already motioning them toward the steps. He could hardly wait to show it to them. That became the trend for the day. People walked in the kitchen, then disappeared downstairs. Everyone: Jazzi's parents, Jerod's mom and dad, Olivia and Thane—who actually came on time—Walker's family, Radley and Elspeth, and even Gran and Samantha. While they gawked and praised, Jazzi set up food and drinks on the kitchen island.

When she was ready, she called down, "If you're hungry and want hot food, you'd better get up here!"

They trudged up, in single file. Her dad grinned when he saw the Hungarian goulash with pork, and Olivia got excited about the Greek salad. Before long, they were all seated and gossiping.

"Have you learned anything more about that poor girl who died?" Gran asked.

Jazzi explained about the Halloween entry she'd read the night before.

Mom waved that away. "Kids do stupid things. Her brother sounds like a spoiled brat, but that doesn't mean he killed her. Remember when Jerod got mad at you and locked you in Gran's chicken coop for half an hour before we found you?"

She'd forgotten about that. Walker laughed. "Sounds like something you'd do," he told Jerod.

"I was eight. And she was being bossy."

"Was not. You couldn't catch me to throw an earthworm down my shirt."

He glanced at Gunther and Lizzie. "Don't believe a word she says. You can't trust her."

"Dad!" Even Gunther knew the score.

Olivia changed the subject. She looked at Gran and Samantha. "Are you coming to the Halloween party next Sunday? And are you dressing up?"

"We're coming as two witches," Samantha said. "We both have black dresses and shoes and we bought pointed hats that have long, stringy gray hair attached to them. We'll be old crones."

"Perfect!" Olivia raised an eyebrow at Jazzi. "Have you two decided on something yet?"

Ansel grimaced. "Haven't had time, but we'll think of something."

She looked skeptical. "You can't cut eyeholes in two sheets and come as ghosts."

"I hadn't thought of that. Good idea." When Olivia glared at her, Jazzi laughed. "We won't do anything elaborate, but we'll come up with something."

River pulled on Didi's sleeve. "Can I invite my friends? They'd have fun, too."

They'd heard a lot about the two boys who lived close to Walker's house. They spent quite a bit of time together. Before Didi could say no, Ansel sidelined her. "It's all right with us if it's all right with your parents."

Walker's lips curled with pleasure, and Jazzi realized that even though River wasn't Walker's biological son, he thought of him as his. He was so devoted to the boy, she thought of him as River's dad, too.

"Can I?" River asked.

Didi looked at Walker, who shrugged. "Sure. Why not?"

His answer even made Gunther and Lizzie happy. "Two more friends!" Lizzie cried.

The conversation shifted to Mom and Olivia's hair salon as Jazzi and Ansel cleared the table.

"We can't take any new clients," Mom was saying. "Our books are always full, so we're thinking of hiring someone new. We have room for another station."

Jerod frowned. "Would the new girl work for you or rent her space?"

"We thought we'd let her rent her station. It would bring more people into the salon, and that would be nice."

"I think you should leave well enough alone," Dad argued. "You and Olivia get along, and your clients are happy. Why push it?"

Mom raised both eyebrows. "Really? You have to ask? We'd make more money, and some of our clients are getting up in age. It might be nice to attract more young people."

Dad sniffed. My father rarely argued with Mom about anything, but when he didn't agree with her, he let her know.

Gran took offense, too. "We old crones like to look decent, even if young people don't consider us stylish."

Jazzi's mom gasped. "Mom! I don't neglect any of our clients, but it never hurts to stay up-to-date and trendy."

The debate went back and forth until Jazzi and Ansel carried the Black Forest cakes to the table. Jerod got up to bring the coffeepots. Once people bit into the cake, they settled down to enjoy their dessert.

As soon as the table was cleared, the men and kids disappeared back into the basement. Jazzi watched them go, then got another glass of wine and poured one for Gran. The women headed into the living room.

Eleanore, Jerod's mom, held baby Peter. Frowning, she asked Jazzi, "You've never said whether this Jessica who died had any family besides her parents and brother. In a small town like Merlot, you'd think she'd have aunts and uncles, too. Did she?"

Jazzi blinked, surprised. "I don't know. No one's mentioned it, but that's a good idea. I'll find out."

"Some families support each other. Others feud," Eleanore said. "Maybe Jessica didn't get along with her cousins either if she never mentioned them."

A new thought. Maybe a cousin did something worse than lock her in a chicken coop. Maybe he pushed her off the balcony. At the very least, family members usually knew one another's dirty little secrets. Jazzi decided she'd make a point of looking them up, if they existed.

Chapter 29

On Monday, the three of them were working upstairs, gutting bathrooms, when someone knocked on the front door. Jerod looked at her. "You're our official greeter."

Yeah, it was starting to look that way. She grimaced. If it was Ruth Goggins, she was turning around and coming back up the steps. But it was a young woman she'd never met, who was a little taller than she was, with a dark brown, chin-length bob and brown eyes. Jazzi opened the door to greet her.

With a nervous smile, the woman rushed into speech. "Hi, I'm Felicity, a friend of Jillian's. She said you were renovating Jessica's house and looking into her murder."

"I'm reading her journals, and they made me curious." Jazzi wanted to clarify. "I'm not a detective or anything."

Felicity nodded, glancing around the room. She smiled. "This is nice. Jessica would love it. You're not changing her bedroom, are you? She loved the color pink."

Jazzi bit her bottom lip. "We'd like to keep everything neutral. Buyers prefer colors they can work with."

Felicity sighed. "Probably better. It hurt when I heard you'd cleaned out her room and were going to redo it. But it's time. None of us have let Jessica go. Probably because the killer was never caught. Her death feels unfinished, unresolved. It's festered. And even with a new owner, the house felt stuck in the past. I'm glad you're making it new for someone else to give it a fresh start."

She sounded like she was trying to convince herself of that. It was obviously hard. Jazzi held out her hand. "By the way, I'm Jazzi Zanders Herstad."

The woman grimaced. "I'm Felicity Kellman Smythe. I was one of Jessica's best friends."

"I know. She mentions you in her journals."

Felicity's eyes misted and she blinked away tears. "Look, I stopped here because I think Darcie got killed doing serious digging about what happened to Jessica. Those two were close, like sisters. They'd been tight since second grade. I live outside Merlot, but I met them in middle school. Someone murdered both of my best friends, and I want whoever it was caught and thrown behind bars to rot."

Jessica's friends were passionate, Jazzi would give them that. "Darcie stopped here to talk to me before she died. She wanted to find out every person who was at the party and who they were with when Jessica died. That way, she could cross off people who couldn't have pushed her."

"I was with RJ in the kitchen at the dessert table. I know his name came up a few times in the investigation, but he was with me. I'll never forget Jessica's scream. Never. Most of the others were outside. That's where the food table was set up, and there was music. A few people even danced on the patio."

"Do you remember if Jessica's dad was at the grill when she fell?"

Felicity frowned and shook her head. "He was at the grill when I got to the party, but I don't remember if he was there when she died."

"What about Tilly? Was she in the food line?"

Felicity let out a breath of frustration. "I don't know. RJ had come inside to hide from his aunt. He'd told her over and over again that he and Jessica were still friends, that he'd wanted to break up with her and she made it easy for him. But his aunt didn't see it that way. She took it as an insult to their entire family, that RJ wasn't college bound and wasn't good enough for her, so she dumped him."

"Do you know where she was when Jessica fell?"

"No, sorry."

"What about Alwin? Was he home for the party?"

She shrugged. "Even if he was, he wouldn't associate with us. He didn't mind coaching the basketball team, but since he was in college, he didn't have time for high school kids. All I know for certain was that RJ was with me, so he couldn't have pushed her." She glanced at her watch. "I can't stay long. I'm on school lunch break, and my aide's covering recess. I have to get back soon."

"Just one more thing. Did Jessica have any other relatives in Merlot? Aunts, uncles, or cousins?"

"Jessica's mom's sister lives near the river, but Jessica hardly ever got to see her. She couldn't stand Jessica's dad, so she was never invited to the house unless he was gone. Even then, Ruth Goggins told him every time she came, and he had a fit."

Ruth Goggins again. What a gossip!

"Jessica's dad's younger brother came to visit twice a year at holidays. The men were two peas in a pod. Hodgkills walked on water." She snickered. "The brother's son turned out to be a rotter. The last I heard, he was in jail again."

"What's the aunt's name?" Jazzi went to the card table to write it down.

"Lydia Jenkins. I liked her. So did Jessica." She started toward the door. "I have to go, but if you have any other questions, give me a call. I'm in the phone book."

"Any grandparents?" Jazzi called after her.

"None in town. Retired and living where it's sunny."

"Thank you." Jazzi waved her away. When she and Ansel got home tonight, she could mark two more *x*s on the house plans Ansel had drawn. She zipped upstairs to get back to work and told the guys what she'd learned.

Ansel was carrying the medicine cabinet he'd ripped out of the wall to the big black trash can in the hallway. He tossed it in. "We'll stop to visit the aunt when we leave here tonight."

"Hey, cuz, give me a hand!" Jerod motioned to the toilet he'd drained. He took one side, and she took the other. Part of the glamour of renovating. They carried it down the stairs and out the back door. The bathtub already sat in the grass. That must have been fun to get down the steps. Thankfully, Jerod and Ansel were both big guys.

Jerod glanced up to see where the sun was. "Gotta be close to noon. We're doing heavy work. I could break for lunch early. I'm starving."

She nodded. "I'll call up to Ansel."

They'd turned off the water upstairs, so they washed up in the half bath off the first-floor hallway. When Jerod walked in the kitchen and saw the slow cooker, he grinned and took a deep breath. "It smells like soup."

He'd been upstairs when she'd carried it in, so she'd caught him by surprise.

"White chili," Ansel said, grabbing one of the bowls she'd brought. She had a set of melamine dishes that she lugged to worksites.

Gaff knocked on the door and let himself in while they ate. He found them in the kitchen and grabbed a bowl for himself. "I got your message about Alwin, and no one can vouch for him when he took his minivacation in Brown County. No one saw him after he left a restaurant at six or until he showed up for lunch the next day."

"So he could have driven to Merlot and shot Darcie," Jerod said.

"He could have, but we can't prove it."

"No one I've talked to can remember if he was at Jessica's graduation party or not," Jazzi said. "Even if he was home, he wouldn't have mingled with her friends. The rumor is that since he was in college, he thought they were beneath him."

"Pretty typical," Gaff said.

Probably.

"Thanks for checking on him for me." Jazzi opened another sleeve of crackers. The men had finished the first one.

"No problem. You've been talking to people who didn't have much to say when my friend asked them questions. He's starting to like working with you as much as I do. Are you coming up with anything new?"

She told him Darcie's plan and how she was marking people off who could alibi one another.

"When you finish your list, will you share it with us?"

She nodded. "Right now, I can tell you that Damian, Jillian, RJ, and Felicity are in the clear."

He took out his notepad and wrote down their names. Then he carried his bowl to the sink. "Gotta go. I have an afternoon court date. One of my regulars was out on parole, but it looks like he wants to be behind bars again."

She'd heard about people like that, who'd spent so much time in jail or prison, they couldn't function in society. It was sad.

After Gaff left, they finished lunch, then went back to work. By five, they'd gutted all three bathrooms. That was the easy part. Putting them back together again was what would take time.

They were grubby and dirty when they left the job, so Ansel asked, "Do you still want to stop to see Jessica's aunt?"

"Might as well. We won't look much better any time this week."

He laughed. "You've got a point." So he headed toward the edge of town to the houses that bordered the river. The college was on the north edge of Merlot, the river on the other. She was surprised at how big and lovely the houses were.

For whatever reason, she'd assumed Jessica's mother didn't have money until she married Jessica's dad. Now, she reconsidered. These houses screamed old, wealthy lineages. Had Jessica's mother married into the Hodgkill family because of true love? If so, could it possibly have lasted? Did she still love her husband? How was that possible?

Chapter 30

They left George in the van and walked up the sidewalk to the tall, Federal-style house. It was topped by a widow's walk. Jazzi leaned back her head to appreciate the railed walkway that encircled the top of the roof.

"It's impressive, isn't it?" a voice asked from the house's open front door.

Caught off guard, Jazzi jerked her attention to the speaker. A tall, thin woman with stooped shoulders stood, smiling at her. Her gray hair was pulled back in a no-nonsense bun. "Sorry to bother you—" she started, but the woman cut her off.

"Two attractive blondes. I've been hoping you'd show up here. I've heard so much about you." When Ansel blinked, she laughed. "Merlot's a small town. If a person slows down to sneeze here, we know about it, but I'm sure you have questions you want answers for. Come in. My husband's already poured wine for us ladies, and he has beer for you men."

They followed her into a formal foyer and past that to a cozy living room. Two overstuffed, flowered sofas faced each other, with wingback chairs on each side. A tray with drinks sat on the coffee table.

The aunt gestured toward her husband. "Clyde's a professor at the college—English lit and Greek myths. Don't bring up a subject he's interested in or you'll never get out of here."

Jazzi laughed, then looked around the room. "You have a lovely house." Big rooms with high ceilings and polished wooden floors. An arch led to a huge dining room with lots of built-ins.

The aunt's expression softened, pleased. "It was my parents' house, and they left it to me after Lorraine married that awful Hodgkill man. By the way, I'm Lydia. My parents liked alliteration."

Clyde's blue eyes twinkled. "And thank goodness they liked me, or we'd have been disinherited, too."

Jazzi couldn't hide her surprise. "They disinherited Jessica's mother?"

"My sister. Yes." Lydia took a sip of her wine. "They loved us all, but none of us could see any good coming from leaving anything worthwhile to Lamar. Never met anyone so greedy and status hungry. That's why he married Lorraine. Our family comes from a long line of judges and lawyers. My brother practices law in Chicago. So do his two sons."

Ansel frowned. "And none of you could put enough pressure on anyone to find Jessica's killer?"

Lydia sighed. "We tried, and we can't fault the law or detectives for coming up empty. At the time, everyone who was at Jessica's party was so stunned and shocked, they couldn't give very much useful information. And those horrid, fork-tongued vipers—Ruth Goggins and Lila Mattock—spread so much untruth, no one was sure of anything."

Clyde focused on Jazzi. "But it seems you've caused quite a stir, and people are serious about finding the truth this time. We hope you do."

Jazzi sighed. "But another woman died because of it."

"Not your fault, dear. Who could have guessed the killer felt so insecure after all this time? All the deaths stopped after Jessica fell." Lydia shook her head. "Her death ruined Merlot for my poor sister. She couldn't bear living here, knowing the killer might walk up to her and smile without her ever knowing."

"Did she ever mention any suspicions she had of who might have pushed Jessica?"

Clyde cleared his throat. "It was my opinion that a small part of her feared it was her own husband, but thankfully, he was grilling at the time. She could put that worry aside."

Jazzi wasn't as sure of that as he was, but she meant to find out. "Had Jessica shared any secrets with you that might shed light on her death?"

Lydia sadly shook her head. "Not many people really knew my niece or understood her. My sister, of course, thought the world of her. Lorraine and Jessica shared a zest for life. You'd never think it, but Lorraine loved to laugh, loved to entertain and throw parties. What she ever saw in Lamar, I'll never know."

It was a mystery to Jazzi, too. "Were you close to Alwin?"

Lydia and Clyde shared a glance. Lydia sighed. "We sympathized with the boy. He loved his mother and his sister, but his father put him in an impossible situation. I'm sorry to say that Alwin wasn't an especially strong individual and could be browbeaten easily. He never stood up for himself.

Or for anyone else. He lacked the intelligence and sparkle of Jessica, but Lamar was determined to mold him into a keen businessman. It was a daunting task, and poor Alwin often floundered."

Ansel finished his beer and sat back patiently until Jazzi smiled at him. She told Lydia, "I promised Ansel I wouldn't take up much of your time. We have more errands to run tonight, but thank you for talking to us."

"Our pleasure." Lydia stood to usher them out of the house. "Both of us wish you luck, dear. And if you have any more need to question us, please feel free."

"Thank you."

They returned to their van and headed to River Bluffs. On the way home, Jazzi remembered that Ansel had wanted to stop to shop for Halloween decorations. "We have time before we go home," she said. "Want to look for your witches?"

He pulled into Lowe's, and when they left, he had three witches stirring a black cauldron when their motion sensor went off. Then he stopped at a party store and bought motion-sensored owls that hooted to put on each step leading down to the basement, along with orange and black crepe paper, paper plates, and serving platters shaped like caskets.

Once home, they carted the witches into the basement and put them in the back corner. Then they fixed a quick supper and settled in for the evening.

More determined than ever, Jazzi went through more of Jessica's journals, working her way through her eighth grade.

Mom was so proud of me when I showed her my report card with straight As that she decided to bake a special cake to celebrate. Alwin loves chocolate cake, too, so we all worked on it together. When Dad came home and Mom served it after supper, he flew into a rage. "Where's your report card, Alwin?" he yelled. When Alwin showed it to him, he shook his head. "All Cs. Is that the best you can do, boy?" Then he pointed at me. "And you? Do you always have to show up your brother?" He ripped my report card off the table, tore it into pieces, and threw them in the trash. Then he took Mom's cake and threw it, upside down, on the table. We all stared at him in shock. Mom rose from her chair, grabbed her purse, and told Alwin and me to get in the car. "Where are you going?" Dad yelled. "To a restaurant to buy my children whatever they'd like for dessert. You're not invited." Dad stared at her, but I'd never seen Mom so angry. He stormed to his den while she drove us to town. But when we returned, he swore he'd never touch anything of Mom's again."

Jazzi wanted to stand up and cheer, *Yay, Lorraine!* But she knew this was just a small victory against an impossible man.

Chapter 31

We were laying floor tile and installing a whirlpool tub in the master bathroom upstairs, huffing under the heavy load and trying to position it correctly, so none of us heard the doorbell ring. It wasn't until a voice called upstairs that we realized someone was there.

"Hello! Is anyone home?"

Jerod gave me a nod, so I went to see who it was. Felicity was standing at the top of the stairs with another woman in tow. When she saw me, she grimaced. "Sorry. I caught you in the middle of something, but I wanted to introduce you to Molly Kroft, another one of Jessica's friends."

Molly was five ten with flaming red hair in a pixie cut that accented her delicate features. "Felicity said that you're trying to place who was at the graduation party and who they were with. I was on the back patio and couldn't get away from Nadia Ashton when Jessica fell past us. I'll hate Nadia forever. She looked at Jessica's broken body and said, 'It couldn't have happened to a more deserving person.'"

Jazzi stared. "You're kidding."

"There's nothing funny about Nadia. She has a nice life now but can't let the scholarship thing go, hangs on to it like a pit bull with a bone. She didn't go to college; she moved in with her life partner, Stephanie Osgood. A truly lovely person. They run a grooming shop together and are doing well."

"So she's happy."

"Until she talks about the past."

There had to be more to it than that. Jazzi had met a few people like that. Maybe home life wasn't too great for Nadia and she needed someone to blame for her misery. "That means I can cross off Damian Dunlap, Nadia, and RJ, along with you, Jillian, and Felicity."

Molly sniffed, giving Felicity a sideways look. "RJ wasn't the great guy everyone thought he was, but he genuinely liked Jessica, even if he used her."

"Used her?" Felicity frowned. "How?"

"Grow up!" Molly snapped. "He only asked Jessica out as a ploy. He'd been wanting to get into Tilly's pants the entire time he dated her. He thought if he broke up with her and went out with Jessica, Tilly would put out to get him back."

Felicity's shoulders sagged. "That was pretty rotten of him."

"He's a guy. They were all hormone-crazed in high school. But once he got to know Jessica, he really liked her."

Jazzi interrupted. "Can you place anyone else at the party?"

"I saw Alwin. When the police asked his dad about him, Lamar swore he wasn't there, but I saw him. He was home from college for the weekend."

"Do you know where he was when Jessica fell?"

Molly shrugged. "He came to grab food and then he disappeared. I think he went up to his room to hide from us."

"And his room was upstairs?" Jazzi asked.

Molly blinked, as if she'd just put that together. "One door down from the balcony. I was surprised he didn't mingle more. The little slimeball loved to hit on Jessica's friends. We nicknamed him Hands."

That was news. Jessica never mentioned it in her journals. "Did he ever get lucky?"

"Have you seen him?" Molly shook her head. "Not even Nadia would let him corner her. Not that Jessica's dad was much better. He never touched. He just leered. I swear, he needed a drool bib when any of us stopped by Jessica's house."

A whole new spin on father and son. They left a bad taste in Jazzi's mouth. "Did you notice Tilly in the food line, or Ruth Goggins? I can't place Lila Mattock either."

Molly sneered. "Maybe she was curled under a rock."

"Molly!" Felicity gave her a look, but Molly shrugged.

"Ruth might have joined her there," she added.

"But you didn't see them?"

Both women shook their heads. Felicity looked at her watch again. "I'm almost out of time, but Molly and I were wondering if we could have a quick tour of the house."

"Sure." Jazzi took them from room to room. When she finished, Molly smiled. "I'm a decorator, you know. You three couldn't have done a more beautiful job. I hope someone buys this house who will love it as much as Jessica did."

Everyone mentioned how attached Jessica was to it. "That's what we're hoping for."

Molly and Felicity said their goodbyes, and Jazzi went back to the master bathroom to help Jerod and Ansel. They installed two pedestal sinks before breaking for lunch. George hadn't appreciated the white bean chili yesterday and trotted over to beg when he saw sandwiches again.

When Jazzi told them what Molly had shared, Jerod wrinkled his nose. "Jessica's dad just gets better and better. Sounds like he was a pervert, too."

"Alwin doesn't come off too well either." Ansel tore off a piece of ham to feed to George.

Eyes glinting, Jazzi tilted her head to study her Norseman. "Your sister must have had lots of friends. Were you in to any of them?"

"After I listened to them all blabbing together? All they talked about were boys, hair, and makeup. They drove me nuts."

She laughed. "And your conversations were a lot more meaningful?"

He gave a lopsided grin. "Guess not. We talked about sports, girls, and cars."

Jerod grabbed another sandwich and more chips. "None of my friends were very intellectual in high school. I never could understand the kids who joined political groups or took up causes. How did they get so serious, so fast?"

"Some kids are born that way, I think." She thought about her friend Leesa. "Leesa was in Future Teachers of America and did canned good drives to feed the homeless."

"I can see that," Ansel said. "She's the brainy type. Probably always loved school and got good grades."

Jazzi frowned. "I loved school and got good grades. There's nothing wrong with that."

"Jaz never spent time in detention with me," Jerod said.

"How did she end up slumming, flipping houses with us?" Ansel asked.

Smiling, Jerod started cleaning up after himself. "She couldn't sit at a desk for eight hours a day. That made it easy for me to talk her into slinging a hammer instead of fussing over a computer."

"You're forgetting my work environment." She stood to put things away. "How could a girl pass up two such good-looking and charming coworkers?"

They laughed as they trudged back upstairs to hopefully finish the bathroom before they left. But they ended up working later than usual to do it. By the time they left the house, they were ready to head home. No stops on the way. That proved a blessing when she and Ansel walked inside their roomy, cozy cottage, because Leesa pulled into their driveway before they even made it upstairs to shower.

Ansel went to clean up and change while Leesa and Jazzi holed up in the living room to talk about everything Jazzi had learned so far.

"You're making progress," Leesa told her when she got up to leave.

"Slow progress, but a little," Jazzi agreed. "Did Damian say much about Jessica's brother, Alwin?"

"Only that the poor guy wanted to be liked but had no social skills. He tried to fit in, but his dad pretty much warped him. Damian kept telling him not to sweat it, he'd grow into himself. He'd get better with age."

"Did he?" Jazzi asked.

"Who knows? The family moved right after Jessica died."

Once Leesa had gone, Ansel grilled two smoked pork chops, and Jazzi made rice and a quick broccoli salad. Ansel loved anything broccoli.

Jazzi didn't open any journals in the evening but stretched on her sofa opposite Ansel's. They watched *The Great British Baking Show*—his choice—until calling it a night. As she climbed the stairs to bed, she realized that even complicated pastry recipes didn't seem as difficult as keeping track of possible suspects in Jessica's murder.

Chapter 32

Jazzi and Ansel sipped their morning coffee at the kitchen island as he poised a pen over a grocery list.

"We need to decide what food to make for the party on Sunday."

She blew out a long breath. "You wanted to keep it fun, didn't you?"

He nodded. "I was thinking things like popcorn balls and caramel apples."

"People are going to be hungry. The party's in place of the Sunday meal. We have to have something for adults, too." She chewed her bottom lip, a bad habit when she was thinking. "I could make meatballs in marinara sauce. I saw a recipe once where the cook put round slices of mozzarella on top of each meatball with a sliced olive with pimentos in the center so they'd look like eyeballs floating in blood."

"I like that." Ansel wrote it down.

"Mummy hot dog? You wrap the hot dog in strips of Crescent rolls."

That went on the list, too.

She didn't think Mom and Gran would enjoy meatball eyeballs and mummy hot dogs as much as Ansel and the kids. "I think I'll make pumpkin soup and pumpkin bread, too. Olivia loves brie wrapped in puff pastry. Maybe I could make that look a little like a mummy wrapping, too."

"Anything else?"

"Mulled cider and plain cider for the kids?"

He put down his pen, satisfied for the moment. Then they packed up everything to drive to work. He carried George to the van, and she carried the cooler. When they stepped through the French doors to the patio, the wind about knocked them off their feet. They had to lean into it to fight their way to the garage.

Once in the van, Jazzi cranked up the heater. "You know, a covered walkway won't protect us from the wind. We passed a house a few days ago with a portico off its side door. If we built one of those, we could park the van under it, and the house would protect us a little."

"But we'd still have to walk to the garage and back," he argued.

"True, but we could unload groceries and supplies without getting wet. And it would be a straight shot to build a covered walkway from the portico to the garage."

His blue eyes lit up, a sure sign he liked the idea. "That would be a lot easier than building a whole new garage and deciding what to do with the old one."

They reached the "Welcome to Merlot" sign and passed a few shops before turning on the street to their fixer-upper. As they pulled in the driveway, Jerod pulled in behind them, and they all entered the house together. Ruth Goggins was outside, near the stone wall, working on her flower beds but turned her head to avoid them. Thank heavens for small favors.

Jerod glanced at the cooler Jazzi put on the kitchen counter. "Must be sandwiches today."

"'Fraid so," she told him. And they were, but not the ordinary kind. She'd loaded hoagie buns with all sorts of cold meats and toppings to make Italian grinders.

"The cold weather isn't inspiring you to cook enough," he told her. "You usually go all domestic goddess this time of year."

She laughed. "Maybe after the Halloween party."

They climbed the steps to start work on the second bathroom. It was nearly as big as the master. They were only installing a regular tub and shower enclosure, along with a double vanity, and a toilet. No fancy tiles in the shower. But first things first. They dropped to their knees to lay a light gray, plank-style porcelain tile that looked like weathered wood.

Tomorrow, when they worked on the last upstairs bathroom, it would be even easier. They'd do a combined bathtub and shower, a sink, and a toilet. They stopped a little before noon for a lunch break, and when they walked down the steps to the kitchen, Gaff was tapping on the front door and stepping inside.

He grinned when he saw them. "I was on the southwest side of River Bluffs anyway, so I decided to drive here to give you the news."

They settled around the card table in the kitchen. "Anything exciting?" Jazzi asked.

"Not yet, but it sure is interesting." He took a bite of the grinder she'd given him. "Mmm, this is good."

Jerod nodded in agreement. "Sorry I doubted you, cuz."

She shrugged. "It's not hot. Next week, I'll have to find my soup and stew groove."

He grinned at the mention of two of his favorites, then glanced at Gaff. "So, what's up?"

"I called the police department in Carolina where the Hodgkills live and asked them to verify Mr. Hodgkill's alibi for the morning Darcie died."

"And?" Ansel went for a cup of coffee and brought her back one, too.

"A detective went to Hodgkill's place of business and asked around to see if he was there that morning. Seems he missed a meeting and didn't get in until late afternoon that day."

"Is that enough time to have driven here and killed Darcie?" Jazzi asked.

"It's possible," Gaff told her.

Ansel frowned. "But wouldn't his wife have noticed he wasn't home the night before and didn't leave for work in the morning?"

Gaff's lips curved in a satisfied smile. "Seems the two have separate bedrooms, and Mrs. Hodgkill fell asleep before her husband returned home after a late business meeting that night. When she went down to the kitchen in the morning, she found a note propped on the table that said he'd gone into work early."

Jazzi pressed her lips together in a tight line, reluctant to ask, "And Mrs. Hodgkill? Did she have an alibi?"

Gaff shook his head. "She was alone all night and all the next morning."

Ansel sent her a meaningful look. "No one ever mentions her, and no one seems to know where she was when Jessica fell."

Gaff reached for his notebook. "None of the reports include any information on her. She must be easy to overlook."

Jazzi jumped to her defense. Jessica was too close to her mother for her to be a suspect. "She was probably busy, going back and forth, cooking and refilling food and drinks."

Jerod gave her a look. "Jessica's dad was grilling, Jaz. All the food was out, buffet style. If she'd been bustling around, someone would have mentioned it."

"Or else they didn't think about it. I'll start asking people directly."

The men let the subject drop. It was obviously troubling her. But they were right. She should find out where Lorraine was and put an *x* on the spot to rule her out. Jazzi returned to Jessica's father. "Did the detective question Mr. Hodgkill? Did he tell him where he was when Darcie died?"

Gaff finished his lunch and glanced at his watch. "The man's so confident of himself, all he'd tell them is that he couldn't remember."

Ansel blinked. "They questioned him the next day, didn't they?"

"Right after I called them. They're easy to work with, I'll say that. But the details slipped Mr. Hodgkill's mind. His memory keeps proving to be very selective."

Jerod finished his second sandwich and leaned back in his chair. "Do you think that means he killed Darcie? That he's the one who killed Jessica?"

Gaff shrugged. "Too soon to tell. But something's going on there. It doesn't mean he murdered someone, though." He pushed to his feet. "When I hear more, I'll tell you. You do the same."

Jazzi nodded, and Gaff left. They cleaned up their lunch things, then went back to working on the bathroom. They were assuming this one would probably be shared by kids, so they made it brighter and more fun. They painted the vanity base a bright blue, and the overhead mirrors had blue frames. They installed towel hooks shaped like seahorses lower and hung a shower curtain decorated with seashells. They normally kept things as neutral as possible, but they thought one room should be a little more fun.

They finished on time for the day. Again, as they locked up and left, Ruth Goggins turned her head, snubbing them. Jazzi hoped she'd snub them for the rest of the job.

"Maybe it's more," Jerod said, keeping his voice low. "Maybe she's afraid if she makes eye contact, you'll ask her where she was when Jessica fell and if anyone can vouch for her."

Jazzi turned to look at her, and Ruth caught her at it. Abruptly, she turned on her heel and hurried into the house. Was Jerod right? Was Ruth worried Jazzi would ask her about Jessica's party? Or maybe she didn't have an alibi for the night Darcie died. Jazzi made a note to check into that, too.

On the ride home, she realized that the longer they looked into Jessica's death, the more questions and fewer answers they had. But she meant to at least assure herself that Mrs. Hodgkill shouldn't be on the suspect list. So once they walked inside their home, and after they'd fed and played with their pets, she called Jillian Hendricks while Ansel showered.

"Sorry to bother you," Jazzi said, "but I've never thought to ask anyone about Jessica's mother. Did you see her during Jessica's party?"

"We all did," Jillian told her. "She was on the back patio, chatting to everyone and making them feel welcome."

"Was she there when Jessica fell?"

There was a slight pause. "No. I glanced out the window and saw her walking down the driveway to the front of the house. Her sister's car had pulled up to the curb, and she went to get the graduation present she'd brought. Aunt Lydia never came to visit when Mr. Hodgkill was home, so she just dropped it off."

Jazzi couldn't keep the relief out of her voice. "So her mom had a solid alibi?"

"I can vouch for her," Jillian said, her tone amused. "I wouldn't want it to be her either."

"Thank you."

"Any time. I mean that," Jillian said. "When we heard the scream, Jessica's mom rushed to the back patio. We all did. Her mom threw herself over Jessica's body and began to wail. I've never heard anything so desperate, so sad. I'll never forget that either."

"Who called the police? Do you know?"

"Molly did. She was always the practical one in our group. They got there really fast, roped off the patio and her body, then started asking questions. All of that's pretty much a blur for me. I think we were all in shock. I just felt numb, like the fall couldn't have happened. It didn't feel real."

"I understand. Thanks again."

When they hung up, Jazzi climbed the steps to shower and change, too. "Jessica's mom didn't do it," she told Ansel and explained.

He wrapped his arms around her and gave her a gentle hug. "Good. You can cross that worry off your list."

She shook her head. "At least Mrs. Hodgkill didn't have to watch Jessica fall. She was walking toward the car when it happened."

"I'm glad she's not a suspect anymore." He kissed the top of her head and left her to go downstairs.

She stood under the shower for a long time, letting the hot water soothe her emotions and her muscles. She shampooed her hair extra-hard, as if washing away the parts of Jessica's death that bothered her. By the time she slipped into her PJs and went to join Ansel in the kitchen, she was in a better mood.

He looked at her and grinned. "You have that look."

When she wanted to push everything out of her mind, she cooked. "Are you in the mood to make some soups and freeze a few for later?"

"I vote for a few desserts, too." He walked to the kitchen pantry and pulled out a box of brownie mix.

George sat up, watching her take ingredients out of the refrigerator for serious cooking. His stub of a tail wagged. Even the cats stayed close.

"I need wine," she decided. She liked to sip between chopping and stirring. She reached for her old, tattered soup cookbook. The pages were frayed, with spills wiped off them. She had to use a giant paper clip to hold it together.

Ansel poured her a glass of Riesling and they got started. By eight, they had a pot of sausage and cabbage soup, a beef stew, old-fashioned vegetable soup, and chicken with wild rice, along with brownies, cherry-coconut bars, and blondies.

They'd nibbled on everything as they went, so neither of them wanted a supper. Neither did George.

At the end of the day, they finally sagged onto their favorite sofas and turned on the TV. Ansel surprised her by asking to watch *In the Kitchen with David* on the QVC channel.

She scowled. "We don't need any more kitchen gadgets."

"I saw a chopper advertised on there. After dicing all the vegetables we needed tonight, I'm all for buying one."

She couldn't argue with that. They'd chopped and diced a large amount of onions, celery, and carrots. And that was just for starters. Ansel was in luck. The chopper was featured on the show that night. By the time they climbed the stairs to bed, they would soon be the proud owners of a square glass dish with a chopping unit they could attach like a lid.

Better yet, she hadn't thought of Jessica or suspects or gossip once, and she pushed away the thoughts now. They could keep until morning.

Chapter 33

The three of them stood, huddled together, staring at the tight space of the third bathroom. Jerod finally shook his head. "There's no way all three of us can work in here." He raised his eyebrows at Jazzi. "Would you mind painting ceilings today instead?"

"It's either that or me in back with a great view of both of your fannies while we lay tiles."

Ansel looked offended. "I thought you liked my backside."

"Yours is fine." She rolled her eyes toward her cousin.

Jerod laughed. "I'd be worried if mine turned you on. But really, you're okay painting?"

"No problem." She left them and began laying drop cloths over the master bedroom's wooden floor. She didn't mind painting ceilings so much since they bought extra-long handles for their rollers. She went to the kitchen, where she'd left the scarf she used to cover her hair and wrapped it up as best she could. Then she opened the can of white paint and got busy. First, she used the ladder to paint around the ceiling's edges. It was a big room. It took a long time. It took her until Jerod called for a lunch break to finish it. She had four more to go.

She glanced at the kitchen clock when she got downstairs. Only eleven thirty. "You called off work early." She frowned at her cousin.

He winked. "I saw the slow cooker and knew you'd brought soup. That made me hungry. Then Ansel said it was beef stew and brownies, and I couldn't stand it."

She rolled her eyes. Men and their stomachs. She waited her turn at the sink to wash up, removing her head scarf. It was covered with splatters.

Better the scarf than her head. As her hair tumbled down over her shoulders, Ansel shot her a hot glance. Her Norseman loved long, unruly blond hair.

"No time for that." Jerod shook his head at them, bringing his bowl to the counter. "I'm ready to dish up."

Jazzi shared a suggestive glance with her hubby when Jerod's back was turned. George got excited every time he smelled beef, so he planted himself beside Ansel's chair. They'd just sat down when a tap sounded at the back door, and Gaff walked in. He saw the stew and went for a bowl to join them. Once he was settled, he looked at Jazzi. "You've caused a firestorm in Carolina."

"Really? How?"

He grinned. "The detective I talked to went to see Jessica's father again, and this time, he expected to have answers. Either that or he told Mr. Hodgkill he'd start digging for them. He'd question everyone he knew or ever talked to until he could account for the man's time."

Jazzi gave him a fist bump. "Hooray for him! Did Jessica's dad talk?"

"Oh, yeah, but he wasn't one bit happy about it. He told our guy that he hadn't been home that night and came into work late because he was with another woman."

Ansel stared. "He's been having an affair?"

"Nothing that nice. No, Hodgkill said he sleeps with young women off and on because they don't expect anything to come of it. They're happy enough if he buys them an expensive piece of jewelry; then he never has to see them again."

Jerod made a face. "Does his wife know?"

"No. That's why he wanted to keep it a secret. He said that he loves her, but she doesn't meet all his needs. Basically, our guy said, she's not twenty-two, so it's not scintillating enough."

Jazzi finished her stew and stood to bring the brownies to the table. "One of Jessica's friends told me that Jessica's dad leered at them all the time. He must have a thing for young women."

Gaff snorted. "He wanted to have it all. His wife, all their money, and play time on the side. He said that he didn't want Lorraine to know because he didn't want the drama. But that blew up in his face. Our guy interviewed his one-night stand, and she didn't appreciate having to explain herself to a cop, so she called Hodgkill's wife. And then the crap hit the fan. Mrs. Hodgkill filed for divorce."

Jazzi couldn't believe it. "She put up with all the abuse he threw at Jessica, and now she wants a divorce because he cheated on her?"

"That was probably the last straw," Ansel said.

"Hodgkill's furious, because he used a lot of her money to invest in his business. Now she's asking for half of everything."

Jerod snickered. "What bothered him more, losing his wife or losing her money?"

Gaff looked pretty amused, too. "He's going to miss them both. Rumor was that he invited anyone he needed to impress home for dinner, and everyone was charmed by Lorraine. People who didn't want anything to do with him, liked her. She smoothed a lot of things over for him."

As much as Jazzi loved the idea that Hodgkill had finally pushed too far, she thought about Jessica's brother. "How's Alwin taking it?"

Gaff buttered a piece of bread to sop up the stew's last dregs. "I don't know. Our guy didn't interview him after news of the divorce. He'd done what he wanted to do: found evidence that proved Hodgkill didn't kill Darcie."

Of course. That would be all he was interested in. Jazzi felt sorry for Alwin, though. Would his dad make him choose between him or his mother? She could see Lamar doing that.

Gaff glanced at his watch. "Gotta go. I just thought you'd be interested in the news. And now you can mark Hodgkill off your suspect list."

With reluctance. The man was a real scumbag. But it did narrow the list. She put a brownie in a bag and gave it to Gaff to eat later. "Thanks for coming."

"Thanks for lunch. And let me know if you hear anything."

They all sat at the card table a while longer after Gaff left. "I don't have one warm feeling for Hodgkill, but somehow, this news was still a little depressing," Jazzi said.

Ansel and Jerod nodded. Jerod reached for another brownie. "I don't feel sorry for Hodgkill, but I sure sympathize with his family."

Ansel finished his soda, then shook himself. "I wonder what Lorraine will do once the divorce is final."

"She's a devoted mother. I can't see her leaving Alwin on his own in Carolina." Jazzi stood and tied back the scarf over her hair. "I'm going to start painting again. I don't want to dwell on this."

The men stood, too, but before they climbed the stairs to start work again, another car pulled into the drive. Fists pounded on the front door.

"What in tarnation?" Jerod went to yank it open. "What the heck do you want?"

A woman with really short brown hair and a lean, muscular build stalked inside the house. George raised his head and growled. Jazzi stared at him. George never growled at anyone. He liked people, but he must have sensed the antagonistic vibes rolling off whoever this was. She stopped, hands on hips, to look at all three of them, slanting a challenging glare at Jerod and Ansel.

"Lila called to tell me that some of Jessica's squeaky-clean best friends stopped here to give you guys an earful. I don't trust Jillian, Molly, or Felicity, so I came to set the record straight. I'm Nadia Ashton, and I hated Jessica's guts, but I didn't kill her. Ask your little Girl Scouts; they can tell you. I was on the back patio with half our class when Jessica hit the cement with a splat."

Jazzi stepped forward, and George padded over to stand next to her. She'd have to give him an extra treat later. Ansel's pug was doing his best to support and defend her. "Can you give me a specific name of someone who can vouch for you?"

"Lila was with me."

Like Jazzi would believe either of them. "You both hated Jessica. I wouldn't trust either of you. Is there someone else?"

Nadia's lips twisted in a snarl. "I'm not sure. Someone should remember that we turned to give each other high fives when blood gushed from Jessica's ears, nose, and mouth."

Ansel's hands curled into fists. "You hated her that much, just because she beat you, fair and square, at tennis?"

"Jessica had everything. Looks, money, brains, and guys gushing all over her. All I had were tennis and the hopes of that scholarship. She took that away from me."

Jerod's voice turned cold, with none of his usual laughter. "If you couldn't beat a fellow student, you didn't have much hope of going to state or getting a sports scholarship."

"That shows what you know. Jessica was one of the best tennis players around. She'd always had private lessons, a personal trainer for a while. I had to work odd jobs to pay for any lessons I got, and my parents weren't happy I spent my money on them."

"Your parents didn't support you?" Ansel asked.

"I don't talk about them."

Just as Jazzi suspected. A terrible home life. "So, you blamed Jessica instead."

"She didn't have to beat me."

The woman wouldn't let it go. "You wanted her to throw the match. Did you ask her to?"

"I wouldn't stoop that low. No, if she was half as smart as everyone said she was, she would have known."

"She didn't." Jazzi clasped her hands together, tempted to smack the girl. Why couldn't she move on? "I'm reading her journals. She was surprised when you hated her so much for winning."

Nadia sniffed. "That was her problem. She never thought about the rest of us, what it was like to struggle for money or be invisible at school. She even had to get better grades than I did."

"But she did think about other people," Jazzi said, defending her. "She sympathized with a lot of them. She just didn't know you."

"She didn't try."

Jerod looked like he wanted to shake her. "Is there a reason she should have? Did you make any attempt to be her friend?"

Nadia stared at him as if he were insane. "Why would I? She had her little clique."

Jazzi was out of patience. She'd heard enough. "Molly Kroft already told me she'd seen you on the patio, so I'd already crossed you off as a possible suspect."

"Then why did you ask me for an alibi?"

"I didn't. I asked if there was someone who could vouch for you. Then I could eliminate another possible person who could have pushed Jessica."

"Lila was with me. Molly probably didn't mention her."

Jazzi frowned, studying her. She got the distinct impression that Nadia was just as intent at providing an alibi for Lila as she was for herself. Had Lila called and gotten her so worked up that she'd barged in here, so angry and aggressive? "I'll call Molly and ask about her."

"You do that, but she'll probably lie. She didn't like Lila." Nadia turned on her heel and slammed away.

When her car tore out of the drive, Ansel shook his head. "Some people can nurse a grudge for a lifetime."

"I think Lila put her up to this." Jazzi bent to pat George's head. "Thanks, boy. You had my back."

The pug looked happy with himself and returned to his dog bed.

Jerod glanced at his watch. "Let's forget work today and call it a loss. Between Gaff's news and meeting Nadia, I'm ready to go home."

"Works for me." Jazzi was going out with the girls tonight. She wouldn't mind time to relax before she had to get ready.

They cleaned up their work messes, and when Jazzi packed the food to leave, she snuck George a few pieces of meat. Then Ansel carried George to the van. With a wave, they and Jerod went their separate ways. Jazzi called Molly Kroft once they left Merlot. She told her about Nadia's visit and asked about Lila being on the patio.

"She's right," Molly said. "She was there, too. I remember now. They high fived each other when Jessica hit the cement."

Nuts. Jazzi had had high hopes for Lila. But that confirmed, she texted Gaff that Molly and Lila could alibi each other. Then she sat back to relax. The sky was a deep blue today, with big, puffy white clouds. The temperature had climbed, too. She only needed a sweater to ward off the chill.

By the time Ansel reached Highway 24, the beautiful fall day had revived her. "It's still early, so why don't we make another stop at the party store to look for costumes? When I see Olivia, she's going to ask me *again* if we have ours, and she's going to give me grief for waiting till the last minute."

"I love the party store," Ansel told her. "Maybe we can even find a costume for George."

Jazzi turned in her seat to look at the pug. Would he tolerate a costume? He was pretty low-key, and he loved attention. He might trot around the kitchen, thinking he was hot stuff. Would Inky and Marmalade like being Halloween cats? Who was she kidding? If she tried to put a costume on Inky, he'd never forgive her—*if* she lived through it.

When they entered the store and walked down the rows of costumes, Jazzi worried that they'd find anything to fit Ansel. Not too many men who were six five probably shopped here. And his tall, muscular build *did* limit their choices, but they found a black-and-white-striped prison outfit—a shirt and pants set with a hat—that would work.

"If I'm going to be a prisoner, you should share my jail cell," he said.

She chose an orange prison jumpsuit. Not the most complementary color for her, but prison guards didn't care about that, did they? Last, but not least, they found a devil's outfit for George with horns, a pitchfork, and a pointed tail. Satisfied, they headed home.

She was grateful they'd made the stop when she walked into Henry's on Broadway for girls' night out. The first thing Olivia asked when she saw her was *did you get a costume?*

Jazzi grinned. "We even bought one for George."

Didi laughed. "Gran's making a superhero costume for River because she didn't like the ones she saw in the stores."

Gran had a thing for that little boy. She was always going out of her way to buy or fix him something. She was forever sneaking him extra dessert.

The waitress had already brought their drink orders when Elspeth slid into the last chair at the table wearing a huge smile. "Our house passed the inspection, and we get to move in two days before Thanksgiving."

"Congratulations!" They waited for Elspeth to get her wine, then raised their glasses in a toast.

"Don't expect to be invited over for a while," she warned them. "It needs a lot of work, but we can't wait to get started. Maybe by Easter, we'll have a few walls knocked down and the kitchen and dining area will be big enough for everyone to eat at our place."

That veered the talk to the party on Sunday. "What are you wearing?" Didi asked Olivia.

"I rented a barmaid's dress like they wear in old TV Westerns, and Thane's dressing like a cowboy."

"I'm coming as a pumpkin," Didi said. "It will go around my belly. And Walker's wearing overalls and a straw hat to be a farmer."

"And you?" Olivia asked Elspeth.

She smiled. "Radley and I are coming as aristocrats. I bought lots and lots of satin and lace, and I've been sewing like mad."

"That's a lot of work." Didi reached for a breadstick. She was always hungry these days.

"You're going to make the rest of us feel like peasants," Jazzi teased.

Elspeth raised a hand, declaring, "Let them eat cake!"

The giggles and laughter just got better after that. By the time Jazzi returned home, she found Ansel in as high spirits as she was. He'd ordered in BBQ and sides from Shigs 'n Pits, and he and the guys had spent the night in the basement. They'd get tired of that eventually. Maybe. But they were enjoying it for now.

Before they went upstairs to bed, Jazzi went to the house plans Ansel had drawn and marked three *x*s on the back patio. Lila, Nadia, and Mr. Hodgkill at the grill. He couldn't have killed Darcie, so she doubted he'd killed Jessica. Her list of nonsuspects was growing longer. Finally.

Chapter 34

On Friday, when they met at the Merlot house, they were all ready to finish the upstairs and be done with it. The men went straight to work on the small bathroom, and Jazzi dipped her brush into the white paint to start the edges of the rest of the bedroom ceilings. Once those were done, they could make quick work of the rest with their rollers.

They completed their projects before they broke for lunch. Jazzi had packed deli sandwiches, and they ate them quickly, returning to work as soon as possible. With all three of them painting, they finished the rooms before quitting time at five. Hurrying through cleanup, they tugged on hoodies and were walking to their vehicles when a black Lexus pulled into the driveway, blocking them.

A man in a powder-blue Polo golf shirt and crisp white pants walked toward them. He was probably five ten, in his early thirties, and thin. His build would have looked athletic except for his stooped shoulders and weak chin. His sandy hair was thinning and his nose was too large for his face. His pale blue eyes narrowed when he saw them. "Look here." He tilted up his head at Jerod and Ansel and took a step back. "I drove here to take care of this problem myself."

Jerod gazed down at him. "Okay, what's the deal?"

Ruth Goggins had just come out of her house, looked over and saw them, and ran forward, gushing, "Alwin! What brings you home?"

Neither Ruth nor Alwin wore a sweater or jacket. It was warm for this late in October, but too chilly for shirtsleeves. Alwin didn't seem to notice. He scowled at her. "Now, Ruthie, this is *not* my home. It holds no good memories for me. You should know that. And I'm here to warn these busybodies to stay out of my family's lives."

Ruth's smile grew even wider. She gave Jazzi an I-told-you-so look. But Alwin didn't notice. Instead, he stabbed his finger at Jazzi.

"Your interference has caused my mother to file for divorce." His voice turned whiny. Jazzi gritted her teeth. She hated whining. "Do you know how much that will cost my father and our company?"

Jazzi stared at him. "That's what's important to you? Not solving your sister's murder? Not that your father cheated on your mother?"

Ruth gasped. She turned to hear Alwin's reply. But Jerod laughed at him. "Jazzi didn't cause their divorce. Your dad did. He can't keep his pants zipped."

Color suffused Alwin's pale face. "My father makes important decisions every day. He's under a lot of stress. Occasionally, he needs relief."

"Some play golf or racquetball," Ansel said. "They don't bribe young girls to go to bed with them with expensive jewelry."

Ruth's eyes almost popped out of her head, but Jazzi wasn't interested in arguing about Mr. Hodgkill. "No one cared about your father's habits," she told Alwin. "All anyone wanted to do was rule out people who couldn't have killed Darcie Winters. If we find out who killed her, we'll probably have the person who killed your sister."

"My sister's been dead a long time." Alwin wrung his hands. "We've finally put that behind us. We don't need to relive that day." He glanced at the patio and hurriedly glanced away.

Jazzi put her hands on her hips. "Some people still want justice for her, even if you don't. Darcie Winters was determined to find out who pushed her. That's what got her killed, so someone obviously is still worried he'll get caught."

"Why a he?" Alwin countered. "Lots of people hated my sister."

"You knew that and never did anything to defend her?" Jazzi had formed a different picture of this man from listening to Jessica's friends. She'd thought he cared more about her.

"Of course I knew. Lila and Nadia made it obvious. And I tried to talk to her about it, but Jessica was strong and independent." He shook his head. "She went at everything full throttle. She didn't care if people were jealous of her. But more women resented her than men. Why do you think a man must have pushed her?"

"Because another woman was killed the same year Jessica died. That makes us think a man killed both of them."

"I see. You don't have absolute proof, though."

"No. That's why Darcie was trying to determine who was at Jessica's graduation party and who they were with. That way, we can eliminate a lot of possible suspects. We've accounted for eight people so far."

Alwin glared at Ruth, still hovering by the wall. "Have you asked her? She wasn't even invited, but she snuck into the house to find RJ when he disappeared inside."

Ruth's jaw dropped. "You're accusing me of pushing your sister?"

"Why not? All you did was spread ugly rumors about her. You were obsessed."

Ruth's happiness at seeing him turned to anger. "You'd know I was there, because so were you, even though your father swore you weren't home, and you hid in your room so the detective wouldn't see you."

Jazzi turned on him. "Where were you when Jessica fell?"

Face flushed, he said, "In my room. I got sick of hearing everyone congratulating Jessica for being named valedictorian."

Jazzi hadn't expected him to admit that. "Did you look out your window and see anyone else? It faces the backyard, doesn't it?"

"I can only see part of it from there. Jessica's room had the best view. I didn't look. I can't tell you who was where."

"What about you, Ruth? Where were you when Jessica fell?"

Ruth lifted her chin. "I'd started inside the front door when Lorraine rushed down the driveway to a car parked at the curb. I turned to watch her. It was that horrid sister of hers, the one married to the college professor. She doted on Jessica. They were so much alike."

"Did anyone see you there?"

Ruth pressed her lips together. "No. From my vantage point, I could watch Lorraine and see into the house."

She was spying on people. "So no one can vouch for you."

"Why would I need someone to do that? I was only checking for my nephew."

"Because," Alwin pointed out, "the stairs are only a short distance from the front door. You could easily have waited until the coast was clear and zipped up them to push my sister."

Ruth gaped. "I'm not a murderess. And besides, why would I kill another girl besides Jessica?"

Alwin sneered. He might wilt under pressure, but he gladly turned on others. "Maybe they turned down your precious nephew, and you took that as a family insult."

Ruth's face contorted with anger. "I never knew you could be such a vile person." She turned on her heel and marched away.

Alwin returned his attention to the three of them. "My family left here to put Jessica's death behind us. You're stirring everything up again. We almost came apart at the seams when it happened. Please, leave us alone."

Jazzi was unimpressed. "Damian had to leave Merlot, too, and he still has to live with the gossip and stares every time he returns home to visit his parents and family. He can't put her death behind him either. People won't let him. He asked us to help clear his name."

Alwin blinked in surprise. "You know Damian? I liked him. But his best bet is to stay far away from Merlot. As long as Lila and Nadia live here, they'll never leave him in peace."

She couldn't argue with that. Instead, she asked, "Did you hear any gossip about the blond cheerleader who died during Jessica's senior year of high school?"

"The police questioned us about her, but none of us had seen anything. I'm not sure her death and Jessica's are related."

"Did you and your father ride to that out-of-town game together?"

His frown returned. "No, I had to drive straight to the game from college. I had a late test that day. I saw Dad in the stands, though."

"Did you get together after the game?"

"For a little while. We went for a late supper at some local place. I had to go to the locker room with the team first, though, and couldn't talk to him until they boarded the bus to go back to Merlot."

"So he was alone after the game?" Jazzi pressed.

He shrugged. "There were a lot of people at every basketball game we played. Dad knew most of them. A lot of people came to the party, too. Again, no one saw anything."

He wasn't going to be any help. Jazzi waited for him to make the next move. Finally, he sighed. "I wish you'd leave the past alone, but you're not going to, are you? My family's going to be torn apart by this. I hope you're happy." He stalked to his car and drove away.

Ansel wrapped his arm around her shoulders. "That guy has some serious issues. So does the neighbor."

"Like father, like son."

They loaded their things into their vehicles and headed for home.

Chapter 35

On the drive home, they actually cracked their windows to let in fresh air. Once the sun set, the temperatures would dip, but at the moment, the crisp fall air felt good.

Ansel glanced at the houses they passed. The farther they got from town, the farther apart they spread. "All we have to do now is work on the basement at the Merlot place. We should start looking for our next fixer-upper."

Jazzi had started thinking about that, too. She knew Jerod had been scouring Realtor books and online sites for a couple of weeks now. "I hope it's in River Bluffs. It's going to be cold soon, and the roads can get bad in December. I'd rather have somewhere closer to drive."

He nodded. "There's not much in the paper or online. If we see something, we'll have to move fast. Houses don't last long in this market."

"We should start looking every day." The basement at the Merlot house would take a decent amount of time to fix, but hopefully, they'd find something before they finished it. Jerod and Ansel had gone down to take a closer look at it while she finished painting the last ceiling. They'd decided to fix the moisture problem; they'd have to dig a trench around the outside edge of the entire house and install tiles to drain water away from the house. Time-consuming. But that was why the walls and floors were crumbling and needed a new coat of cement. On top of that, they had to replace the furnace and central air. They'd be lucky if they could put the house on the market before Thanksgiving.

They reached the highway and turned left toward home. Hillegas Road had been closed for repairs for the last two months, but it was finally open. They could take that to the north side of town. They passed the street that led southwest to her parents' home but kept driving. Mom and Dad always went out with friends on Friday nights lately. Since she and Olivia had moved out, their social life had exploded. Mom hated to cook and loved people—one of the reasons her hair salon was so popular. They were always doing something or going somewhere.

Instead of passing Jefferson Point, Ansel turned in and stopped at Pier 1. "The kitchen and living room could use some fall touches," he said.

George sat up on the back seat. He recognized the pet store next door, where they often stopped. People walked inside with dogs on leashes. Ansel shook his head. "We'd better let George find a new toy first."

She'd buy something for Inky and Marmalade, too. Ansel attached George's leash to his collar and lowered the pug to the pavement. George didn't like to be carried into the store. It looked bad when all the other dogs trotted in on their own. He almost swaggered as he walked through the door.

Jazzi tried not to laugh. The pug didn't have a problem with self-esteem. He padded straight to the dog toys and inspected them. When he stopped to stare at a stuffed animal with a long neck made out of rope, Ansel picked it up. Jazzi chose a cube that opened up with holes for cats to peek out of for her two furry friends. Then Ansel bought a bone for George to chew on while they shopped in Pier 1.

They found forest-green throw pillows for their butter-yellow living room grouping and gold throw pillows for her red-leather grouping, along with a myriad of decorations for the tables and fireplace mantel. Ansel even bought huge baskets of fake mums to place by the front and patio doors. Then they loaded up their purchases and hurried home.

"If we clean the house and decorate tonight, we can spend all day tomorrow cooking," Jazzi said.

"I'm a whiz with a dust mop." Ansel parked at the back patio so they could unload all their purchases. George wouldn't give up his bone, so Ansel carried the pug into the house with it still gripped in his teeth. When the cats saw his new toy, they waited for Jazzi to take theirs out of its package and open it up. Then the fun began. They chased each other through the tunnels and pounced on each other when they popped their heads out any of the holes.

The pets happy, Ansel went to park the van in the garage, and she carried pillows to scatter on the sofas and chairs. Their living room was huge, with two leather furniture groupings—the butter yellow and the red. By the time Ansel came to see how the decorations looked, she'd put the cornucopia, spilling its bounty on the fireplace mantel, along with the tiers of red, gold, and dark green candles. The black runner with orange and gold leaves was on the farmhouse table. And hollow ceramic jack-o'-lanterns filled with candy corn were on the side tables.

He grinned. "Perfect."

They didn't bother to shower and change but began cleaning. It was after seven before they called for a pizza. They were waiting for it to be delivered when Lydia Jenkins called. "I thought you might like to know my sister Lorraine's coming to stay with us for a week while the dust from her divorce settles. She needs some TLC. Lamar won't stop arguing with her. He doesn't want to give her a penny in the settlement. She's hired a good lawyer, and he said he'd call her in Merlot if he needs anything, but he thought it was a good idea for her to get away from Lamar and block his calls."

"Do you think she'd mind talking to us?" Jazzi asked.

"I'll do my best to persuade her. She might not be up to it, though."

Jazzi wouldn't push her. She doubted if the poor woman could tell her where people were when Jessica fell anyway.

After the phone call, they settled at the kitchen stools to enjoy their supper. Jazzi sipped wine, and Ansel drank a beer. Jazzi let her gaze scan the large room. She didn't think she'd ever get tired of its robin's-egg-blue cabinets, stainless-steel countertops, and the island with its butcher-block top. And she knew she'd never regret paying extra for its fake tin ceiling, painted white.

George came to beg for pieces of pepperoni and bits of sausage, and Ansel tossed scraps to him. Jazzi got out two felt mice stuffed with catnip to throw for the cats, who batted them around the whole room.

At ten, satisfied with what they'd accomplished, they climbed the steps to shower and change into their pajamas. Jazzi was sliding between the sheets when her cell phone buzzed.

"Hello?"

"Have you checked the coat pockets yet?" Gran demanded.

"I haven't found a coat yet."

Gran sighed. "No worries. You will, and that will give you the answer you need. I'm going back to sleep now." She hung up.

Jazzi stared at her phone. "Gran must have had a vision in her sleep." She told Ansel about it.

He grinned. "I'd better never try to slip anything past you. Gran will know and tell on me."

"Keep that in mind."

They rolled to face the walls, their butts bumping, and drifted to sleep.

Chapter 36

They were sipping coffee, and Jazzi was writing out a grocery list, when a tall, lean man with hair graying at the temples knocked on their back door. When Jazzi answered it, he said, "I saw the lights on back here, so I thought I might have more luck coming to the kitchen door. I'm Jillian's husband, Dexter. I got called in to the hospital today, and she told me to stop to talk to you on my way home." He glanced inside and smiled. "Nice place."

"Thank you." Jazzi led him to the kitchen island. "Coffee?"

"I wouldn't mind." He took a stool a few spaces down from Ansel.

She glanced out the kitchen window and saw a silver Mercedes parked in the drive. The man wore an expensive watch. No wonder Jillian sported a big diamond on her finger. He wasn't handsome, but he looked so pleasant, Jazzi immediately felt comfortable with him.

When she handed him his coffee mug, he said, "Thanks for making time for me. I always do what my wife tells me to do."

"Are you a doctor?" At his nod, Jazzi tried to picture him with Jillian. He was tall. She was short. He looked serious. She came off as artsy, a little eccentric. They probably balanced each other. She poured more coffee for herself and took the stool beside Ansel's. "Why did Jillian want you to stop by?"

He sighed. "I was at Jessica's graduation party, too, and we were talking about it. I wasn't with Jillian. She didn't even know I was alive in high school, but I had a terrible crush on her. I wasn't very sociable back then, but I knew Jillian would be there to celebrate with Jessica, so I went. And I was trying to build up the courage to ask her out."

What a sweet man. "Did you do it?"

He pulled a face. "Finally. Glad I managed before Jessica was pushed. She said yes, and we kept dating every time we were back in Merlot after that. I really had to work at it, though."

Jazzi smiled. "I'd say you both got lucky."

"I would, too." He stopped to drink his coffee, clearly trying to collect his thoughts. "That day, I mostly hung out on the patio. A few people I knew were out there. Jillian and I ran in different circles. I was in the chess and Latin club. She was in drama and art."

"More coffee?" Ansel offered when his cup was empty.

He shook his head. "The thing is, I was standing with my back to the balcony, talking to Tilly in the food line. Jillian said you'd asked about her."

Jazzi nodded. "Good. Thank you. I can mark her off the suspect list."

"There's more, though. Nadia and Lila were a little farther away. Nadia was badgering poor Molly Kroft, and Lila was getting bored, so she started asking me a lot of stupid questions, trying to flirt. I didn't want to bother with her, but I didn't want to leave where I was because I thought Jillian would eventually get in line for food, and I could talk to her again. But Lila kept annoying me. That girl always followed money, and my parents were well-off. All of a sudden, though, she stared up at the balcony and stopped talking. I was going to turn to see what she was looking at, but just then I heard Jessica scream. I jerked out of the way right before she hit the cement on the other side of me." He squelched his eyes shut, as if blocking out what he'd seen.

Jazzi stared at him, horrified. "She died right next to you?"

"Right at my feet. It was awful. I watched her eyes go blank and the blood gush from her nose, mouth, and ears. When the police questioned me, that's all I could think about. I completely forgot about Lila."

A frisson of energy shot down Jazzi's arms. Her stomach fluttered. "Do you think Lila saw who pushed Jessica?"

"I think she might have. I'd never have remembered if Jillian and I hadn't been talking about who was where."

Jazzi pushed her coffee cup aside. "We have to talk to Lila."

He shook his head. "Jillian already tried. She's out of town right now. She drove to visit her parents in Carolina."

"Close to where the Hodgkills moved?"

He blinked and shook his head. "I don't remember exactly where either of them are now. Sorry."

"Don't be sorry. Thank you so much for stopping to tell us this." Disappointment warred with excitement. They might not be able to talk to Lila until she got back, but they had a new lead.

The man stood. "Thanks for seeing me so early on a Saturday morning. I wouldn't have bothered you, but Jillian said it was important."

"It is. Thank you." Jazzi walked him to the door and waved him off. The minute she was back in the kitchen, she called Gaff and shared the news.

"She's on a trip?" He sounded as frustrated as she was. "To Carolina? I'll have to look into that. While I'm at it, I think I'll do some digging into Miss Mattock."

"She's still single?" Jazzi asked.

"Divorced. She took back her maiden name when she and her husband split."

It must not have been a friendly parting, then. When she hung up with Gaff, she went for more coffee. Pulling the grocery list back to finish it, she bit her bottom lip. "I've lost my concentration."

"Why wouldn't you?" Ansel said. "If Jillian's husband is right, Lila Mattock knows who pushed Jessica, and she's never told anyone."

"I wonder why." Was Lila protecting a friend?

"With her, maybe she'd rather try to make Damian miserable. She probably wanted to reward whoever did it."

That sounded about right. Jazzi turned her attention back to the groceries. If she didn't have party food when everyone came tomorrow, she might as well wear sackcloth and paint her face with ashes.

They left a half hour later and returned after filling their cart, ladened with groceries. The cats loved it. More sacks to play in. Even George looked hopeful. That many bags had to hold something he'd like.

They spent the rest of the day cooking and prepping food. George was their official taster. He approved of the meatballs, not so much the sauce. He even liked nibbles of pumpkin bread. And he always begged for popcorn, even though he wasn't fond of it as popcorn balls. Jazzi didn't even bother trying to give him pumpkin soup. The pug had high standards, and soups without meat weren't on his list of favorites. He did like the caramel sauce, though, just not the caramel apples.

When they were finishing up, Ansel said, "It's going to be easy to do the rest in the morning. We've cooked enough, and you've been a good sport about the party. I want to take you out for supper tonight."

He didn't have to ask twice. They went upstairs to shower and change. Before getting dressed to go out, Jazzi said, "You've never tried on your prison garb. You should see how it fits."

"It had better. I don't think I can find anything else this close to Halloween." But he slipped on his black-and-white outfit, and as always, he looked great. He raised his eyebrows at the fake handcuffs included with the costume.

"Are you thinking about handcuffing me?" She was sliding one of his favorite dresses over her head.

"I've heard you've been naughty. I might have to frisk you."

There could be an upside to being on the lam.

He laughed at her expression. "You have no shame. But right now, I'm hungry. And you look great in that dress." It was dark green, with a deep plunge. "How does the Outback sound?"

"They have my favorite salad and burgers in the world."

"Then let's go." He pulled on a pair of Dockers and a deep-blue, button-down shirt that accentuated his sky-blue eyes.

George pouted when they left him behind, but he'd had enough snacks; he wouldn't suffer too much. The cats jumped in the window to watch the pickup back away, then Jazzi was sure they'd return to their naps.

She was glad she'd worn her lightweight leather jacket when they walked from the parking lot into the restaurant. Ansel wore his black leather, too. He looked scrumptious in it. A small breeze had blown up, and it made the cool temperatures even chillier. They were seated in the bar, enjoying their suppers, when Jazzi looked up and tried to hide a gasp. Ansel frowned and turned to see who'd walked in.

A man, six foot with dark hair and a year-round tan, spotted her and left his two buddies to stalk toward her. When he reached their table, he glared at Ansel. "Who's this?"

Jazzi raised her eyebrows. "Chad, this is my husband, Ansel Herstad. Ansel, this is my ex-fiancé, Chad."

Chad's frown deepened. "When did you get married? I didn't see it in the paper."

"We had a small ceremony at home. The reception, too."

He pressed his lips together. "You could have at least told me you were tying the knot."

"Why? You got married without telling me. You probably have kids by now."

"No such luck." His voice was brittle. "All I wanted was a family. Ginger can't have any. Found out she got an abortion when she was fifteen and now she's sterile."

Jazzi winced at his tone. "You can always adopt."

"And get some loser's cast-off? I don't think so."

She stared. When had he grown so bitter?

Narrowing his eyes, he studied her. "I thought maybe you'd worked long enough that you were starting to think about having a family."

"Not ready yet. I'll probably work even after I have kids."

"You wouldn't!" Chad looked at Ansel. "Are you okay with that?"

"That's her choice. Lots of women manage it these days."

Chad snorted. "You look like you'd have a backbone. She's got you cowered, hasn't she?"

Ansel's expression turned dangerous. He started to push out of his chair when one of Chad's friends called, "Hey, bud, we're holding a stool for you at the bar. The place is filling up. Get on over here."

Chad turned on his heel. "See you, Jaz."

Jazzi reached across the table to pat Ansel's hand. "Don't let him ruin our evening. Things haven't worked out for him like he planned."

Ansel slowly sank back onto his chair. He glowered in Chad's direction. "Your ex is a real douche."

Jazzi laughed. "What was your first clue?"

That made his lips turn up. He shook his head at her. "How did you end up with a jerk like that?"

"We met when he came to landscape a few houses that Jerod and I were flipping. I didn't know squat about yards and plants back then. I learned a lot from him. He was fun while we worked together and hung out, but the minute I moved in with him, his priorities switched. He constantly nagged me to give up flipping houses to stay home and have his babies." She bit her bottom lip, feeling pensive. "It's sad. He was obsessive about it. He's gotten worse with time."

"That's why you were so reluctant to get serious when we moved in together."

"Chad made me pretty wary, that's for sure."

Ansel nodded understanding. "I get it, and I can't say much. I lived with Emily, and she made my life miserable."

She reached for her wineglass and finished what was left. "Neither of us chose too well our first time out."

"That's for sure." He chuckled. "At least we learned from our mistakes. You ready? I don't want to share a bar with your ex."

She only had a few bites of her burger left, and she'd been struggling to finish it. They paid their bill and left. On the way home, she thought about how lucky she was that she and Jerod had found the stone cottage to fix up and that Ansel had come into her life. They both might have had rocky starts, but they'd sure hit the jackpot when they finally teamed up.

Chapter 37

Everyone came a little early. They were as excited about the party as Ansel. He'd spent the morning in the basement, setting up games for the kids while Jazzi finished cooking. He had bobbing for apples, pin the black hat on the witch, a black cat piñata, musical pumpkins—they were big enough to sit on when the music stopped—and wrap your dad as a mummy with toilet paper. He had enough small prizes for everyone. The games were his thing. She was staying out of it.

While people lingered upstairs, admiring one another's costumes, the kids found the candy corn in the Halloween pumpkin dishes. She had cheese cubes on skeleton toothpicks for them, too, and she'd decorated a cheese ball with black licorice "legs" to look like a spider for the adults. Franny came as Little Orphan Annie. It suited her orange-colored hair and freckles. And Jerod came as Huck Finn, with bib overalls, a flannel shirt, and a straw hat. When Walker walked in, dressed similarly to be a farmer for Didi's pumpkin, they laughed at each other.

River was so excited to have his two friends with him, he got Gunther and Lizzie excited, too. Ansel, in his prison garb, had to blow a whistle to get them to calm down. The weather was mild enough, he said. "I bought pumpkins and carving kits for each one of you. When you finish your jack-o'-lanterns, you can take them home." He, Jerod, and Walker led the kids out onto the patio.

Didi grinned at Jazzi's jumpsuit. "You don't look much better in that color than I do," she teased. At least her pumpkin had green leaves on top to soften the neon orange. Gran and Samantha came next, dressed as two old crones. Gran had even applied a wart on her nose. And bat wings stuck out from the sides of Samantha's pointed hat. Olivia, as always, looked wonderful with her dark blond hair pulled up in a Gibson style and her brown eyes lined with black liner. She'd painted a beauty mark on her cheek. Her barmaid's outfit made the most of her willowy figure. Thane, big and bulky, had his auburn hair pulled back in a ponytail with a hole for it to fit through in his cowboy hat. His badge read "Sheriff." But the real stars of the party were Elspeth and Radley when they arrived as aristocrats. Their outfits looked like something off the covers of Jazzi's favorite Regency romance novels. Elspeth even wore a white pompadour wig.

Jazzi's mom and dad were overshadowed as a flapper and a gangster, and Eli and Eleanore were even more anticlimactic as stodgy Puritans. All they needed was a pitchfork to look like the somber couple in Grant Wood's *American Gothic* painting. They were all eclipsed, though, when George trotted to the kitchen island, dressed as a little devil. The kids came to fuss over him. The adults told him how adorable he looked, and George loved every minute of it. Jazzi had to admit, everyone had gone to the bother to dress up, and it was fun. Next year, she and Ansel would have to try harder.

People snacked until everyone had arrived. Then they gathered around the table to eat. The kids got a kick out of the mummy hot dogs, and Olivia was excited about the wrapped brie with fig jam and fancy crackers. There was a lot of food, but it quickly disappeared. Before Jazzi brought out the candy apples and popcorn balls, the men herded the kids into the basement.

The women grabbed wine or mulled cider and relaxed in the living room, but the noise and laughter in the basement eventually drew them to see what was happening. Kids were on their knees, grabbing for the candy that had spilled from the piñata. Then it was time for the mummy contest. Jerod couldn't work with both Gunther and Lizzie, so Gunther grabbed Ansel to decorate with toilet paper. River claimed Walker, so one of his friends nabbed Radley. The other yanked Thane over. Every man was too tall, so they had to kneel on their knees so the kids could wrap their faces and necks. When Ansel said, "Go!" the kids sprang into action. Inky and Marmalade joined in the fun, attacking toilet paper as the kids threw and draped it. Gran got to call the winner. They all finished at about the same time, but of course, she chose River. Gran had no problem about being partial. But no one cared, because Ansel had a huge candy bar for each of them.

Didi shook her head. "Those kids are going to have so much candy between today's party and actual trick-or-treating, their teeth are going to rot."

Ansel had planned bobbing for apples next to let the kids calm down a little before the last game—musical pumpkins. While each kid took a turn bobbing, the others sat on the large throw rug, sorting through their winnings. They'd all received yoyos, and Walker was patiently trying to teach River and his friends how to use theirs. Gunther was trying to hit the small rubber ball attached to his paddle, and when he connected, smacked Jerod in the face with it. He looked horrified, but Jerod only laughed. Thane was busy helping Lizzie color a picture with the colored pencils she'd won.

Watching them, Jazzi swallowed a lump in her throat. All good guys. Keepers. Then Ansel called River and his friends to bob for apples, and when River was having trouble bending over the tub far enough to reach one, his buddy, dressed as a pirate, reached forward. Jazzi held her breath. In her mind, she saw Jessica's brother plunge her head under water and hold it there, but the little boy grabbed River's shoulders to steady him so he could lean farther.

That's what good kids did. They helped one another. And that was how good fathers acted. They paid attention and encouraged. Jazzi let out a breath and shook her head. Jessica had been cheated.

Once the games were over, everyone headed back upstairs for caramel apples and popcorn balls. After that, energy lagging, people started to leave. When Gran and Samantha, the last to go, finally started toward the door, Gran stopped to wrap Jazzi in a hug.

"What a fun day, Sarah! Your cooking was as wonderful as always."

Samantha gave Jazzi a secret smile. Gran only reverted to the past, where Jazzi became her dead sister Sarah, when she was too tired or too stressed. This time, it was probably because she'd had too much fun. Jazzi hugged her a little more closely than usual. Gran was a treasure. She hoped she'd stick around a long time.

Finally alone, Jazzi and Ansel looked at the aftermath of the party. Not as bad as it could have been. They'd designed this house for entertaining. They'd installed two dishwashers, so it was easy to rinse and load all the dirty dishes and silverware. They'd bought a vacuum to keep in the basement, so Jazzi dragged a black trash can back and forth to toss all the scraps of paper and toilet paper in, and Ansel swept the area rugs.

In forty-five minutes, the house was put back together. They changed into their pajamas and stretched on their couches to relax. Tomorrow, she'd call Gaff to see if Lila Mattock had returned home. She was looking forward to paying her a visit.

Chapter 38

She and Ansel dragged a little on Monday morning. It had rained sometime during the night. When they looked outside, the yard and driveway were wet. They'd gotten lucky that the weather had stayed dry for their party. The gray sky encouraged second cups of coffee, so that they had to hustle to make it to the Merlot house on time. When they got there, Jerod was sitting at the card table, waiting for the coffee urn to finish brewing.

"I need some black magic this morning," he told them.

They could use more. Even George was tired. He went straight to his dog bed, flopped down, and closed his eyes. Being a devil was hard work.

Once they'd drained their mugs, Jerod pushed to his feet. "I'd like to give the upstairs one more look before we start work on the basement. I liked the colors in the rooms and hallway, but they always look different when they dry."

She was curious, too, so they climbed the elegant staircase to the second floor and walked from room to room. The master bedroom, painted Martha Stewart's sharkey gray, was so big that the color worked well in it. They walked down the hallway, stopping in each doorway, and agreed the honeysuckle off-yellow was the perfect airy feel, and neutral enough to go with anything. The next room was Alwin's, and then, lastly, they'd check Jessica's. Jazzi frowned at the wall that adjoined them.

"There's a spot that dried funny," she said, walking closer to inspect it. At first, she thought maybe it was just the way the light spilled in from the window, but when she studied the quarter-size circle, it looked flatter than the paint on the rest of the wall. She reached out to touch it, and the surface felt funny, too.

Jerod stood beside her, scowling. He pressed his finger on it and shook his head. "It's not drywall." He pressed harder, and the circle moved. As they watched, a plug fell into the space between the walls. He stared. "Wasn't this where we figured a picture had been hanging?"

Ansel nodded. "The paint around it had faded. You could see the shape of the frame."

"Someone cut a hole here. This is way too big for a nail." Jerod walked out, and his voice came from Jessica's room. "The same thing happened over here." He made a scraping noise, and a round hole opened up on her side, too. Then they heard his footsteps returning to them.

He held out his pocketknife with a gummy substance jammed on the tip. "Someone plugged the holes with toothpaste and let it dry before they painted over it."

They would have missed that. Madeline had owned the house long enough after the Hodgkills left that the entire walls were mottled, with faded areas where pictures, mirrors, or posters had hung. Jazzi blinked, confused about the hole, and then her jaw dropped. "Alwin could peek through the hole and watch his sister."

Ansel looked stunned. "You mean..."

Jerod knocked the plug of toothpaste into the trash and slid his pocketknife back into his jeans. "Alwin was a dirty Peeping Tom. He could watch anything and everything Jessica did. Probably watched her get undressed when he needed a little boost."

Jazzi pressed a hand to her stomach. For a brother to watch his own sister...Goose bumps covered her arms.

"He really was a pervert." Ansel scraped his hand through his hair, clearly upset, making it stand up in spikes.

"I think you should call Gaff." Jerod went to look out the window. She could hear him count to ten under his breath. Ansel looked like someone had knocked the air out of him, too. She was still trying to process it.

When she called Gaff and told him what they'd found, silence greeted her. "Are you there?" she asked.

"I'm here." There was a short hesitation, then he said, "Wendy looked like Jessica, remember?"

"Same coloring and build," she replied.

"Makes me wonder." His sigh carried over the phone. "I need to start digging again, but I have to tell you, things are starting to look bad for Alwin."

"I thought you were asking around about Lila." She was sure Lila had seen something the day Jessica died.

"I have been, and that's interesting, too. Lila lives large for the salary she makes as a paralegal. She got married right after she got her degree and had two sons. When she and her husband divorced, the dad got both kids. Now, Lila works part-time for a lawyer in Merlot, but she can afford a house near the golf course and she belongs to its clubhouse. She's not getting alimony. She has to pay it, and her family didn't leave her any money, so where's the money coming from?"

"An affair?"

Gaff snorted. "Or blackmail."

Jazzi would never have thought of that. But what if Gaff was right? "You could trace that somehow, couldn't you?"

"If a judge gave my friend permission to look into her finances. That might be tricky."

Jazzi hesitated. "Who do you think she's blackmailing?"

"Someone who has enough money to keep her in the lifestyle she likes. But Merlot has a decent number of well-off people. It doesn't have to be Alwin."

Maybe it was time for Jazzi to start asking about more people who'd been at the party. Jessica's entire class had been invited. "Would Ruth Goggins be rich enough?"

"She lived next door to the Hodgkills, didn't she?"

"And she loves status. Takes it seriously."

"Thanks for the info, Jazzi. I'm going to call my detective friend and pass it on."

She knew a dismissal when she heard one. When she hung up, the guys were staring at her.

"Blackmail?" Ansel asked.

Jazzi repeated what Gaff had told her. Jerod stared for a minute, then shook his head. "Let's get to work. I'd rather think about crumbling cement than Jessica's friends and family. We'll fix the bedroom walls later and repaint them."

By mutual agreement, they all started to the basement. Once there, they stopped and stared. Water had seeped in from the sides and corners, staining that cement darker than the rest, and there hadn't even been a downpour during the night. Hands on hips, Jerod shook his head. "I thought it was dry."

"It has been," Ansel said. "But this must be the first time it rained enough to leak in."

Jazzi cursed under her breath. There was no water standing in puddles, but they couldn't in good conscience call this a dry basement. This would take more work than simply patching crumbling cement. Still, it was just as well they knew they had a problem now rather than later. "We'll have to dig a trench and drain the water away from the house."

Ansel nodded agreement. "The soil looks like clay. It's going to be a pain to dig."

"First things first." Jerod picked up his garage broom. "We'll clean the crumbles off the walls and floor first and spread the new cement. Once it dries, we'll seal it; then we can tell Thane we're ready for him to install the new furnace. He can work in here while we work outside."

They spent the rest of the morning sweeping cement bits off the walls and floor to clean them. After lunch, they'd lay a thin layer of cement over all of them to seal what was there. Then they'd dig the trench to dry out the basement so the new cement would stay solid.

"What are we eating today?" Jerod asked as they climbed up to the kitchen. He'd seen the slow cooker they'd carried in but was more interested in coffee this morning.

"I thawed some of the soup Ansel and I froze ahead."

They washed up and were enjoying the creamy chicken and wild rice when her phone buzzed.

Jerod's brows shot up. "Gaff's fast today. He must have found out something."

Without looking, she pulled it out of her pocket. "Hello."

"You just won't leave things alone, will you?" Alwin sounded furious. "You found my peephole. Good for you. Did you have to tell your pet detective?"

"It doesn't make you look good."

"It doesn't mean I pushed Jessica either. My father secretly hates women, but I love them. And I always admired Jessica. I couldn't show it, or Dad would have disowned me, so I watched her."

"And you don't think that's wrong?"

"She was a beautiful girl. Is that against the law? To enjoy a beautiful body? Who's going to press charges? And can you prove anything?"

"It's still wrong." And icky. She didn't add that.

"Don't judge me. But know this: If I'd have pushed my sister, my fun would have ended." He hung up.

Jazzi stared at the phone. Then she frowned and turned to the guys, who'd heard every word of the conversation. "And if Jessica had left Merlot, his fun would have ended, too. I'm betting he thought about that."

Chapter 39

There's no joy in mixing bags of concrete and spreading them on walls and an extremely large floor. The basement had a musty smell, and even with the kitchen door open to, hopefully, allow fresh air downstairs, it was a dirty, smelly job. They started on the far end and had worked their way to the behemoth old furnace before quitting time for the day.

Just before five, Jazzi's cell phone buzzed. She glanced at the ID. "It's Lydia, Jessica's aunt."

When she answered, Lydia said, "I know this is last minute, but Lorraine's agreed to talk to you. Can you drop by our house before you leave Merlot?"

"We're done at the fixer-upper. I can be there in a few minutes."

Ansel shook his head. "*We'll* be there in a few minutes. You're not going anywhere in Merlot without me."

She covered her phone. "Nothing will happen to me at Lydia's house."

He crossed his arms, and Jazzi corrected herself. She told Lydia, "We'll be there soon. Ansel's coming with me."

"I heard, and he's right. We'll have drinks and snacks when you get here."

Jazzi put the leftover soup in the refrigerator so that it wouldn't have to sit in the van. It was cold enough outside, it probably wouldn't matter, but this way, they could have it for lunch any time they wanted. It only took them five minutes to reach Lydia's house near the river, and when they started to the door, Lydia stepped outside to greet them. She saw Ansel crack the window for George.

"Bring him in," she called to him. "Clyde loves dogs. He's behaved, isn't he?"

Ansel nodded and lifted George to carry him inside. Lydia led them to the sitting room again, and Clyde let out a hoot. "I've always had a fondness for pugs." He patted the side of his chair, and Ansel set George there. George, being a dog who believed he deserved undivided attention, was happy to be fussed over.

Ansel took a chair beside him, and Jazzi sat on the other side of the coffee table, near Lydia and the woman who must be Lorraine. Now she knew where Jessica got her beauty. Lorraine's silky, platinum hair was pulled back in a knot, showing off her oval face and high cheekbones. She was tall and moved gracefully when she handed her a glass of wine.

Lydia had gone to a lot of bother. A three-tiered tray held tiny pimiento cheese sandwiches, éclairs, and tarts. "This is lovely," Jazzi told her. "I feel too shabby to eat it. We came straight from the job. We look a mess."

Lydia laughed, dismissing her. "Both Lorraine and I love to entertain. So did our parents. Clyde insisted we feed you something this time instead of only offering you drinks."

Clyde scanned the offerings. "I doubt there's anything George would like. Should I get him some cold meat?"

Ansel grinned and shook his head. "He's happy with pie crust and pastry."

"A dog with refined tastes. Good boy." Clyde patted him even more.

"Everything on offer came from a shop. I used to bake more, but we don't eat as many sweets as we used to. Do you like to cook?" Lydia asked.

"I love to entertain," Jazzi admitted. "But I rarely bother with anything this elegant. Thank you."

"Our pleasure." Lydia motioned toward her sister. "I'd like to introduce you to Lorraine. We're so pleased she's come to visit us. I tried to talk her into stopping by her old house, but she didn't want to see the changes you've made to it. You understand."

"I certainly do." Jazzi turned her attention to her. "I'm so sorry I stirred up sad memories for you."

"It bothered me at first," Lorraine admitted. "But now I'm grateful. One of the reasons we left here was because I couldn't bear the idea of my daughter's killer smiling to my face, and I'd never suspect. If the killer had been caught, I could have handled things better."

Again, Jazzi understood, but how would Lorraine feel if the killer ended up being her son? Instead, she said, "Then I'm sorry we exposed your husband's affair. We never considered that."

Lorraine's green eyes glittered. "How could you? I'm grateful for that, too. Lamar's never been fun to live with. I'd have left him years ago, but he swore he'd fight me, tooth and nail, for custody of Alwin. Alwin needed me while he was growing up. His father was too demanding, expected too much. I couldn't in good conscience leave my poor boy to withstand Lamar on his own."

"And now?" Jazzi asked.

She grimaced. "After all these years of supporting him, his only concern when I filed for divorce was that I was ruining his future by demanding funds from the business he runs with his father. He's a grown man. He can decide if he wants to see me or not. If money matters more to him than I do, he deserves his father."

Jazzi grinned. She'd pictured Lorraine as a bit of a weakling for tolerating a domineering husband for all these years. She was wrong. Lorraine had decided her son needed her and stuck it out, but it was possible she'd held her own in the household.

Lydia asked, "What will you do after the divorce is final? Have you decided?"

Lorraine took a sip of wine, considering the question. "You and my oldest, dearest friends are all in Merlot. It would be nice to return to the area, but I could never settle in town again. Depending, of course, on whether Jessica's killer is caught this time."

Lydia locked gazes with Jazzi. "We're counting on you, dear. Poor Darcie's already died trying to find the answers. We're hoping you can finish what she started."

Nothing like too much pressure. Jazzi pinched her lips together. "We went to see Lila Mattock to ask her questions, but she's in Carolina visiting her parents. She didn't happen to stop by to visit your family, did she, Lorraine?"

"If she did, I wasn't there. I might have been at my lawyer's office when she came."

"Were she and Alwin close?"

Lorraine reached for a tart, her forehead creased. "I doubt it. She was Jessica's age, too young for him. Besides, Alwin despised how she treated his sister. He wouldn't have wanted to spend time with her."

Jazzi finished her éclair and wine, then glanced over at Ansel. He nodded.

"Thank you for your hospitality, but we'd better go." He started to stand when Jazzi's cell phone buzzed. She glanced at it.

"Gaff," she said.

Curious, Lydia leaned forward. "Your detective friend?"

Jazzi nodded as she took his call. "Hi. We're at Jessica's aunt's house right now, talking to her and Jessica's mother."

"Good. Put the phone on Speaker."

She frowned but did as he said. "All set."

"Lila Mattock died in a car crash early this morning. She was driving home from Carolina after visiting her parents and swerved off the road, down a ravine, and wrapped her car around a tree. She died instantly."

"Something feels fishy," Ansel said.

Gaff heard him. "It sure does. She wasn't on the highway. She was on a side road that led to the hotel where she was staying."

"She was staying at a hotel?" Jazzi asked. "She didn't stay at her parents' place?"

"That's the thing. Her parents thought she'd left two days ago. They didn't know she was still in the area."

"Anything else?"

"Another car left a lot of rubber on the road a few feet from where she swerved off."

"They saw the accident and braked to help her?"

"It looked more as if another driver and Lila were playing a game of chicken."

"So she was forced off the road?"

"That was the opinion of the cop who worked the accident scene." He paused. "Any opinions, people?"

"I left our house a few days ago to fly to see my sister," Lorraine said. "Lila would never stop to see me. She knew I despised her. My husband used to be fond of her, though. He liked anyone who was cruel to our daughter. And Lila called him often to tattle on people in town. You should ask him if he met with her."

"And your son?"

"He didn't like her either."

"I'll ask your husband, then, and thank you." Gaff hung up.

Jazzi returned her cell phone to her pocket. She felt numb. "Do you think…" She looked at Ansel.

George could tell she was upset and came to rest his head on her knees. She gently stroked between his ears—his favorite spot.

Ansel glanced at Lorraine. "Gaff learned that Lila lived way beyond her means, and he thought she might have been blackmailing someone. It's just conjecture."

Lorraine reached for Lydia's hand, and the two women gripped each other fiercely. "I can't believe it," Lorraine said. Her face and lips were stiff. "Lamar was a tyrant, but he'd never…" She stopped, suddenly uncertain. "He always accused me of having an affair, swore that Jessica wasn't his."

Lydia snorted. "Transference. He would think that because *he* was having affairs."

"People have told me that he was working the grill when Jessica died," Jazzi said.

Lorraine brightened, but then fretted again. "He left for a while. I saw him. He'd splattered BBQ sauce on his good shirt and hurried upstairs to change. No one would have noticed if he was gone a short while once the food was served."

"Was that close to when Jessica fell?" Ansel asked.

Lorraine frowned. "I can't be sure. It's been so long."

Ansel cringed, hesitant. "There's something else."

Lorraine's other hand gripped the edge of her chair. "Yes?"

Ansel told her about the peephole.

Color drained from her face, but then she frowned, troubled. "I often saw Lamar leave Alwin's room once Alwin was away at college. I always thought it odd. When I asked him about it, he said he liked to go in there. It made him feel close to his son."

Lydia pressed a hand to her forehead. "Oh, Lord, he was a peeper, too."

Her voice broke, and Clyde stood to go to her and hug her. Soon, all three of them were hugging one another.

"We'll leave now," Jazzi said, standing, too. "You have a lot to think about. And thanks for talking to us."

Clyde turned to walk with them to the door.

"No need," Ansel said, carrying George.

"But there is." He patted Jazzi's shoulder. "It's bothered you that you've upset us, but we'd rather know now than receive bad news as a complete surprise later."

She nodded and followed Ansel to the van, but she felt terrible. She hadn't expected to like Jessica's mom, but she did. And she really liked Lydia and Clyde. And what had she done? She'd been the deliverer of bad news, all the way around. If they never wanted to see her again, she'd understand.

Chapter 40

It was a cool day, but sweat dripped off Jazzi's chin as she helped dig the trench around the Merlot house. They'd finished the cement in the basement and moved outside to work. When they'd started, they all wore hoodies. After an hour, they'd removed them. Even her long sleeves felt too warm, so she crammed them up to her elbows. After another hour, Jerod went to fetch them cans of soda and was returning when a car pulled into the drive. Stifling a groan, Jazzi quickly sipped from her can. Visits hadn't gone well on this job. They'd been yelled at more often than not.

A young man in his early thirties got out and walked toward them. "I'm sorry to bother you. I heard this house is for sale, but there's no sign in the yard."

Jerod motioned to the trench they were digging. "That's because we haven't finished renovating it yet. We still have the basement to go."

"Everything else is done?" When Jerod nodded, he asked, "Can I see it? It's a beauty. My wife and I both travel a lot for sales, and we do a lot of work from home. This would be a perfect location for us."

Jerod's eyes lit up. A potential buyer. With a smile, he motioned toward the kitchen door. "Come on. I'll show you around."

They disappeared inside, and Ansel grinned at her. "We should have fixed the peephole in the bedrooms."

She shrugged. "Jerod has to tell him someone was murdered here. It's only ethical. If that doesn't stop him, neither will a peephole." Not that Madeline had told them about Jessica. But maybe the Hodgkills hadn't told her the entire truth either.

They went back to digging. Jerod was gone quite a while before he led the prospective buyer out to see the patio and backyard.

"I love it. Can I bring my wife by to see it when she gets back in town tomorrow?"

"We're here from nine to five," Jerod said.

"Perfect, I'll give you a call before we come." He drove away.

Jerod turned to them, a big grin splitting his face. "He loved the place. He and his wife are both in sales. They entertain clients a lot. With five bedrooms, they'd each have an office and plenty of room for kids. His wife's four months pregnant. We might have a sale."

"Did you tell them about Jessica?" Jazzi asked.

Jerod nodded. "He said he and his wife love old houses, and they'd guess most of them had someone die in them at one time or another. Said they're not superstitious."

She'd never thought about that, but he was probably right.

Ansel leaned on his shovel and took a long slug of soda. "This place is getting far enough along, Jazzi and I have started looking for the next place to flip."

"Any luck? I've been looking, too. Haven't seen anything I like."

Jazzi took the last swig of her drink and walked to toss the can in the trash. "I looked under 'For Sale by Owner' and saw a Dutch Colonial on the north side of River Bluffs." They usually tried to avoid houses sold by occupants because people often were so fond of their homes, they expected too much money for them. But they'd bought this house directly from Madeline, and it had worked, so it couldn't hurt to drive by the house in Kirkwood Park.

Jerod made a face. "Sure, the north side would be a lot closer to you guys."

She shrugged. "Not that much closer. We live far enough northeast, it's still a drive for us. The neighborhood is close to Coliseum Boulevard and Stellhorn. I've driven by it, but I've never driven through it before."

He nodded, a little less grumpy. "I could take Hillegas to the turn-off for Coliseum. That wouldn't be too bad."

"Besides," Jazzi pointed out, "you picked this house, and it's not exactly an easy drive for us. You picked the house in Auburn, too."

Jerod raised a hand. "I get it. You're right. Beggars can't be choosers. Our choices are limited."

They agreed to check it out on Friday morning. Maybe they'd have the trench dug by then. But it wouldn't dig itself. They got back to work and were all happy when it was finally lunchtime and they could stop for a while.

Jazzi's back ached when she bent to pass out ham and cheese sandwiches. She'd brought her panini maker and pressed each one so they were warm and the cheese was gooey.

"You should open a restaurant," Jerod said. "These are good."

George liked them, too, but Jazzi shook her head. "Cooking wouldn't be fun if it was a job. Most restaurant owners put in long hours, longer than I'd want to."

"Guess you'll just have to enjoy yourself cooking for us, then," he teased.

She'd half expected Gaff to drop by today and had made two extra sandwiches in case, but when he didn't show up, she told Jerod to take them home.

"Have I told you that you're my favorite cousin?" he joked. "If I open a can of soup, we can each have half a ham and cheese sandwich to go with it for supper."

"You'd better never let Olivia hear you say that, but whatever makes your life easier." She cleaned up their things, then they started digging again. They were trying to be as careful as possible so they didn't ruin any of the house's landscaping.

By the end of the day, they were exhausted. The clay soil was dry and rock solid, making the trench hard work. But they'd finished one side of the house and most of the back. Another day and a half and they could lay the drainage tile.

They didn't even put their shovels away, just leaned them against the back wall before they left. Jazzi promised herself a hot bath when they got home. They'd kept the claw-foot tub in their master bath, and it was perfect to soak in. Gaff didn't call until they were a few minutes from home. "I'm close to your place. Can I stop by in half an hour?"

Her bath would have to wait. "Sure, we'll be home by then."

"Should I give you a little longer to take your showers? Every time I stop by the Merlot place, you're both a mess."

Jazzi snorted. "We're even worse tonight. We've been digging all day."

"Then I'll give you an extra fifteen minutes." And he hung up. Detectives must do that. Once their business was done, the phone went dead.

She sighed. So much for a long, hot soak. The first thing they did when they walked in the house was feed and play with the animals, or there'd be no peace. Inky expected attention after being left alone all day. Marmalade, her orange cat with a sweet disposition, was happy whenever they took time to pet her.

Ansel showered first, then Jazzi. Her hair was still wrapped in a towel when Gaff arrived. He shook his head. "You're not the turban type." He took a stool at the kitchen island, and Ansel brought them all drinks.

"Beer okay?" he asked Gaff.

"Yup, I'm off duty. I got Jazzi's text message last night about Jessica's dad. Guess it looks like he and his son are both in the running as top suspects, but Ruth Goggins has inched up the ladder, too."

"How's that?" Jazzi went to the refrigerator and took out what was left of the cheese ball from the party and a sleeve of crackers to munch on while they drank.

"Your friendly neighbor was on a trip, too, when Lila died."

Jazzi didn't miss the sarcasm. "Really? Where did she go?"

"To visit her sister in Virginia, not that far from North Carolina. The sister confirms the visit, but Ruth left in plenty of time to lie in wait for Lila in Carolina."

Ansel rubbed his head. "Would Ruth have the nerve to play chicken on a highway?"

"If she thought her reputation was at stake?" Jazzi nodded. "She's really single-minded."

Gaff smeared cheese on a cracker. "I think we have three top contenders. Unfortunately, we don't have any proof." He popped the snack in his mouth and smiled. Jazzi would bet he'd eaten a quick lunch and was hungry by now.

Jazzi pursed her lips, thinking about proof. "I don't suppose the tire marks can identify a certain model of car."

"Sometimes that works," Gaff said, making himself a few more crackers. "If the tires are different sizes or have some distinguishing flaw. We didn't get that lucky."

Of course not. That would have been too easy. "Jessica's dad couldn't have killed Darcie, though, right? He spent the night with the young woman."

"You're right. He had a solid alibi that night. Unless..." He paused, thinking. "What if he pushed Jessica, but Alwin killed Darcie to protect him? The detective working the Carolina end says those two have a weird bond of some kind."

"Maybe it started when they shared the peephole to watch Jessica."

Gaff grimaced. So did Ansel. Finally, Gaff stood to leave. "Eventually, we're going to find the one thing that gives us an answer. We're getting there."

Jazzi watched him drive away, then sighed.

"Is it that bad?" Ansel asked.

"Every time I think we're narrowing things down, something new comes up that confuses me."

He patted her arm. "Gaff has faith in you. So do I."

That was a good thing. They had more faith in her than she did.

Chapter 41

On Wednesday, the young couple came and walked through the Merlot house with Jerod. In less than an hour, they bought it. Jerod was ecstatic. They got full price.

On Thursday, the three of them finished digging the trench. Another reason to celebrate. And after work that night, the trundle daybeds Ansel had ordered were delivered. They looked perfect against the walls of the kids' space in their basement. That made him ecstatic. He had a place for his family if they came to visit.

Jazzi should have been happy, too, but when she left to drive to Olivia's favorite Mexican restaurant on Jefferson for girls' night out, she didn't feel up to it. Gaff had called to tell her that Lila Mattock's funeral was at two on Friday afternoon and asked her to go with him. She wasn't looking forward to it. She especially didn't want to see Ruth Goggins, who would undoubtedly be there, or Nadia Ashton. But Gaff wanted her there. He hadn't met any of the suspects, only knew them by name, so she'd go. The one redeeming factor was that she, Jerod, and Ansel would still have plenty of time to look at the house in Kirkwood Park before she had to be in Merlot. Fingers crossed it would be a good candidate for their next fixer-upper.

Olivia was already holding a table for them when Jazzi walked inside the restaurant. A miracle. Olivia was never the first person at anything. Her sister took one look at her face and raised her eyebrows. "This would be a good night for your favorite—a strawberry margarita."

The waiter raised his pen, and Jazzi nodded. "The middle size." The bar offered small, medium, and large drinks. The large might make her a little too carefree.

Olivia waited until she sat across from her. "Thane called Ansel today. They're meeting at your house again this Thursday. You might regret buying so many boy toys for your basement."

Jazzi smiled. "The novelty will wear off. Eventually, they'll be ready to eat out again."

Didi and Elspeth walked into the bar area together. Didi was moving a little slower lately. She only had a month and a half until the baby was due.

Once they were settled and gave their drink orders, Olivia leaned forward, bursting to share some news. "Mom and I hired a new girl who's going to start working in our shop the first week in November."

Jazzi blinked. That was only a few days away. This coming Sunday was Halloween. Last year, she and Ansel had met Jerod and his kids at Olivia's house to help with trick-or-treating. This year, Walker and River were going with them, and Didi was staying with Olivia to pass out candy. That meant the new girl would be starting work next Tuesday. "Why so sudden? You and Mom have co-owned the shop ever since you graduated from beauty school. I thought you were happy having the shop to yourselves. Someone new might change the atmosphere, the camaraderie."

"We thought about that, but we both interviewed Misty, and we both liked her. We have plenty of room for another work station, and Mom and my books are so full, we can't take on any new clients. This way, we can bring new people into the shop."

"That's what you want? New clients?"

"Some of ours are getting up there in years. It might be nice to attract a younger crowd, to be able to do some trendier stuff and stay up-to-date."

Jazzi shrugged. Who was she to argue with how they ran their shop? Their drinks came, and the conversation stopped while the waiter took their food orders.

Once he left, Olivia made a face. "Dad's not too happy about it. He gave Mom some grief when she told him. He didn't change his mind, even after Mom told him the new girl would rent her booth. We'd make more money."

Jazzi could understand his concerns. "Dad's hired lots of part-time workers at the hardware store over the years. He knows everything that can go wrong with a new employee."

"Hair is different," Olivia argued. "The more, the merrier."

"Did you check her references and credentials?" Elspeth asked.

Olivia looked put out. "Of course we did. She moved here from New York, worked in a flashy salon there. She gave us the name of its manager, and we called her. She gave Misty high recommendations."

Didi jerked and pressed a hand to her stomach. The baby must be kicking again. "I'm glad I work from home. All I have to concentrate on is finishing my medical transcriptions every week."

"I'd get lonely," Elspeth chimed in. "I like an office atmosphere. Some of the women at the insurance company work from home a few days a week. I wouldn't like it. Unless I have to drive in bad weather. Then, I work on my laptop in my pajamas."

Their food came, and the conversation turned to small talk. By the time they walked out of the restaurant together, Jazzi was in a better mood. But the weather had turned grim while they were inside. The wind howled and a drizzle made everything wet enough to be uncomfortable.

On the drive home, streetlamps and headlights disappeared into dark, wet cement. She had to keep her windshield wipers on the entire way. If a car followed her tonight to force her off the road, she'd never notice until it was too late. Shivering, she pushed the thought away. With relief, she pulled into their driveway and parked her pickup in the garage, then raced to the kitchen door. Warmth greeted her when she stepped inside. So did the aroma of chili. The soup pot was upside down on the drying rack.

"It was so crappy out, the guys and I decided to make chili. It sounded better than takeout."

"Did they help you cook it?" Jazzi hung her leather jacket on the coat tree by the door.

"They even wrote down the ingredients so they can make it at home." He grinned. "I used your recipe this time. I learned my lesson trying to download one of my own." It had been so hot and spicy, they couldn't eat it.

"Did you give George the crumbled hamburger before you added all the spices?"

Ansel glanced at his pug, watching them from his dog bed.

"I forgot, and you might want to wear a gas mask for the rest of the night."

Jazzi shook her head. The last time Ansel gave the dog chili, he'd passed so much gas, they had to turn on the vent over the stove. That wouldn't help once they settled in the living room. Oh, well, what was done was done. She couldn't do anything about it now.

"Did you have a nice night?" she asked him.

He nodded. "Thane's getting excited about his gazebo. It's almost done. Radley's excited about getting the keys to the house they bought. And Walker's getting excited about the baby."

They went upstairs to change, and Jazzi told him about Mom and Olivia hiring a new girl for their shop and Dad's concerns about it. Ansel gave her a look. "Were you and Jerod worried when you hired me on as a contractor?"

"It was for one job. We figured if you didn't work out, we'd look for someone else at our next house."

"But I did work out, and look what happened. We made a great team all the way around, and I was so wonderful, you married me."

She laughed and wrapped her arms around him, leaning her head against his chest. "We wouldn't have hired you if you weren't so gorgeous."

Chuckling, he dropped a kiss on the top of her head. "You didn't even look at me back then. You were engaged to Chad."

"See what I knew?" She stepped back to look up at him. "I'm glad we finally figured things out."

Glancing at the alarm clock, he gave her a smirk. "It's still early. We have plenty of time to celebrate smart business practices." He closed their bedroom door, then turned off every light except the one on the nightstand.

Her night was going to get lots better. She stepped into his arms again.

Chapter 42

They got to sleep in on Friday. There was no reason to drive to Merlot and then return to River Bluffs to see the house. They'd agreed to meet the owner at ten, so they had time for extra cups of coffee and relaxing before they left. Inky and Marmalade loved it, rubbing against their legs, expecting more attention. Ansel even dragged their string around the kitchen, pulling it over the chairs in the sitting area and on the countertops so they'd have to jump for it.

The weather was worse than last night's. Gray clouds piled on top of one another, hunkering over the city, and rain fell in a steady rhythm. Jazzi didn't pack anything to take for lunch today. They'd stop and grab fast food after they looked at the Dutch Colonial.

Ansel bent over George to keep him dry as he carried him to the garage. On their way to Kirkwood Park, he glared at the ominous sky. "A perfect day for a funeral—dismal and gloomy."

She was wearing her black slacks and a black sweater. Her raincoat was red, not appropriate, but she'd hang that up at the funeral home.

"Did you remember to bring your work clothes?" he asked.

She nodded. "On the back seat." She hoped the service would go so fast, she'd have plenty of time to change and help the guys on the job. "Did you talk to Thane last night? Is his crew coming to install the new furnace and central air today?"

"Yeah, we're going to help him with the vents. And Jerod and I thought we'd fix the peephole and repaint those walls today."

That would keep them out of Thane's way. It was too wet to work on the drainage tile.

When they pulled to the curb in front of the house, they saw an SUV parked in the drive. Jerod's truck pulled in behind them. "Stay," Ansel told George. The pug glanced at the rain and settled more comfortably on the back seat. Then the three of them walked to the front door together.

A young man opened it to invite them in. If he was over twenty-one, Jazzi would be surprised. He pinched his lips together and motioned to the rooms they could see. "No one's fixed anything here for years. My gran lived at home until I had to put her in hospice. I live in Idaho and asked her to move to a nursing center close to me, but she wouldn't do it. Always did love her independence."

Jerod frowned. "What about your parents?"

"Both died before her. Smoked like crazy. Cancer got them. I'm all she had at the end, but I have a family and a job out there. I couldn't come home very often to see her, but at least I was with her when she passed."

He sounded like a good kid. Jazzi liked him.

"Gran left everything to me. All she asked was for me to find someone who'd make sure her house got a good family who'd take care of it. That's all I want, to keep her last wish. I looked up you guys after you called me, and you do that, don't you? You fix a house so it gets good owners?"

"We do the best we can," Jerod told him.

The boy nodded. No, not a boy. He had to be older than he looked if he had a family, but Jazzi would bet he got carded at liquor stores all the time. He shook his head at a stain where a window leaked. "I know you have to make money, so I'm keeping the price low enough, this might be worth your time."

"Can we go through it before we decide?" Jerod asked. Otherwise, they wouldn't buy it.

"Oh, sure! Sorry. I don't usually handle things like this." And he turned to walk them through the place.

It needed a lot of work. No one would know from its exterior. That had been kept in perfect shape—a new roof, new paint, and great landscaping—but the interior had been neglected. Two ceilings sagged. Every window needed to be replaced. The kitchen might as well be a closet, and the bathrooms were straight out of the fifties. There was no master bathroom at all. No surprise. Those were a more recent must-have. But the foundation was in good shape, the basement dry—even with the rain—and when he told them the asking price, Jerod raised his eyebrows for their opinions. Ansel and Jazzi nodded their heads.

The kid grinned. "Then it's a deal?"

"It works for us." Jerod extended a hand, and they shook.

"This is such a relief," he said. "I can tie things up here pretty fast now and drive home."

Jerod made arrangements to finalize the details, and they left. She was in charge of providing lunches, but her cousin took care of all the paperwork, so he'd meet with the kid and their lawyers and go from there. It was still early, only eleven fifteen, so they decided to drive through the neighborhood to check it out before driving to a restaurant for lunch.

Jerod crowded into their van, sitting beside George, and Ansel wove his way up and down streets. The neighborhood proved wonderful. Houses were well-kept. There was a park a few blocks away with a baseball diamond. Schools were close by, even grad schools. Ivy Tech was on one corner and the Purdue extension campus on another. Shops, a post office, and restaurants were only a few streets away. The location was convenient to everything while still maintaining a neighborhood charm. Ranches, two-stories, and Cape Cods mingled together.

Happy with their choice, they drove to a coffee shop on South Anthony that served lunch. It was after one before they finally pulled into the drive at the Merlot house. Thane and his crew were already there, working in the basement. When they went down to see him, he grinned.

"I took a peek through the house. Talk about a beauty. Once we get the new heating and cooling system in, it looks like you're pretty close to done, aren't you?"

"All we have to do is lay the drainage tile," Jerod told him.

Thane glanced out a high window and shook his head. "And you're not doing that today?"

Jerod grunted a response. "I don't mind getting wet, but I don't like to be half-drowned."

"Need any help with vent work?" Ansel asked.

"I never turn down free help." Thane pointed to a huge, metal arm that came off the old furnace. "If you guys can get rid of that, we'll install a new, smaller one."

Jerod and Ansel got busy, and Jazzi wandered upstairs to wait for Gaff. She flipped through different products on her cell phone that she thought might work at the Kirkwood Park house. She'd made a list by the time he pulled in the drive. Then she tugged the hood up on her raincoat and braved the rain to run to his car.

"Have you been looking forward to this as much as I have?" he asked.

She rolled her eyes. "I've already met Lila's friends. They're as nice as she was."

He snorted a laugh. "Do you think lots of people will show up?"

"Not if they're smart." It was only a ten-minute drive to the funeral home. A respectable number of cars were parked in the lot. She and Gaff hung up their coats and entered the room for Lila's service. A man stood near the back of the room, a few steps away from the casket, with a boy on one side of him and a younger girl on the other. The boy did his best to smile and greet people like his father, but the girl shifted impatiently from foot to foot. There were only a few floral arrangements, but their sweet, sickly scent hung in the air.

Gaff studied them. "That must be Lila's ex and their two kids. From what I've heard, Lila didn't have much to do with them, rarely took them for weekends."

Jazzi studied them more closely. Neither kid looked heartbroken. They'd glance at the open casket once in a while when a visitor said something, but their expressions didn't show anything more than polite curiosity. Their dad obviously had brought them to pay respects to their mother, but she must not have been a strong presence in their lives.

A line of people waited to shake his hand and offer condolences. From their demeanors, he must be well-liked. An older couple stood slightly behind him. Lila's husband resembled his father—a high forehead and a square jawline. The little girl left his side for a minute to go to her grandmother, leaning into her for comfort. Another older couple stood close by, and the woman had the same long red hair and eye color as Lila.

Jazzi motioned her head to four people clustered together on the other side of the room, two men and two women, standing away from the others. She kept her voice low. "I'm surprised to see Alwin here."

Gaff stared. "Which one is he?"

"The one in the navy-blue suit." Jazzi pointed out Ruth Goggins, and Nadia Ashton, too. "I don't know the older man." He was taller than Alwin, with a solid, stocky build. His lips were turned down in a sneer as he scanned the room. His gaze stopped on them, then he turned to talk to Nadia.

She and Gaff were making their way to seats near the back of the room when Nadia stalked toward them. "Uh-oh, get ready," Jazzi warned.

Stopping in front of her, Nadia barked, "What are you doing here?"

Gaff extended his hand. "I asked her to accompany me. She's met people in Merlot. I haven't. I'm a detective assisting with the case."

Nadia ignored his hand but stared at him long and hard. "What case?"

"The authorities have talked to Lila's ex-husband. They believe Lila's death was suspicious and are investigating it as a homicide, along with Darcie Winter's murder."

Nadia blinked. "A homicide?"

He nodded. "But this isn't the appropriate place to discuss it, and I can't go into details."

Nadia would have pressed him anyway, but music started, and everyone took their seats. She turned and rushed back to her friends. Soon, their four heads were bent together as they whispered furiously.

Alwin, Ruth, Nadia, and the man sat together in one row. People kept their distance from them.

"Do you think that's Alwin's father?" Jazzi asked Gaff.

"I'd say that's a good guess. I'll find out after the service."

The service was long and dreary. The minister was doing his best to make Lila sound better than she was. Jazzi's mind wandered. Midway through a hymn, the sun came out, filling the windows with light and making the room overly warm. Then there were scripture readings and more homilies. When the final chords of the organ eventually played, pallbearers appeared to carry the casket to the waiting hearse. Then anyone who was following the hearse to the graveside ceremony was directed out the same door.

Gaff and Jazzi rose and walked in the opposite direction, to the lobby. They started to the exit when a greeter called, "Sir, did you leave your coat? And ma'am, is this one yours?"

Grateful for the reminder, Jazzi returned to slip into her red raincoat. The rain had stopped, and the day had warmed up enough, she would have forgotten it. Gaff grabbed his car coat but stepped back inside the viewing room to look at the register. He pointed. "Lamar Hodgkill."

"I never expected to see him here." Jazzi frowned at his sharp, angular signature. The letters looked like stabs.

When they left the room, the greeter had been called away, and she glanced at the man's coat that had been hanging next to hers. Cashmere. She lifted the collar to look at the name brand. Expensive. Ansel would look wonderful in a coat like that. It started to slip off the hanger, and she grabbed it to hang it more securely and noticed an inner pocket.

Gran's words returned to her. "Look in his pocket."

She couldn't help it. She reached inside and felt a slip of paper. Gaff watched her, his brows raised, but he didn't comment. When she pulled out the paper, she looked at it and smiled. She went to show it to Gaff. A receipt for a gas station in Merlot for the same night that Darcie died. Signed by Alwin Hodgkill. "Alwin swore he wasn't in Merlot that night."

Gaff pinched his lips together. "I can't use that. We didn't have a warrant, wouldn't have been able to get one. It's inadmissible evidence."

"Except..." She raised her eyebrows.

Gaff grinned. "If the gas station has security cameras, my detective friend can ask for the footage." He pulled out his cell phone and made the call.

By the time Alwin returned with his father for the coat, the receipt was back in his pocket, and Gaff and Jazzi were leaving the funeral home. The detective Gaff knew was waiting for him. "Alwin Hodgkill?" he asked. "I'd like a word with you."

Chapter 43

Gaff drove Jazzi back to the fixer-upper. When she entered the house, she told Ansel and Jerod her news. It was late enough, Thane and his crew were gone, and the two of them had finished repairing the walls upstairs. It was too wet to lay field tile, so they decided to lock up and leave early.

They usually went out for supper on Friday nights, so on the drive home, Jazzi called Leesa to ask if she and Brett would like to meet them somewhere, because she had news.

"Damian and Kelsey are on their way to stay the weekend with us. Can they come, too?"

"Even better." Damian's relief would triple hers.

By the time they finally walked into their own kitchen, Jazzi felt like a great weight had been lifted from her shoulders. She'd never known Jessica, didn't really know Damian, but they'd finally found justice. She didn't know all the details, but the case was closed.

She didn't need a shower, so she fed and played with the pets while Ansel got ready to go out. When he walked down the stairs, she stopped to admire him. Her Norseman wore black slacks, like she did, and a charcoal gray, button-down shirt. He looked good in dark colors. They complemented his white-blond hair and blue eyes.

Before she could savor him properly, Gaff called to tell her that Alwin had confessed to the murders of Jessica and Wendy Roeback, the cheerleader he'd met randomly, Darcie, and Lila. Gaff stayed on the line long enough to answer all her questions before he had to return to his paperwork. "And the detective I worked with wants me to thank you from him."

Jazzi sighed with relief as she finished the call. "It's wrapped up," she told Ansel.

"Finally. You can fill me in when you tell Leesa and the others." He threaded his arm through hers and led her to the pickup. The Lucky Turtle Grill was only a short drive from their house at a busy intersection. They had to circle to find a parking spot in the strip mall's lot.

They were the first to arrive. The place was getting crowded, so they claimed a table for six and ordered drinks. Jazzi already knew what she was getting—the plump, juicy red shrimp, shell on, with drawn butter. It was an appropriate splurge for solving Jessica's murder.

Once everyone had arrived and ordered, Damian said, "Did you find out who pushed Jessica? Can I finally prove I didn't do it?"

Jazzi nodded. "It was Alwin. He didn't mean to kill her. He pushed her in a fit of temper."

"His own sister?" Leesa pinched her lips, unhappy with the thought.

"He'd obsessed over her since they were little. Even drilled a peephole so he could spy on her in her room."

"Her bedroom?" Brett asked to clarify.

Jazzi nodded and went on. "He tried to find someone like her but couldn't. Every girl as pretty as she was, and as smart, rejected him."

Damian lowered his face into his hands, fighting to compose himself. When he looked up again, he said, "Sorry. It's been so long, such a strain. It's almost overwhelming to know it's over. Do you think Alwin was all there? You know, mentally all right? I always felt sort of sorry for him."

Jazzi shrugged. "He was as sane as he could be with his father constantly berating Jessica and browbeating him."

Kelsey grimaced. "I never knew. Jessica never complained, never felt sorry for herself. I should have been nicer to her. I feel bad, the way I treated her. I was just so jealous of her."

"A lot of people were," Jazzi said. "It didn't do her any favors. She was actually a really neat person."

Brett frowned, trying to piece everything together. "But why kill Darcie? Could she really have found anything after all these years? Did she threaten Alwin that much?"

"Alwin thought she could. After all, Lila had seen him push Jessica."

"Wait! Really?" Anger flashed in Damian's eyes. "And she spent years telling everyone it was me?"

"That worked in her favor," Jazzi explained. She stopped, and they grew silent while the waitress delivered their drinks. Once she left, Jazzi said, "Lila was blackmailing Alwin. He was paying her a lot of money to keep quiet. By blaming you, she diverted the blame from him."

"And that's why he killed her?" Leesa asked.

Brett still wasn't satisfied. "But why lose his temper with Jessica at her party? What made him snap?"

"A good question." Jazzi took a sip of her wine. "He couldn't stand the idea that Jessica was going to move away as soon as she got her diploma. She wasn't waiting until classes started in the fall. She was escaping her father as soon as she could. Alwin had tried to convince her to stay home, to study at Tri-States with him, but she wanted to be as far away from Merlot as she could get."

Damian shook his head. "I feel sorry for both of them, Alwin and Jessica. Hodgkill ruined both of their lives."

"Pretty much." She had to admire Damian. He'd suffered a long time because of Alwin's sins, and he could sympathize with him. "Their mother tried to run interference, but it wasn't enough."

Kelsey laced her fingers through her husband's and gave them a gentle squeeze. "Are you going to be all right?"

"Better than all right." He forced a smile. "But it wasn't Alwin who tried to pin the murder on me. It was Lila and Ruth Goggins."

Ruth's name left a sour taste in Jazzi's mouth. What would the woman gossip about now?

Damian sighed. "What did Alwin and Jessica argue about that made him push her?"

"He told the detective he'd begged her not to go. He said she looked so beautiful that day, so happy and proud of herself, that he lost control and grabbed her and kissed her."

"On the mouth?" Leesa stared.

"She pushed him away in disgust, and he lost it and shoved her. He said it almost killed him to hear her scream, to watch her fall, and then he looked up, and Lila was smirking at him."

"Lila." Damian spat out her name. "I can't feel sorry for her at all."

Neither could Jazzi.

Ansel looked around the table, at the misery on every face, and shook his head. He raised his glass of beer in a toast. "To Damian! He's finally free. You can return home to no whispers."

Kelsey squared her shoulders, her eyes glinting. "What about Ruth Goggins? Does she get out of this unscathed?"

It didn't seem fair, but Jazzi thought that might happen. "I doubt anyone will press charges, but you can sure shut her up."

"How?" Damian asked.

"Threaten to sue her for defamation of character, for spreading false rumors and lies when she obviously didn't see you climb the stairs to Jessica's balcony."

"She'll deny it," Kelsey snapped. "She'll say it must have been a mistake, that she could have sworn it was Damian."

Brett's smile was scary. "But everyone in town will know. They won't believe her, and I'll make sure to spread the word she's a liar. That woman deserves to be put in her place."

"How did old man Hodgkill take it when his son was charged?" Damian asked.

"He swore to fight it. He's hiring a top-notch lawyer."

"A waste of time and money," Leesa said. "But that man would never give up without a fight."

"Who'll take over his company when he retires?" Brett asked.

"He doesn't have anybody," Jazzi said, "unless he remarries and starts over. Even then, he'll be lucky if his business isn't worth a lot less than it is now. Lorraine's asking for half of it in the divorce settlement."

Ansel grinned at that and raised his glass again. "To justice!"

This time, they all joined him, and the mood at the table changed. They were finally ready to celebrate.

Chapter 44

The day after Jazzi, Ansel, and Jerod finished work on the house, Jazzi drove back to Merlot alone. She was meeting Molly, Jillian, and Felicity, along with Lydia and Lorraine, at Jessica's grave. They all brought roses.

They met at Jessica's grave and bent to place the flowers on it together.

"Are you going to be all right?" Jillian asked Lorraine.

Her face was strained, and she had to blink back tears, but she nodded and reached for her sister's hand. "Jessica's been at peace since the moment she died. It's taken the rest of us longer, but I believe we'll find ours now."

Lydia's brow crinkled with sympathy. "She's moving back to this area, settling a few towns over. She'll be close by. There are a lot of people who love her here."

Lorraine hunched her shoulders. Voice tight, she said, "There's no point in returning to Carolina. I don't want to see Lamar, and Alwin will be in prison somewhere in this state. I know he pushed Jessica, but he didn't mean to kill her. He'll need someone to visit him."

Jazzi's heart hurt for Lorraine, but she thought of the three other women Alwin had killed besides his sister. Still, Alwin was Lorraine's son. A mother probably loved her child, no matter what.

They stayed for a short time, paying their respects, and then they all headed to their individual cars and left. On the return home, Jazzi thought about families and their bonds. Her family was so close; could she ever give up on one of them? How big would the crime have to be before it scarred their love?

Even when Bain was a suspect in Donovan's death, Ansel had never lost faith that his brother was innocent. How could he? Who knew a person better than family?

If every shred of evidence pointed to Olivia committing a crime, would she believe it? Hopefully, she'd never find out.

Please turn the page for some yummy recipes
from Jazzi's kitchen!

Recipes for *The Body in the Past*

Sauerbraten

Preheat oven to 350 degrees.
Combine for marinade or sauce:

> 2 c. beef stock (I prefer Kitchen Basics)
> 1 c. burgundy
> 1 c. red wine vinegar
> 3 t. minced garlic from jar
> 1 t. dried thyme
> 2 bay leaves
> 1 t. coarse black pepper
> 1/2 t. cloves

In a Dutch oven:
Sear a 3–4 lb. chuck roast in olive oil.
Season with salt.
Remove from pan and add:
2 sliced onions
Half a small bag of baby carrots
2 slices of celery, cut in chunks
6 small potatoes, cut in half
Cook until tender. Then add 2 T. flour and stir to coat vegetables.
Add the roast and sauce.
Cover and roast in oven until tender, about 2-1/2 to 3 hours.
When finished, plate the roast and vegetables on large platter, simmer the sauce in Dutch oven.
Add 1 more cup of beef stock. Remove bay leaves.
Add: 2 T. crushed gingersnap cookies and stir 'til thickens.
Pour over roast and add more salt, if needed, then serve.

Pork Goulash

Cut 2 lbs. of pork loin into cubes.
In a Dutch oven, cover bottom with olive oil and heat.
Add the pork in single layers and sear.
Add:

    2 c. sliced onion
    1 t. minced garlic from jar
    3/4 c. ketchup
    2 T. Worcestershire
    1 T. brown sugar
    2 t. salt
    2 t. Hungarian sweet paprika
    1/2 t. dry mustard
    Dash of cayenne
    1-1/2 c. water

Cover. Simmer for 2 hours.
Blend 1–2 t. of cornstarch with 1/2 c. water to make slurry.
Add to sauce and heat to thicken.
Serve over buttered noodles.

Greek Salad

Tear 1 large head of romaine into bite-size pieces.
Add:

    3 green onions, diced
    2 medium tomatoes, seeded and cubed
    2 Persian cucumbers, sliced
    1/2 c. black olives, sliced
    1/2 c. feta cheese, crumbled (2 oz.)

Dressing:

    3 t. minced garlic from jar
    1 t. kosher salt
    Dash ground black pepper
    1/4 c. red wine vinegar
    1/2 c. olive oil
    1/2 t. Dijon mustard
    1/2 t. oregano
    (and, for me, a tad of sugar)

Easy Buffalo Chicken Wings

Preheat oven to 400 degrees.
Rub:

 1/4 c. brown sugar
 2 T. chili powder
 1 T. Hungarian sweet paprika
 1 T. garlic powder
 1 T. onion powder
 1 T. oregano
 1 t. kosher salt
 1 t. coriander
 1 t. coarse black pepper
 3 lbs. chicken wings

Line 2 large, rimmed baking sheets with parchment paper.
Spray.
Layer chicken wings on baking sheets, so single layer on each.
Sprinkle with rub and coat each wing.
Roast in hot oven for 1 hour.

Remove from oven and toss in buffalo sauce:

 1 c. melted butter
 1 c. Frank's Hot Sauce

Printed in the United States
by Baker & Taylor Publisher Services